THE
SONGBIRD'S
$\mathcal{S}$EDUCTION

Also by Connie Brockway

HISTORICALS
Promise Me Heaven
Anything for Love
A Dangerous Man
As You Desire
All Through the Night
My Dearest Enemy
McClairen's Isle: The Passionate One
McClairen's Isle: The Reckless One
McClairen's Isle: The Ravishing One
The Bridal Season
Once Upon a Pillow, with Christina Dodd
Bridal Favors
The Rose Hunters: My Seduction
The Rose Hunters: My Pleasure
The Rose Hunters: My Surrender
So Enchanting
The Golden Season
The Lady Most Likely, with Christina Dodd and Eloisa James
The Other Guy's Bride
The Lady Most Willing, with Christina Dodd and Eloisa James
No Place for a Dame

CONTEMPORARY ROMANCE
Hot Dish
Skinny Dipping

ANTHOLOGIES
Outlaw Love, "Heaven with a Gun"
My Scottish Summer, "Lassie, Go Home"
The True Love Wedding Dress, "Glad Rags"
Cupid Cats, "Cat Scratch Fever"

THE SONGBIRD'S SEDUCTION

CONNIE BROCKWAY

Published by Montlake Romance, Seattle

www.apub.com

Amazon, the Amazon logo, and Montlake Romance are trademarks of Amazon.com, Inc., or its affiliates.

ISBN-13: 9781477824894
ISBN-10: 1477824898

Cover design by Mumtaz Mustafa
Illustrated by Dana Ashton France

Library of Congress Control Number: 2014905947

Printed in the United States of America

For Ann Hovde,

*Beloved sister-in-law, fellow loony,
best of friends.*

Man, I really fell into it.

CHAPTER

1

Wilfred Martin Whinnywicke expired Tuesday
last. Stop. Bernard DuPaul, Junior

Late September, 1908
Robin's Hall, twenty miles northeast of London

At the base of the faded, moss-softened façade of what had once
been a dignified, old stone manor house, a pair of elderly, smock-
clad ladies worked industriously, attempting to hold at bay the
encroaching woodlands from what they fondly imagined to be—or
perhaps, more to the point, remembered as—a tiny formal garden.
They were sisters, though no one would guess as much. One was
tall, hawk-nosed, and as spindly as a stair rail, her head crowned
by a wealth of silvery down. The other was short, soft as fresh butter, and round as a dumpling, her straight hair obstinately refusing
to lose the middling brown color that never had been one of her
few chief recommendations.

Both had lived their entire lives, with one notable and short exception, from within the manor's walls.

Indeed, they had reached the humble heights of their feminine attractiveness at the same time that the house had enjoyed its own salad days. Alas, the years had piled on far past this zenith, the ladies' dwindling prospects marching in time with the house's deterioration, but at so slow and regular a pace that no one really noticed.

Indeed, it was only when the sisters answered the front door to a stranger on the buckled front entry steps that they recognized in the unknown person's expression the condition into which they had fallen. This, in part, accounted for their very wise decision not to open the door to strangers at all, the other part being that those same strangers often came in response to unpaid bills. Happily, no one had troubled them for some months now and so they were quite content transplanting tulip bulbs in anticipation of another spring.

They were nearing the end of this endeavor when a jubilant cry rang out from the second-story window of the house, attracting the attention of the elder sister, Miss Lavinia Litton. She sank back on her bony haunches and looked up just as a young female voice burst into song—and a most engaging voice it was, too—noting that the singer was also waltzing with joyful abandon directly in front of the open window.

"I say, Bernice," the older lady fretted, "do you think it quite safe for Lucy to be dancing about so near those open windows?"

"Dancing, is she? I daresay she'll be all right," Bernice said, handing a bulb to Lavinia. "She's in fine voice this morning, isn't she? And a merry little tune she's after, what? Though I can't quite catch the lyrics."

"I believe she's singing, 'He's dead, he's dead, bless him, he's dead,'" Lavinia explained patiently. Despite her strenuous protestations to the contrary, Bernice was a tad hard of hearing.

"Oh." Bernice frowned in puzzlement. "Is she rehearsing for a new role?"

Lavinia listened a moment longer. "I don't think so. I believe she's making it up as she goes."

"Why do you think that?"

"Because that's *all* she's singing and I can't think a real song would have only four words to it."

"Well, whatever she's singing, it's nice to hear her sounding so happy." Bernice commenced digging another hole.

"Is it?" Lavinia, who had always prided herself on having an elevated sense of propriety, asked a trifle nervously. "Do you think she is referring to an actual *event*? And if so, do you think she ought to indulge in such an effusive demonstration of her feelings?

"I mean, what if she is referring to Mr. Gouge?" she went on, naming their small town's perpetually expiring deacon. "Certainly one could empathize, especially after he alluded to Lucy as a Flora Dora girl in last Christmas's sermon, but some degree of decorum is always—"

"Don't be silly, Lavinia. If Mr. Gouge had died Lucy would simply gloat in silence like any decent person. Obviously whoever 'he' is, he deserved to die, and as Lucy is clearly unconcerned that her, er, enthusiasm regarding 'his' demise will garner censure—because otherwise she wouldn't be dancing about and singing, would she?—neither need we. Lucy is generally a prudent girl"—she lowered her voice—"for all that she is in the theatre." Though Bernice publically and vociferously supported Lucy in her chosen profession, privately it was still a source of some consternation for her.

"Operetta, second principal," Lavinia corrected absently. "You are so sensible, Bernice. And of course, you are right. I am ashamed I doubted her, even for a moment. Still, it begs the question: Who do you think 'he' is?"

"Haven't the foggiest," Bernice replied, companionably patting the dirt around her last tulip. "Probably that tomcat that's been having his way with Pauline." Pauline was the sisters' overindulged Manx tabby. "I haven't seen him in several days."

Bernice nodded. "Or perhaps—"

"There you are, my darlings!"

The sisters' speculation was cut short by the sudden appearance of a young Rapunzel hanging out the window above, her long, cocoa-brown tresses shadowing a pretty gamine face with hazel-colored eyes that reflected back both the gold of the turning aspen leaves above and the lichen below. It was their grandniece, Lucille Eastlake, the only child of their deceased sister's only child, the last tiny twig on what had once been a proud and robust tree. Lucy had come to them as an orphan when she'd been eleven years old and though nearly a decade had since passed, both sisters still caught their breath at the sight of her, so vibrant and lovely and, well, *exuberant*.

And dear.

But mystifying.

The preadolescent girl they'd taken into their home and hearts had been an enigma to them and in many ways still was. And while it was often very exciting to live with Lucy, it was sometimes rather bewildering.

She waved excitedly. "He's dead!"

Like now.

"Yes, dear," Bernice said, climbing to her feet and beaming up at her great-niece. "So we gathered. Do tell us, who is he?"

"Why, Wilfred Whinnywicke!"

"Did she name the tomcat?" Bernice murmured out of the corner of her mouth.

"She names every creature," Lavinia whispered back.

"Aha!" they called up brightly, attempting to muster what they considered suitably sanguine expressions.

Lucy was not deceived. "Come now. You remember."

"No, dear," Lavinia admitted, grateful to not be required to pretend otherwise. As far as she could tell, Lucy was the only member of the family to carry a Thespian gene. It must have come from her father's side of the family—the side Bernice preferred not to acknowledge. "I'm afraid we don't. To whom are you referring?"

"Not whom, precisely, but *what*. The tontine thingie with the rubies!"

"It's not a true tontine—" Bernice started to correct Lucy but was cut short.

"I'm referring to the fortune that goes to those left holding the bag, as it were, in India fifty years ago. The horrible Mr. Whinnywicke has died, very probably performing the only considerate—not to mention timely—act of his life, leaving you, Aunt Lavinia, one of only four people left to share the booty."

Enlightenment dawned in Lavinia's blue-gray eyes, once and still her chief attraction. "Oh! *That* Whinnywicke. *Sergeant* Whinnywicke. I haven't thought of him in years. Dead, is he?" She sniffed at some memory. "Well, I'm not surprised. Drank like a fish throughout the entire siege. On the sly, as you young people say, but everyone knew it. Disgraceful. Fate was bound to catch up with him."

"Fate riding a hobbled horse," Lucy replied glibly. "He lived over eighty years."

Lavinia ignored this.

"He was that awful fellow at Patnimba with you?" Bernice said.

"Yes. Terrible man. One of those small-minded fellows whose lofty opinion of themselves is entirely without basis. It was small wonder the native soldiers despised him. Not the sort of person with whom one wants to wait out a siege." Her gaze grew pensive as she recalled long-past events.

Fifty-one years earlier, in an effort to marry off Lavinia after she had failed to "take" the previous two seasons, Lord Litton had shipped his eighteen-year-old daughter off to her godparents in India, Lord and Lady Pictard. They'd assured him that, between the civilian and military population, the pickings there were very good for eligible young ladies. Lavinia had fallen happily in with the plan, more thrilled by the prospect of adventure than that of a husband.

She did not receive any offers of marriage; she did, however, have an adventure. Though not one she would ever have expected or wanted. While she was visiting a small military hill station called Patnimba with a party of other "young people," the Sepoy rebellion broke out. Besides herself, the besieged party had been composed of Lady Pictard; a pair of young Englishmen, Lord John Barton and Kimberly Mills; a French banker named Bernard DuPaul and his daughter Arnette; and the eighteen-year-old son of the Portuguese ambassador, Bento Oliveria, along with his school friend, Luis Silva.

For long months the small garrison of soldiers and their officers held off sporadic attempts to overrun the compound, the roads around being held by rebels.

"So . . . *not* the tomcat," Bernice finally murmured, breaking Lavinia's reverie.

Lucy, who'd been leaning on her forearms out the window casement as she patiently waited for her great-aunts to return from wherever their imaginations had transported them, straightened. "Beg pardon?"

"We'd been speculating on whose demise you were celebrating and Lavinia proposed it might have been that tomcat who's always bothering Pauline. I confess, for a few seconds I was afraid you might have—what is the theatrical parlance? Oh, yes—*done him in* yourself."

Lucy's eyes widened in surprised amusement and perhaps, to a lesser degree, chagrin.

"Better than thinking you might have disposed of the deacon," Lavinia said.

The merriment in Lucy's hazel eyes turned to confusion. "The deacon?"

"Yes. I considered that you might have been, er, eulogizing the deacon. I hear he's taken to his bed again."

"That's ridiculous. If the deacon were dead I would gloat silently like any—" She broke off and shook her head as though to clear it. "My darlings, do you understand how close we are to being *saved*?"

Bernice leaned slightly toward her sister, a little alarmed. "Were we in danger?"

"I believe she is referring to our financial circumstances," Lavinia said, "not what you and I would call danger. Lucy undoubtedly has a different understanding of the term."

"You think she is being dramatic?"

"Of course, dear," Lavinia replied. "She is an actress."

"Did you hear me?" Lucy called down.

"Yes, dear. And we are most gratified!" Bernice called back up to her, happy, as always, to humor Lucy.

"I shall be down forthwith to explain."

"That would be lovely," Lavinia said, sinking gingerly back down to her knees. They tended to ache these days. "I've only a few more tulips to plant and I should hate to stop now."

Lucy, in the process of lowering the casement window, abruptly stopped. A spark of devilry appeared in her eye. "Great-Aunt Lavinia?"

"Yes, dear?"

"You know that notion you had about my having a part in the disappearance of that awful tomcat? Not that he *has* disappeared," she added, "only that if he *were* to have disappeared and I should want to dispose of the, er, evidence, I should . . . well, you're not going to plant anything near the rhododendron, are you?"

The two ladies froze.

Lucy let them suffer a full ten seconds before bursting into laughter. "Sometimes, my darlings, given your rather odd ideas about me, I really do wonder that you ever let me in the front door. I am *teasing!*"

She shook her head and closed the window, leaving her great-aunts to stare after her with the same bemusement that they had worn to one degree or another ever since Lucille Rose Eastlake had arrived on their doorstep.

CHAPTER

2

"Lady Pictard was the first casualty from our little party, the victim of indiscriminate gunfire, but alas, not the last. Kimberly Mills followed closely after, then Arnette DuPaul."

They were sitting around a small wrought iron table in the conservatory overlooking the back garden. It used to be a very nice back garden but, as with the rest of Robin's Hall, time had been quick to take back what two full-time gardeners had once kept at bay. Weeds had sprung between the flagstones and the boxwood hedge had grown into wall that obscured any view of the marble fountain at the bottom of a once-manicured lawn, now an overgrown jungle of vegetation.

At Lucy's behest, Lavinia was relating the story of the siege of Patnimba. It was a tale Lucy knew by heart but never tired of hearing. Her great-aunt paused and Lucy took up the narrative. "There were only seventeen of you left in the little hill station fortress, five civilians and a dozen soldiers, by the time the lookout saw a rider approaching on horseback." She lashed imaginary reins over an imaginary horse's withers.

"He came thundering up the road, shouting for the gates to open. For a few minutes it looked like he might make it, but forty yards from the compound his horse was struck and killed and the rider pinned beneath the carcass."

Lavinia nodded. "I thought he was lost but then without any thought to their own safety, Lord John Barton and Lt. Burns rode out beneath the cover of our soldiers' gunfire and somehow managed to drag him to safety." Her eyes shone with admiration for the bravery of the young men and, Lucy guessed, one young man in particular.

"The rider proved to be very young, more a lad than a man, and though he gave his name as Robert Smith, what with his skin being the color of tea and his strangely accented voice, his ethnicity was indiscernible.

"Within a day, he had recovered sufficiently to insist on leaving, emphatic that he had information that was imperative be delivered. There was no stopping him. And so, an hour before daybreak the next morning, he prepared to leave."

Lucy had often imagined the scene, flickering torchlight illuminating a small circle of people surrounding the lad: the pair of Portuguese lads, a middle-aged banker, a young English lord, and a brave girl standing alongside those few soldiers not manning the stockade.

"What happened next?" Lucy prompted, though she knew.

"While Mr. Smith was packing supplies into his saddlebag, he dislodged a pouch. His expression grew tight, as though recalling something he'd as soon have forgotten. He hesitated a moment then handed the bag to Monsieur DuPaul."

"The banker?"

Lavinia nodded. "'I can't take these with me,' the boy said. 'It would be disastrous should they be found on my person.'"

"I wonder what he meant by that?" Bernice pondered at this point just as she had a hundred times before and, just as she had a hundred times before, replied, "I fear we shall never know."

"I asked the boy what was in the pouch but all he said was, 'They're mine, don't worry on that account.' Then he seemed to come to a decision, for he said, 'You've already done so much for me. Would you do one more thing and keep this until I return for them?'

"Lord John and I traded despairing looks at his brave words, neither of us willing to acknowledge what was uppermost in our minds: Mr. Smith wasn't likely to live to return. Hundreds of rebels waited outside in the darkness. But Lt. Burns, then the most senior officer remaining, had no such compunction.

"'But what if you . . .' he started to say but then, looking at the brave lad standing in front of him, faltered.

"'Die?' Robert Smith shrugged. 'So be it. If I do, divvy them up between the lot of you. You saved my life. God willing, you'll have saved a good many more if I can reach my destination.'"

"But Lord John pressed him to give you some name that you might contact in the eventuality of his death," Lucy said.

"Yes," Lavinia said. "Lord John was always scrupulous about doing the right thing, though he got no pleasure in having to remind the lad that his chances of making his destination were slight.

"It didn't seem to bother Smith. He swung up into the saddle and declared with an almost savage pride, 'I haven't got a family.'"

"But then the banker spoke up," Lucy said. "'And just how long are we to wait for you to come fetch these . . . whatever they are?' he demanded angrily."

"I think his anger was more for the situation than the lad," Lavinia explained. "'What are we to do with them if you don't return? The fact is that none of us might make it out of here alive.'

"I felt my flesh grow cold at his words. I knew our chances of survival grew worse with each passing day but until that morning I had never allowed myself to appreciate what might befall me.

"I fear I must have looked faint. But then, I felt a hand brace my elbow and an arm reach around to support me and I heard John say, 'We will,' and his calm confidence restored my courage." Lavinia's gaze had grown distant but then she came to a sense of her surroundings with a start, a soft blush rising in her papery thin cheeks.

"Over the weeks of enforced intimacy, we had become close friends," she said in a hushed voice.

More than friends; Lavinia had fallen in love with the young Englishman.

"Anyway," Lavinia hurried on, "Monsieur DuPaul kept insisting Robert Smith say how long we should hold on to the purse until finally the young man threw up his arms and blurted out a time. 'Fifty years,' he said. And then he spurred his horse through the narrow gap of the gate.

"I watched until he disappeared, silently praying I would not hear gunfire and offering a word of thanks when I did not. But then I heard someone emit a low whistle of astonishment. I turned to find the Portuguese boys staring at a mound of colored stones in Monsieur DuPaul's palm.

"'There's a fortune in rubies here,' Luis Silva said. Then, 'What should we do with them?'"

"And so you made a pact!" Bernice burst in excitedly.

"Indeed," Lavinia said. "It was Lord John who suggested it, more as a way to bolster our courage than of any thought of future rewards. We decided we would honor Mr. Smith's request and when he returned, we would have a celebration, give him his rubies, and demand the story of how he had come by them."

"And if he *didn't* return?" Lucy prompted, though she already knew the answer.

"If he had not returned by the time we were rescued, Monsieur DuPaul was to take them back to France; with all the nationalities represented it seemed the most central location. He would enter them into an account at his bank, registering all our names—civilians, officers, and soldiers alike—as co-owners. And if Mr. Smith did not claim them sometime during the next fifty years, we agreed to meet in in Saint-Girons and divide them up amongst those still living. Like a tontine.

"Two of our number did not live to see the end of the siege and several others died of wounds sustained there. But then a rescue expedition arrived and managed to evacuate the rest of us. We dispersed, each going back to the lives we'd led before." She sighed and it seemed to Lucy a sigh from a place deep within her, from her soul. "I heard some years later that Lord John had married the daughter of an earl," she finished in a softly musing voice.

"Why didn't you write to him afterward?" Lucy blurted out and at once regretted it.

She had never asked aloud the question that had always vexed her. She had always thought that someday Lord John Barton would appear at Robin's Hall and explain himself. Because Lavinia was not a woman given to flights of fantasy and if she reckoned she and Lord John Barton were friends, then they were. Even if he hadn't loved her as she did him, surely he should have kept in touch with her?

But the years had come and gone and Lord John Barton had never appeared. Time had not diluted the emotion Lucy heard in Lavinia's voice every time she spoke of the man but if Lavinia had loved him so much, why hadn't she put forth an effort to win his heart?

"I'm sorry, Aunt Lavinia. I had no right to ask that," she said when Lavinia did not reply.

Lavinia only smiled, a little sadly. "My dear, the relationships one forms during times of crisis are at best suspect. Everything is heightened. Everything seems more precious, more vital." She glanced at Bernice for support. But Bernice had never left Robin's Hall except in the company of their parents and knew little of the world and even less of the sort of experiences Lavinia had encountered. Lucy had always considered her timid for all her blustery ways.

"Besides, I was only eighteen," Lavinia went on when no help was forthcoming from that quarter. "Everything seems doubly tragic when you are eighteen. And afterwards . . . Well, I never was a beautiful woman and our family, while genteel, is not titled and I had no fortune. In short, I had nothing to recommend me to a man who would inherit an earldom. And, of course, I never presumed a relationship born amidst blood and fear. I never considered it. A lady didn't."

I would have, Lucy thought. I would have fought tooth and nail for him.

But then, I am no lady.

CHAPTER

3

"—and if what I suspect is true, we shall have more than enough money to repair Robin's Hall to its past glory and better!" A quarter hour later, guilty over any pain her inquisitiveness might have caused, Lucy had turned the conversation from the past to speculation about the future.

"Bit of a hand here!" a voice called from outside the conservatory doors.

Lucy leapt up and opened the door, stepping aside for their raw-boned, fourteen-year-old maid-of-all-work—and never was an appellation more appropriate—Polly. The girl huffed past under the weight of a crowded silver tray, setting it down on the table before removing a plate of sandwiches. She deposited it proudly in front of the sisters.

"There's cucumber and butter or deviled egg." She stepped back, awaiting the sisters' approval. She didn't even bother looking at Lucy, who she considered only half a step above her in the social hierarchy.

"Look, Bernice," Lavinia said, helping herself to a thinly sliced triangle. "Polly has cut off all the crust. Isn't that nice?"

"Very nice, Polly. Quite like those our old cook used to serve." For some reason, Polly had undertaken as her personal mission the re-creation of an era that she had never known, nor, for that matter, had her mother or grandmother. She considered any comparison of her efforts to those of her long, long dead predecessors to be the highest form of compliment.

She pinked up, pleased, and hooked a strand of frizzed red hair behind a protruding ear. "Mind, don't you go ruining your dinner with too many of them now, Miss Bernice." Alas, the verisimilitude of Polly's re-creation did not extend to the deference those pantry ghosts had shown their betters. "I'll be back shortly," she announced and trudged back into the house.

"I do hope Polly is continuing with her typewriting lessons," Lavinia fretted, lowering her sandwich down toward the waiting maw of their omnivorous feline, Pauline. "I hate encouraging her illusions about her culinary prowess, but I should hate even more to hurt her feelings. But I am afraid once we are gone—"

"You won't be gone for a long, long time," Lucy said decisively. It had been touch and go with Lavinia this past spring and while the doctor had assured Lucy that her great-aunt had made a full recovery, she remembered all too vividly her great-aunt's awful helplessness and the despair in Bernice's square face.

"Yes, dear, but when we are, I should very much dislike Polly to be startled by the revelation that perhaps she is better suited to some other line of work."

"I'll encourage her to keep up with her typing lessons," Lucy promised.

Lavinia sighed gratefully. "Thank you." She reached over for the teapot. "I thought we'd sold all the silver."

"Most of it." Lucy raised the lid on the teapot, releasing a cloud of oolong-scented steam. She peered inside. "I couldn't bear to part with great-grandmother's tea service."

She saw no reason to tell her great-aunts that the decision not to sell had less to do with sentiment than pride. The silver dealer had made an insultingly low offer for the set and she'd already been forced to accept mere pittances for many of the things her great-aunts considered priceless. She simply couldn't stand to part with one more thing they valued, let alone give it away.

Lavinia and Bernice Litton had taken Lucy in when she'd had nowhere left to go. Having been orphaned by her parents' death in a train accident when she was seven, Lucy had spent the next four years being shunted from one distant relation to another, each having less obligation, or interest, in taking her than the last. The Litton ladies, her mother's long-estranged aunts, had been the last possible way station on what seemed an inevitable journey to the orphanage.

Despite their own poverty, Lucy's youth, their advancing years, and their complete lack of experience with children, especially the children of "artistic types," they had not hesitated for an instant before taking her in.

"Soon we shall all be able to afford as much sentiment as we care to indulge," Lucy said now, pouring out the tea. "We shall be able to put Robin's Hall to rights, make all the repairs, buy new furniture, and," she paused, her hazel eyes sparkling, "*hire gardeners.*"

Of all the trappings of a formerly gracious lifestyle, Lucy knew that the dereliction of the garden, even more than that of the house, weighed most heavily on the Litton sisters. And with Lavinia's prolonged illness this past spring, even the small plot they'd managed to maintain in some semblance of its former glory had shrunk to tablecloth size.

"Oh, I *do* hope you're not overestimating the value of those stones," Bernice said.

"From your description I should think not," Lucy reassured them. "Besides, you recall that Monsieur DuPaul had an appraisal done in Paris the last time one of your compatriots was," she floundered for a nice euphemism to make amends for the spontaneous vulgarity of having sung the news of Mr. Whinnywicke's demise, "taken from us."

Lavinia nodded. "Vaguely."

"They were worth nearly a quarter of a million pounds at the time. Undoubtedly, they are worth more now. And now that good old Whinnywicke has had the courtesy to withdraw from the proceedings—"

"Lucy!"

Lucy wrinkled her nose in a manner Bernice had always found both vulgar and adorable. "I am sorry. Don't mean to sound callous, but one can't fault his timing, can one? Especially with the anniversary just a few weeks away, leaving you in the envious position of being one of only four now left to split up the loot."

"Don't call it loot, dear," said Bernice. "It's common."

Lucy waved down this criticism. "All the bright young things speak this way. I daresay you would have too, had you been born in the same year as I, Aunt Bernice."

"Never," she said primly but Lucy thought she seemed secretly pleased.

As a girl, Lavinia had been considered the "spirited" Litton sister, always up for a spot of mischief and as like to thumb her nose at society's edicts—within reason, of course—as abide by them. Bernice had been the predictable, unadventurous sister.

"I don't know that I would trust Monsieur DuPaul's appraiser," Bernice said, returning to the subject at hand. "You know the French are prone to exaggeration."

Lucy, who had her share of French admirers, did indeed, but she was not the sort to let past experience dash her optimism. If she were, she'd have arrived on Robin's Hall's doorsteps a very different sort of girl.

"I daresay we'll see soon enough." She dropped two sugar lumps into Bernice's teacup, surreptitiously adding a third because Bernice liked her tea sweet and was embarrassed by the fact. "Tomorrow morning I will go into the city and make travel arrangements."

The city. It had been seven months since Bernice had sent word that Lavinia was "not feeling quite the thing" and suggested that "if it wasn't too much trouble, a short visit" from Lucy would do "wonders for Lavinia's spirits." She had come at once, in her anxiety forgetting to inform management that she would not be present for the evening's performance. Only a near-mortal illness would ever cause Bernice to send such a request.

She had arrived to find Lavinia even more ill than she'd feared. There had been nothing for it but to send for the doctor. Later that same day she had sent a message to the director of the operetta in which she'd been performing explaining that she would be unable to return to her role until Lavinia was out of the woods.

He had not been pleased; she'd developed a small following since her debut three years earlier and was being hailed as one of light opera's rising stars, whose "angular aristocratic looks are so at odds with her comedic aptitude as to make an irresistible combination" and whose soprano "exhibits a light effortlessness that cannot fail to charm."

She'd been fired.

It had proved costly in more ways than one. Everything she earned had been divided between paying the taxes on Robin's Hall and day-to-day necessities. She well realized that her great-aunts ought to sell the place and move to more modest—and cheaper— accommodations but they had spent their entire lives here. It would kill them to have to leave it.

Now they wouldn't have to.

And as an added bonus, it looked very likely she would be able to audition for the upcoming season's plum roles. She couldn't deny the pleasure of the thought of returning to the stage brought her, of hearing the audience's laughter as she delivered some saucy line, of basking in their applause and approval, their admiration and their cheers.

"How shall we get there?" Bernice asked. She sounded a little breathless. Bernice had only just made her curtsey in society when her father's financial ruin had eschewed any further seasons. She had never appeared to resent it, seeming content to stay at Robin's Hall. Traveling to France might be uncomfortably daunting for her.

"We shall take a train to Weymouth, I expect, and from there a ferry across the channel. Once we are in France, we shall see what is available to us. Perhaps we'll stay a few days in Bordeaux. There's no reason to hurry." She didn't bother to point out that they couldn't afford the cost of the higher-end, faster modes of travel. "On the way back we can take our time as well. Maybe tour the countryside, make a holiday of it."

Bernice and Lavinia exchanged a look.

"It will be fun. You'll see."

"How long shall we be gone?"

"A day to Weymouth and then one to cross the channel, two in Bordeaux and then a few days south to Monsieur DuPaul's little town, Saint-Girons. Call it a week. We'll allot a day to tidy up whatever legalities present themselves—though Monsieur DuPaul has assured me that everything has been taken care of. Then a week or so back. By month's end you shall be in gravy and I shall be auditioning for the soubrette role in Mr. Lehar's new operetta, *The Merry Widow*."

She regarded her great-aunts expectantly, fully anticipating that they would fall in with the plan. Why wouldn't they? There was nothing to worry about. True, she'd never been out of Great

Britain before and spoke barely a word of French but Brits traveled around Europe all the time. How difficult could it be?

She fixed them with an encouraging smile.

"You've been in correspondence with Monsieur DuPaul?" Bernice asked, looking mildly scandalized.

"Yes, of course. It's not as if we haven't been *waiting* for this day. You practically weaned me on the story of Patnimba." And the story of Lavinia's lost love. "You've known this date was coming for fifty years."

"Yes. Of course."

She divided a surprised gaze between them. "You're not offended that I've been in touch with Monsieur DuPaul, are you?"

"Oh, no! Not at all. Most enterprising of you." Both elderly ladies hastened to reassure her. "We have always been impressed by your perspicacity and foresight. Had only dear Papa been similarly blessed in his investments, this entire trip wouldn't be necessary."

They were spot-on, of course, but Lucy felt it only polite to modestly lower her gaze. She frowned as something occurred to her. "Do you feel up to making the trip, Lavinia?"

"Oh, yes. Quite. But feeling *able* to do something is not the same as wanting to do it." She flushed. "Are we really that desperately in need of the funds?"

In point of fact, they were, but Lucy considered it a testament to her acting ability, not to mention her skill in doctoring the household accounts, that her aunts did not know this and, God willing, never would. She did not want their later years troubled by worry.

"The money will allow us those little niceties that make life pleasant," she equivocated. *Like food.* "I really, *really* think we ought to go."

"I realize that, my dear," Lavinia said. "It's just that we haven't been away from Robin's Hall in a very long time."

"Not since Papa was alive," Bernice put in.

"The world has changed so much since then," Lavinia murmured, "and so have I."

Lucy suddenly understood. The last time Lavinia had left Robin's Hall she had been in a siege, fallen in love, witnessed death and sacrifice and courage. Since then she had lived, if not a reclusive life, a much confined one. Now she faced the prospect of once again meeting the only man she had ever loved.

It would be daunting for even the bravest of women to wonder if she would see reflected in his eyes the wasting effects of time and age. Especially since he had not found even in her glowing youth enough favor to marry her.

Lucy could not find it in herself to press her great-aunt into going if she did not want to. She simply would not ask it of her. They would make do. Things always had a way of working out.

"No," Lavinia suddenly said, her tone taking on an unexpected edge of firmness. "No. Of course, we shall go. Bernice and I have always felt terrible that you forsook your Calling to come and live with us last winter, and just when you were on the cusp of achieving Greatness."

"You had *pneumonia*," Lucy said, "and I was hardly on the cusp of achieving great—"

Lavinia held up her hand, cutting off Lucy's protest. "Nonsense. What you do is Art. *You* are Collectible."

Last fall Lucy had made the mistake of mentioning that her picture had been included in a set of cigarette cards of "Rising Stars of the Musical Stage." Confronted by her great-aunts' shock that she would allow her picture to be "manhandled by strange young men," she had blurted out: "It's not like that. It's a *collectible* card. Very respectable. Like stamp collecting. It's quite an honor, really."

Her great-aunts had not only bought into this minor fabrication, they had decided to embrace it as a symbol of Lucy's success.

Lucy simply hadn't the heart to point out that Kumquat the Boxing Kangaroo was also a Collectible.

For all that they'd never seen her perform, Bernice and Lavinia were her greatest fans. They had a scrapbook stuffed with newspaper and magazine clippings that included any mention of Miss Lucille Eastlake, any of which was proof enough that she was simply a secondary singer in lightweight, popular productions. But because they were gentlewomen, and she was a gentleman's great-granddaughter, they would never believe her capable of doing anything common. Which by default meant what she did was Art.

What she really did was sing light opera. Very light opera.

She winced inwardly.

"Well, I don't know that I'd call it *art* precisely, a few runs in the upper octaves and little swag and hop if you—"

"But it is," Bernice broke in determinedly. "*Art*. We know how you have been pining to once more enter into the service of your Muse. Just as we also know you won't be able to give yourself completely to your Muse if you are worrying over finances."

"I haven't been pining," Lucy went on. "Really. I've been quite content pottering about Robin's Hall, though I admit it will be fun to be back in the old limelight."

"We should like to see you on the stage someday, Lucy," Lavinia said. "Perhaps this season when you once again take your rightful place amongst opera's luminaries."

"*Operetta*. And I'm more of a lightning bug than a star."

They totally ignored this. "We won't be content until we do. And neither shall we be content until you are back where you belong, accepting the accolades of your adoring public."

"Adoring" was patently overstating the case, but one look at her great-aunts' faces and Lucy realized this was a battle she would not win. They would put down any protestation on her part as modesty.

"Are you sure, Aunt Lavinia?" she asked gently, holding her great-aunt's gaze.

Lavinia answered with a tender smile. "Entirely. Now then, you go into town tomorrow and make whatever arrangements you deem necessary."

"I shall probably stay over the night. Some of my old theatre pals are getting up a little party at the Savoy to wish a bon voyage to a friend. They have invited me to join them. I thought I might, if you can spare me?"

They could.

CHAPTER
4

Lucy did not enter the Savoy's American Bar at once. Instead she stood to the side by the doorway, drinking in the sounds and sights of London society at play. As always, it was crowded, every table occupied and the bar at the far end of the room nearly concealed by the gentlemen standing three-deep before it, all dressed in standard evening attire: black coattails, white waistcoats, and ties. Their well-groomed heads gleamed with pomade, the younger ones clean-shaven while those in their middle years sported carefully trimmed moustaches.

The music being played in the adjacent dining room filtered in through the open archway and mixed with the busy hum of conversation, punctuated by the tinkle of glass and the occasional laugh.

Ladies decorated the room like single stems of multicolored flowers, full-blown blooms of silk, lawn, and organdy trimmed with lace and beading and flounces. Deeply cut bodices exposed creamy bosoms and swanlike necks, unbowed by mounds of hair teased and piled to amazing heights and further augmented by enormous feathers and flowers.

The women were heavy-lidded and languid, animated by no more than the lift of a perfectly styled brow or the slight turn of a tiny smile, their voices well modulated and discreet. Lucy might have been among their numbers (except for the creamy skin part; she had a distressing tendency to freckle) but a certain maestro in a certain seaside town eloping with Lucy's mother before she had even officially debuted had forever changed his descendants' social status.

Truthfully, Lucy wouldn't have traded her lot for any of those around her. She enjoyed life far too much to learn to smile with her lips closed. Besides, even though her dress was not expensive—having been salvaged from the costume shop—it was at the very cutting edge of fashion, reworked by the magical fingers of Lucy's friend, a theatrical wardrobe mistress, into a facsimile of Mr. Poiret's latest creation, a "robe de Eugenie" of midnight-blue crepe de chine. It eschewed a pigeon-breasted bodice, having instead a low neckline embroidered with gold threads; a higher, more natural waist; and a tighter silhouette around her hips and thighs.

"Ah, there's our girl!" A clear tenor voice rose above the mob's buzzing. "What are you doing playing Shrinking Violet over there, Luce? Come here!"

Shrinking Violet? Not likely. Lucy threaded her way through the crowd toward where Margery—the only performer in the London music halls to be universally recognized by one name—sat on a stool at the end of the polished mahogany bar holding court over a half a dozen of his fellow actors and twice as many fans.

He was a middling man of middling years, his features even but unremarkable except for the brilliance of his light blue eyes, his ginger hair starting to recede even as his belly started to advance. One would scarce credit it, but for nearly twenty years Margery, born Jasper Martin, had reigned over London's vaudeville theatres. Later this week he was leaving on a much ballyhooed tour of France, "starting in the outlying towns and culminating in a command performance at the Moulin Rouge."

Lucy had met him the year she'd made her stage debut. It had been Margery who'd insisted she had far too lovely a voice to waste in music halls and had introduced her to the impresario who'd cast her in her first operetta. Though Margery and she had never again performed on the same stage, they'd remained close friends.

"Here, ducks, make way for our prodigal child," Margery said, shooing several people back so she could slip onto the barstool next to his. He waggled a playful finger. "Now, you wait here while I go see a man about a bottle of bubbly. We're celebrating, eh? I'll be right back."

In all likelihood the man was the maître d'hotel and Margery was going to put the pinch on him. Margery's presence in the American Bar at the Savoy was good for business, and Margery, who had been raised poor and never forgot the feeling, never paid for what he could get gratis.

"A pretty drink for a pretty girl." Jack Darling pressed a cut-glass tumbler into her hand. He was a slight, handsome man who, despite approaching middle years, still managed to secure all the plum second juvenile roles. Only when you stood close and under the unforgiving light of full day did you realize his blond hair was dyed and he was nearer forty than twenty.

She took a sip of her drink. Her eyes widened. "Say, what is this?"

"A new cocktail Ada made up called the Hanky-Panky. Like it?"

Ada was the Savoy's female bartender, an institution in her own right. The drink she'd concocted was sweet as a stolen kiss and went down easily. Maybe too easily. Like cherry phosphate. A soft little buzz tickled Lucy's senses. "Pretty potent stuff for a young lass like me."

"A couple more seasons treading the boards and you'll grow up fast enough. Would you rather something else?"

It *was* strong, but as this was a homecoming of sorts and she was thirsty and it was tasty, she decided to keep it. "No. It's swell."

"Is it true that you're going to audition for Mr. Davenport?"

"That's the plan. Whether he gives me the job is another thing. Keep your fingers crossed for me, will you? Cheers." She tipped her glass back and finished off the sweet concoction.

"I will. There now, your glass is empty! Can't have that." Before she could reply, he'd relieved her of the empty glass and replaced it with a fresh one from the tray sitting at his elbow. "There you go, kiddo. Bottoms up!"

He clinked his glass to hers and lifted it in a toast.

She raised the glass to her lips.

He frowned. "Wait. Something's missing . . ." He snapped his fingers. "Ada forgot to put a cherry in it. It ain't a proper Hanky-Panky without a cherry."

"Really, Jack, I don't—"

"Wait here. I'll be back in a jiff," he said, elbowing his way into the throng near the center of the bar.

She smiled after him. She had forgotten how much she enjoyed the camaraderie of actors and actresses, their energy and enthusiasm, quick wit and easy—all right, sometimes *too* easy—manners. But if actors tended to live only on the peaks or in the valleys, and sometimes ran the entire gambit of moods in between all in the course of a single conversation, they never criticized a person, only his performance. Which for many, she conceded, was one and the same thing.

It was small wonder she felt comfortable with them. She'd been acting since her parents' deaths, performing whatever role her father's far-flung family required of her, hoping against hope she'd be kept on for an extended run. First there'd been Uncle Mikhail, the music hall magician who'd always wanted a son and for whom she'd become a tomboy. Then came Cousin Caroline, who fancied herself a musician, so Lucy had taken up singing. And there'd been old Jonas Neubaum, whose relationship to her she never had figured out, but who loathed coarseness in any form, and for whom she'd learned etiquette. And in between there had been others, all wanting something else. *Someone* else.

None of them had kept her for more than a few months. She didn't blame them. Mikhail had been forced to move into a single-room apartment where there was simply no place for a girl. Cousin Caroline had been hauled off to an asylum. And Jonas Neubaum had accepted an acting job with a touring company. None of her father's many, if always auxiliary, relatives were affluent enough to keep her for long. Then it was off to the next household, the next county, the next audition.

Until she'd flat run out of relatives on her father's side and been forced to apply to her mother's family who, though much better bred, were no better off. By the time she'd arrived at Robin's Hall, only two Littons were left, a pair of spinster great-aunts. Truth be told, she hadn't expected to be allowed past the threshold, anticipating they had been cut from the same cloth as their mother, a woman who'd disowned her granddaughter and died never having spoken to her again.

Instead, she'd been welcomed and loved, if not always, well, *understood*.

She took another drink, enjoying an unaccustomed but pleasant lightheadedness. She really ought to have eaten before coming.

"Here you go." Jack arrived back at her side carrying a single cherry skewered on a toothpick. He dropped it unceremoniously into her drink, then, satisfied, leaned against the bar. "Now, tell me all about it, kid."

"There's nothing much to tell. I've been on vacation. Taking the waters."

"Sure, you have. Where have you really—oops!" He suddenly ducked his head, half turning away from her. "Say, Lucy, be a sport and move over here, right in front of me, will you?"

"And why am I moving here?" she asked as she obliged.

"Because there's a lady sitting at a table across the room with whom I recently shared a"—he glanced at her—"pleasant evening."

"So? I should imagine you would be happy to see her again."

"I would. Except that she's with her husband."

"Oh." Lucy felt her cheeks warm. Silly. You'd think that by now she'd be used to the looser morals that surrounded theatres and music halls. Curious, she turned her head to get a look at Jack's married lady friend.

Her gaze never made it past the first occupied table.

"Thanks, Lucy. You're a peach," Jack whispered. She barely noted his words. She was too busy staring.

Because sitting at a nearby linen-clad table was the most gorgeous man in the room, perhaps in the entire city. He was dark, his sable-colored hair brushed into disciplined order, black pirate's eyes smoldering beneath heavy winged brows. A perfectly chiseled pair of lips was set in a straight line above a square jaw and a wickedly cleft chin. His skin looked nearly bronze above his brilliant white dress shirt, waistcoat, and bow tie.

She figured him to be near thirty and, from his expression, awfully serious for a pirate. Pirates, in her estimation, ought to have a ready and devil-may-care look. Unless they weren't very successful pirates . . .

He was writing something on a paper in front of him. When he finished, he looked up and spoke. Only then did she realize he was sharing his table with two other people: a dark-haired lady of a similar age, very elegant and even more somber, and directly across from him, an equally serious-looking taffy-haired fellow.

"I wonder who died?" Lucy murmured as the gorgeous man reached across the table and took the young lady's hand, not in an intimate way, but more in a gesture of appeal.

Looking vaguely impatient, the woman carefully disengaged her hand, took the paper he'd written on, and rose. The men leapt to their feet, the smaller man pulling out the woman's chair.

". . . unused to being surrounded by vulgar theatre sorts," the woman said with obvious displeasure, looking in the bar's direction.

It took a few seconds for Lucy to realize that the woman was referring to Margery and his pals. Which included her. Not that Lucy cared. She was too distracted by studying the pirate. Purely for the sake of her craft. Musical comedies were simply stuffed with pirates.

He was, Lucy noted, just as yummy standing as he'd been sitting. He had the physique of an athlete, tall, trim, but broad-shouldered and long-legged. The other fellow . . . oh, who cared about the other fellow?

Her pirate said something more to the woman. She shook her head and hesitated a second before reluctantly touching his cheek in a carefully conciliatory gesture. She turned to the other gentleman, who hastily moved to her side and escorted her out the door. Probably her husband. Poor sot.

And the pirate must be her brother, Lucy decided. That explained the mixture of fondness and annoyance in her attitude. And the reason for her put-out expression. She looked like she'd just told him that she didn't *ra-lly* care for polo ponies and would he kindly keep that in mind for future birthdays and while he was at it do something about the one he'd given her as it was eating Grandmama's prize hibiscus. And as an aside, what was he thinking, taking Biff and her (Lucy had decided the taffy fellow's name had to be "Biff") to a place crammed with *theatre* sorts?

She had *that* sort of look. *Terribly* well-bred and *terribly* rich and *terribly* bored with the whole thing . . .

Lucy smiled at her nonsensical flight of fancy just as the gorgeous fellow turned his head. Their eyes met.

For one brief second everyone else in the room blurred into shadows. Sound faded until the only thing she heard was the beating of her heart.

He frowned, looking puzzled, making her aware that she was staring. Like a vulgar theatre sort.

She wasn't vulgar! She had two great-aunts who'd made it their mission in life to see that she wasn't. But she *had been* staring and that *was* vulgar and *that* embarrassed her.

Though it needn't.

With his looks and obvious wealth, he must get stared at all the time by chippy young things on the make. Rather than comfort her, it only made her feel dismal. She didn't want to be just another, well, chippy.

So, she shifted her gaze a fraction of an inch, tossed her head a little, and pretended to laugh as though in response to something going on behind him. The man's black brows dipped into a vee of confusion. She raised a hand and wiggled her fingertips coyly at an imaginary friend, keeping her gaze fixed beyond the pirate's shoulder.

His black eyes narrowed. He pointed questioningly at his chest.

She moved her gaze deliberately back to his face then widened her eyes, feigning surprise. Lowering her lashes demurely, she shook her head and pointed behind him.

He turned around. Since there was no one behind him but an extremely confused-looking waiter, she took the opportunity to do the only sensible thing she could think to do: She fled through the crowd to the other end of the bar.

On her way, she bumped straight into Margery.

"Ah, there you are, lambkins," Margery said as if he'd been looking for her. She eyed him wryly, knowing full well he'd been holding court with his fans and had likely forgotten all about her. While she didn't doubt his affection for her was sincere, she also knew stardom was his first and foremost love.

He led her to his barstool, insisting she take it. Then, noting the slight difficulty with which she climbed atop, he shook his finger lightly under her nose. "You've been drinking cocktails, haven't you? Jack's doing, I suppose." He clucked his tongue. "You're far too young to be drowning yourself in gin, toots. Leave that to the old roués like Jack and myself."

Lucy laughed, forcefully dismissing the gorgeous dark fellow from her thoughts. "Then what should I drown myself in?"

"Why, champagne, of course." He turned to his fans and announced, "Step lively, m'dears! We're celebrating Lucy's return to the fold. You *do* know who she is, don't you?"

"Margery!" Lucy protested, hot blood rushing to her cheeks. None of these people were likely to have the vaguest notion who she was. She'd only had credited roles in three productions—

"I should say I do!" a plug-shaped youngster with fair, curly hair announced in triumphant, if slightly slurred, tones. "That's Miss Lucille Eastlake."

Lucy's eyes grew round with astonished pleasure. Someone had recognized her! She laughed. No . . . much to her horror, she realized she was tittering. She cleared her throat and attempted to look as though being recognized was standard for her. "You've seen me perform?"

"Well, no," the young man admitted. "I don't go in much for warbly stuff. You were in a pack of cigarettes. On the back of a card. I saved it. You were April." He leaned closer to her, eyes wide and earnest. "But"—his whiskey-soaked breath washed over her face—"if I ever were to spend money on a ticket to a show like that, it'd sure be yours and that's the truth."

She tried not to laugh. He earnestly believed he was complimenting her. "Why, thank you."

He rocked back on the balls of his feet, grinning with gratification, clearly more inebriated than she'd originally suspected. But then, so was she. "'low me to introduce meself. The name's Charlie. Charlie Cheddar."

"Charlie?" Margery exclaimed indignantly. "You mean to say you are named 'Charlie' and yet you have never heard Miss Eastlake sing 'In the Moonlight, Charlie'?"

"No," the boy stuttered, nonplussed. "I haven't."

"And never shall now," Margery said ominously, "seeing how the *The Debutante's Complaint* ended after only a five-month run. Too bad. The critics universally acclaimed Miss Eastlake's late second act song in the unappreciated and underutilized role of the maid, Poppy, to be the highlight of the show. The sole highlight, unfortunately. So I'm afraid you've lost your chance. Pity, seeing as your name is Charlie and all."

"Oh!" The boy looked stricken.

"Unless, well, unless you could convince Miss Eastlake to sing it . . ."

"Margery!" She should have expected this sort of nonsense from him. He was a diligent booster of his friends. Even when they didn't want to be boosted.

"Oh, *would you*?" Charlie Cheddar breathed.

"I'm sure the Savoy's orchestra—"

"Ach!" Margery broke in with a derisive snort. "Can barely hear them all they way in here. And what is that they're playing? A dirge? Terrible stuff. Bound to give a fellow indigestion if he listens too long. Come on, ducks. Sing us a tune."

"Oh, yes, please," Charlie begged.

"I—"

"Wouldn't you like to hear Miss Eastlake sing?" Margery asked the group around them. At once, a chorus of yeses answered him. She was not vain enough to think any of them shared an honest desire to hear her sing. Politeness stirred their assent. What else could they do but agree?

Still, it was rather nice that they sounded sincere and since she knew from past experience that Margery was not going to let it alone until she'd acquiesced, she might as well enjoy herself.

"One song," she warned.

"One song it is," he agreed and before she knew it, he'd clasped her around the waist and popped her atop the bar.

CHAPTER 5

Her great-aunts would die of mortification if they saw her perched up here. Simply die.

Luckily, mortification and Lucy had only a negligible acquaintance. She'd been in so many should-be mortifying situations throughout her childhood that if she had taken to fainting whenever anything embarrassing happened she would have spent the vast majority of her childhood insensate.

She took a sip from the glass Margery handed her, inhaled deeply, and as the small circle of people about them hushed, began the sprightly, charming little tune that had first won her the notice of the London critics.

> "During the day I see your face is funny,
> Can't call you handsome when it's sunny,
> But by the moon's much kinder light,
> Girls like me lack perfect sight . . ."

And then she launched into the rousing chorus:

> "In the Moonlight, Charlie,
> You're a dandy,
> Words like honey, lips like candy,
> You may not have a handsome vis
> But by gum, by moonlight, you're swell to kiss!"

It was a ridiculous song, but the tune was bright and catchy and so by the time she finished the last line, everyone around her was joining in to sing the chorus. When she'd finished, she performed a seated curtsey and slipped from the bar lightly to her feet only to be confronted by Charlie Cheddar's rapt, round face.

"That was wonderful," he said. "Wonderful!"

Good heavens, the boy didn't actually think she'd been singing to him? Why, what a sweet kid!

"Thank you."

"Do you think . . . That is, would you be so kind as to, well, give me your autograph?"

"My *autograph*?" No one had ever asked her for her autograph before! "I've never—that is, I would be delighted, Mr. Cheddar."

"Charlie."

"Charlie. But I don't have anything with which to write."

"No?" The young man looked crestfallen.

"Now, now. You mustn't disappoint your public, Lucy." Margery, who'd been watching the little byplay with avuncular amusement, intervened. "I shall return anon with scribbling apparatus. Be patient!" Once more, he vanished into the crowd.

Darling Margery, she thought, accepting the new glass of champagne the curly-haired youngster offered. She smiled at him over the rim. He beamed back.

"Large crowd here tonight," she said when it became clear that her young swain had used up his small store of conversation.

"Yes," Charlie replied eagerly before falling once again into worshipful, and silent, staring.

"What sort of theatre do you like, Charlie?"

"None."

"Oh."

She looked around, hoping Margery wouldn't be too much longer. The American Bar had gotten even more crowded, every table now ringed with elegant ladies and gentlemen who'd stopped for a post-theatre cocktail.

"You are even more beautiful in person than on your card."

Well, if a fellow were capable of only a few words, those were certainly worthy ones. She dimpled, causing his mouth to slam shut again and fiery red color to bloom in his apple-round cheeks.

"Here you go, Lucy." Margery reappeared, holding out a new and expensive-looking silver Conklin fountain pen. Probably a gift from one of his admirers. "And mind you don't misplace that because—"

"Yes, yes. I promise."

"Good, because it's—"

"Is that *the* Margery? But I simply *adore* you!" Whatever Margery had been about to say was forgotten as an ardent female fan seized his arm and pulled him around to face her.

Lucy, well used to the demonstrativeness of Margery's admirers, particularly the female ones, turned back to Charlie Cheddar, the fountain pen at ready. "Now then, where shall I sign?"

The question proved a poser. "I . . . I don't know. Gosh."

"Have her sign your cuff," someone suggested.

"The menu."

"Napkin."

"Will you sign *my* menu, Miss Eastlake?" another young man asked.

"Hey. Miss Eastlake is signing *my* menu," Charlie said with some asperity. "You can wait your turn."

"After you're done with theirs, can you sign my menu, too?" a new voice asked. "I saw you perform the part of Honoria in *The Catch of the Season* last November. You smoked a cigarette on stage! It was . . . swell!"

"I nearly choked every time I set the vile thing to my lips," she confided with a grin.

She'd been warned beforehand that playing the part of a young girl who had yet to make her bow but smoked behind her parents' backs might shock the older audience members. Apparently it had not shocked everyone. And even though she knew that male competitiveness had more to do with her current popularity than an appreciation of her voice—or whatever it was they appreciated—it felt good. No, it felt *grand.*

"Let me get you another glass of champagne, Miss Eastlake," Charlie said and, before she could refuse, hurried off.

Margery leaned close, whispering in her ear. "Go on, ducks. Enjoy yourself!"

So she did. She scribbled her name on the menu a young man handed her and presented it with a flourish. No sooner had she finished with that one than another took its place and then another. She flushed, smiled, and flirted, alternately taking sips of a champagne glass that miraculously never went dry. She traded quips with the various young men handing her items to be signed, her signature becoming bolder with each autograph. It was ridiculous. It was nonsensical. *It was wonderful!*

"Miss? Excuse me, miss."

She turned, her hand already stretched out to accept whatever this new petitioner might want autographed, and froze.

Her pirate stood before her.

He looked horribly self-conscious. "You . . ." Their gazes

caught. Held. He frowned again. He frowned an awful lot, her pirate.

Her pirate. She smiled, floating on the euphoria of public adulation and more alcohol than she'd ever consumed at one time. He looked so nonplussed. Rather sweet, really . . . Why was he standing there?

Oh, yes! She remembered. He was waiting for her autograph. And now that he was here, he was clearly too embarrassed to ask her for it. It was adorable.

She smiled graciously. "No need to be bashful, my good man. I'll be happy to sign your. . . ." She looked around for his menu or card or napkin and didn't see anything she could write on. "What is it you wish me to sign?"

His scowl deepened. "What? I don't want you to sign anything."

She blinked, feeling a little muddled. "You don't?"

Her heart began pattering pleasantly in her chest. He couldn't be . . . Why, he wasn't going to ask her to join him at his table? Well, of course he was! How forward! How naughty! But how *deliciously* tempting! She forced herself to remember her great-aunts.

"Oh, I couldn't possibly!" she fluttered as she wondered if perhaps she could.

"Couldn't what?"

"Accept an invitation to dine from a complete stranger. I mean, I am sure you're a very nice man and all but—"

"*What?*" Deep color swept up her pirate's neck, turning his tanned face an even richer color. "Whatever are you talking about?"

She frowned, all interior fluttering abruptly halting in the face of his explicitly *un*flirtatious tone. "What am *I* talking about? What are *you* talking about?"

"My pen."

"What?"

"You have my pen. I would like it back."

She stared at him. "Now see here. I may have been precipitous in declining an invitation you hadn't yet finished—"

"*Finished?*" he cut in, startled into rudeness. "I hadn't *started* one. Why would you make such an assumption?"

Assumptions? He didn't . . . ? She wasn't . . . ? *He hadn't . . . ?!* Oh, dear. Pride alone allowed her to keep her chin up. "I saw the look in your eye."

"*What?* There was no look in my eye."

"There was," she said. "Which is how I deduced your intention. It's not the first time this sort of thing has happened to me, you know." It was the second time. The first had been an invitation from a middle-aged, overweight financier who'd ambushed her at the stage door and which, needless to say, she'd refused in no uncertain terms. But the gorgeous man with the cleft chin needn't know that. A girl had her pride.

"That was *not* my intention."

"You're self-conscious," she said, with dawning understanding. "I daresay you don't generally approach strange women in hotel bars."

He opened his mouth. Closed it. Opened it again. "No. I do not."

"You don't look the type," she agreed. "Which is why you are now attempting to mask your embarrassment by coming up with an excuse for your impulsive act. One that will, as they say, allow you to save face."

His frown had disappeared, replaced by an expression of amazement. "Incredible," he murmured.

"Yes, I know," she said demurely. "I am good at reading people. It's what I do, after all." She fluttered her lashes just to let him know there were no hard feelings. "Certainly this is not the first time nor, dare I say, shall it be the last that a gentleman has sought an introduction through unusual means. But that's no reason to claim ownership of a very expensive pen that does not belong to you."

"But it *does*." He was openly exasperated now, running a hand through his hair. Just as she'd suspected it would, it tousled up into thick, loose curls. "Are you listening to me, young lady?"

She flushed. As a matter of fact, she hadn't been. "Of course. But if the pen is yours how then could my friend Mr. Margery have loaned it to me, making me promise to look after it?" she asked reasonably enough, because, truth be told, she was becoming a bit annoyed he wouldn't simply own up to being overwhelmed by a desire to speak to her.

"I have no idea," he said, by all appearances attempting to master a nearly equal frustration.

"Of course you don't."

"But it *is* mine and I would very much appreciate it if you would return it to me."

This was getting out of hand. "Now see here, this is a very expensive instrument and I am not going to simply hand over my friend's pen so you can preserve your dignity."

"*What* dignity?" he demanded through clenched teeth. "Everyone is staring at us. And I *know* it is expensive. It is one of the reasons I am willing to make a public spectacle of myself in demanding its return. That, and the fact that *it was a gift*."

She looked around. Those in their immediate vicinity had stopped talking and were regarding them with amused interest. A small group nearby had even turned their chairs for a better view.

Heat swept into Lucy's face and suddenly she was eight years old again and at her great-grandmother's house, being introduced to the Tartar for the first and only time while Uncle Mikhail stood by, hat in hand, extolling Lucy's many virtues as a battalion of servants looked on: She could mimic any bird, sing like a nightingale, sit quiet as a cat at a mouse hole through even the longest sermon, even cook. Some.

"Why she can brew up a pot of—" he'd continued.

"Be still," Gertrude Litton's voice had cut across Mikhail's words like a whiplash. "You're making a spectacle of yourself."

She had turned away without another word.

The butler had ushered them out, and they had passed beneath the amused and pitying gazes of the assembled servants.

Though since then Lucy had turned making a spectacle of herself into a career, she did so on her terms, fully in charge of the role, the stage, and her lines. Now memories of that long-ago encounter washed over her, the feeling of public humiliation biting as acid. Her cheeks grew warm.

"Hey! If Miss Eastlake says thas her pen, then ish her pen." Charlie Cheddar suddenly reappeared. He'd apparently tucked into a few more drinks in the interim and was now prepared to play knight-errant, which was categorically the *last* thing she wanted. "You better clear out if you know whas good fer you, mister."

"Oh, for the love of Mike," the gorgeous man muttered.

"Put 'em up," her blond champion commanded, raising his fists and wobbling slightly where he stood.

"Would you please tell your young man to put his hands down so we can settle this matter?"

"He's not my young man," Lucy said, desperately wanting to escape the growing snickers of their impromptu audience. "And as far as I am concerned the matter is settled. Good evening." She wheeled around and started to move away. He took a step after her.

Riiiippp.

She stopped dead.

Laughter, surprised laughter, the kind people take care to quickly stifle but that invariably burbles up again in spite of one's best intentions, rose all around her. With a horrible sense of foreboding, she twisted at the waist and looked down. The seam up the back of her gown had ripped open, exposing the very sheer petticoat beneath. The hem of her dress was caught under one of his highly polished shoes.

"Ohhhhh!" A wail of distress escaped her throat. She looked up and met his gaze. "*Do something!*"

Without a second's hesitation, he pulled off his tuxedo jacket and wrapped it around her shoulders. "Come on," he said, taking her elbow in hand and moving her forward.

"You cad!"

Before she realized what was happening, Charlie had grabbed hold of the dark-haired man's shoulder and spun him around. She turned just in time to see the youngster's fist collide with the gorgeous would-be pirate's jaw and his eyes go wide.

He crumbled to her feet.

CHAPTER
6

"Mister! Mister!" A frantic female voice called Professor Ptolemy Archibald Grant from blissful oblivion.

It had to be *her*. The strange young lady in the dark blue dress. For some unknown reason she'd been staring at him earlier and then, when caught at it, pretended to wave at someone behind him. A short time later he'd spotted her sitting atop the hotel bar leading a pack of semi-inebriants in what he assumed was some music hall ditty. And *then* she'd taken his pen.

What a peculiar girl.

He stirred. A sharp pain in his jaw greeted him on the threshold of consciousness and oblivion beckoned him back. Though he didn't generally consider himself cowardly, he nonetheless decided to accept oblivion's invitation, it being preferable to what he recalled of the last few minutes before he'd been laid a facer. Or most of the evening before that, for that matter.

That decision, unfortunately, was denied him as the girl calling his name now added a physical element to her insistence by vigorously shaking his shoulder. Lights exploded across the backs of his eyelids. His jaw throbbed.

"Someone help me with him!"

That brought him fully alert. He had already made a spectacle of himself. "*No.* I'm fine. Just give me a second."

He opened his eyes and squinted at the face floating above him. A long coil of satiny brown hair had come down and was spilling over her shoulder. Other than that, he couldn't make out much. Except that she had eyes the color of the green-gold quartz he'd once seen decorating the ceremonial breastplates of an Aztec king.

"You most certainly are not fine. Charlie laid you flat out."

Charlie must be the young man. "He punched me. Where is he?"

"Gone. Let me help you up."

"No. Please." He winced. "Don't do anything. You've done quite enough."

His vision had cleared sufficiently for him to see her lips press tightly together before, ignoring his refusal, she scooted behind him and slid an arm around his shoulders. What did she expect to be able to do? The top of her head barely reached his chin and if she weighed a hundred pounds, he'd be surprised. At six two and nearly fourteen stone—

She heaved him upright with unexpected strength, the sudden movement making his head throb. "Ow!"

"Sorry. Someone get him a glass of water."

"I don't want a glass of water." Holding his head, he climbed painfully to his feet.

She reached out to steady him but he scowled fiercely enough to make her snatch her hand back.

"If you would just kindly return my pen I won't trouble you any longer." He made no effort to hide his sarcasm.

She sighed. "You're not still going on about that, are you?"

"Yes," he said. "I am." The pen had been a gift from Cornelia. He'd hate to think what she'd say if he lost it; he'd lost too many of her other gifts. It didn't matter that he hadn't actually *lost* the pen; his having allowed it to be stolen wasn't going to materially change Cornelia's reaction. Not that she would cause a flap; Cornelia never flapped. But her disappointment was worse. It was so ripe with fatalistic assumptions.

Now that it was clear he wasn't in danger of dying or leaking blood anywhere, the crowd around them had begun to disperse. The girl, still draped in his jacket, hovered, probably due to guilt.

She had a fresh, expressive face crowned by a cloud of rich brown waves. Her clipped chin; wide, delicate lips; straight, thin nose; and bright hazel eyes were too animated and her bones too angular for beauty, but she possessed a sort of high-strung thoroughbred attractiveness. A few freckles dusted the tops of sharp cheekbones. She was quite lovely in an odd, fey sort of way.

"Listen, young man." *Young man?* He was probably over a decade older than her. She looked about sixteen. "No one is paying us any attention now. You needn't keep up this pitiful charade."

He stiffened. That she considered him "pitiful" wounded him in a place he hadn't even realized was vulnerable.

"So, let's just call it a night, shall we?"

Damned if she didn't sound sorry for him.

His pride, rarely entering into many equations—having been taught from the nursery that personal pride was vulgar—nonetheless rose to the occasion.

"No," he said. "We shall not. I have no idea how you have come into possession of my pen but I will give you the benefit of a doubt and assume it was in an innocent albeit highly unlikely manner.

"Nonetheless, by whatever offices, it went missing. I left it on the table when I followed my companions to the doorway. When I returned, the pen was gone. Or rather, not *gone*, precisely. It was in your hand."

Despite his assurance that he trusted her integrity, he could see her take umbrage with what was, if he was being honest—and he was always honest—a very nasty implication.

She drew up all of the few inches she possessed. The green in her eyes became shards of colored glass. "Now see here. This pen belongs to my friend Margery—"

"Oh! Oh, dear. No. It doesn't." A dapper, pleasant-looking middle-aged man edged between them, smiling sheepishly. "I was in a hurry to find something for you to write with and when I saw the pen I . . . well, I borrowed it. I had every intention of returning it, I assure you," he quickly added. He turned to the girl. "I was trying to tell you the pen wasn't mine when we were interrupted. Remember? I *told* you to take good care of it."

Ptolemy listened with a burgeoning sense of vindication. He turned to the girl and silently raised a brow. She stared at the older man for a full ten seconds, a delicate peach hue staining her throat and cheeks and her—well, one could not help noticing a décolletage so obviously meant to be noticed. She swallowed visibly. Then, as he watched, every vestige of embarrassment evaporated as if by magic, replaced by a truly masterful, if patently false, nonchalance.

"Well," she said, thrusting the pen toward him, "why didn't you just say so?"

He gaped, amazed. Not only was she odd, but audacious. Spectacularly so. "I—" He stopped himself. Anything he said to this peculiar creature was bound to be a waste of breath. He took the proffered pen. "Thank you."

"Of course," she replied and then, before he could utter another word, disappeared into the crowd.

CHAPTER
7

"I am sure your grandfather understands that for the next few weeks you must devote yourself entirely to preparing for your interview with Lord Blidderphenk," Cornelia Litchfield said as her father's chauffer threaded the car through London's late-afternoon traffic toward Pimlico where Ptolemy's grandfather lived. "But in case he does not, you must remind him so that whatever this request of his is, it does not interfere with what may well be the most important weeks of your life."

Though Ptolemy wasn't sure he would go quite that far, he figured it would be rude to say as much. Two months ago Cornelia's father, vice-chancellor of St. Phillip's College, had nominated Ptolemy for the Blidderphenk professorship, which came tandem with being named head of the newly minted anthropology department with which Lord Blidderphenk—and his millions of pounds—was endowing St. Phillip's. For a man of Ptolemy's age to even be considered for such a post was a coup and now he was one of only three nominees to have made it through to the final interview with Lord Blidderphenk himself. Truly exciting stuff. He supposed.

"Just think, everything we've worked for is within your grasp," Cornelia said, her fine eyes gleaming with fervor. But not too much fervor; Cornelia was not the sort to gloat.

Ptolemy didn't begrudge her the use of the first person plural. She had been indispensible in the research and compilation phases of his publications as well as organizing, well, almost everything in his life, thus freeing him to concentrate on his passion: cultural anthropology. They'd met four years earlier at St. Phillip's annual reception for its incoming staff. Her father had left them standing together to greet a late arrival. For want of anything else to say, he'd mentioned how hard it was to find decent apartments. She'd immediately offered her assistance. And she had continued to offer her aid, in all sorts of useful ways, ever since.

"You only need to stay focused, Ptolemy," she was saying now, as she rifled through a thin portfolio of papers on her lap, "and not allow yourself to be distracted."

She had a point but then she always did. He did tend to run off on tangents when his interest had been piqued. He relied on her to keep him on the straight and narrow even if the straight and narrow sometimes felt a little claustrophobic.

"Especially by anything someone of your grandfather's nature might propose." Cornelia did not approve of his grandfather, whom she considered irresponsible.

"I'm sure whatever my grandfather wants can be dealt with expeditiously." Actually he wasn't at all sure of this. His grandfather rarely asked him for favors, let alone to perform a service, so this was uncharted territory of a sort.

"Hm." She did not sound convinced. "Well, just keep in mind how important the next few weeks are."

Having delivered this judicious bit of advice—or maybe it was more of a judicious directive, it was so often hard to tell the difference—she turned to him and, seeing the bruise on his chin, *tch*'d her tongue lightly.

"Ptolemy. However did you manage to walk into a door?" she wondered aloud for the fourth time. Ptolemy had decided earlier that it wasn't worth the effort to explain the truth of how'd he come by that bruise and so had made up a rather lame story about walking into a door swinging out unexpectedly.

"You . . . you didn't overimbibe after Lionel and I left, did you?" A trace of horror touched her voice.

"No!"

"I should hope not. You know that the main requisites Lord Blidderphenk has for anyone being named the Blidderphenk professor is that the candidate be temperate, sober, and in possession of an impeccably moral character."

"I would think he might want his professor to know a bit about anthropology, too," Ptolemy said drily.

Cornelia peered at him uncertainly. "Well, yes. That, too."

Cornelia's one fatal flaw was her complete lack of humor. He supposed it was too much to ask. Being the daughter of one of St. Phillip's vice-chancellors came with certain expectations of dignity and serious-mindedness—qualities Ptolemy, whose parents had always driven home the importance of dignity, respected but suspected maybe he ought to have appreciated more. As a boy, he'd often been accused of having a little too much humor. He recalled more than a few instances when his glibness had won him a session with the headmaster's switch.

And really, what purpose did humor serve except as a distraction from serious thought?

Why, he bet the girl from the Savoy last night hadn't spent five minutes this morning in serious thought . . . Where had *that* come from? He frowned, dismissing the girl from his mind.

"So what *were* you thinking?" Cornelia prodded. "No. Don't answer. Clearly, you were daydreaming.

"I do hope," she went on when he didn't reply, "that when you sit down with Lord Blidderphenk you do not allow yourself to drift while he is speaking."

He made a noncommittal sound before broaching a less dangerous subject because he did have a tendency to drift when people rambled on. "Do you suppose if I were to be named the Blidderphenk professor it would be, er, seemly for me to organize and lead my own expedition using his lordship's endowment? Wouldn't it be grand, if I should? Why I might even return to the Pearl Islands."

"Excuse me?"

Cornelia was frowning. He had no idea why . . . Perhaps she was distressed by the intimation that he would leave her behind? It seemed unlikely but perhaps . . .

"My pardon. Would you . . ." All at once, his heart started racing and his throat tightened. He stared at her. He had meant to propose to her last night but what with one thing and another . . . or rather one person or another . . . No that wasn't true, either. There hadn't been *another* person, just the one. That girl. That hazel-eyed . . . pip—at any rate, he hadn't gotten around to it. But now, here was a likely opportunity to achieve what he and everyone else he knew assumed to be a foregone conclusion. He might as well jump in feetfirst . . . mightn't he? Yes. Yes.

"Would I what?" Cornelia asked impatiently. "What is wrong with you, Ptolemy? You look most peculiar. Are you sick?"

He took a deep breath and forced the words past the unnatural constriction in his throat, "Would you like to come, too?"

"What? Oh, Ptolemy." She gave an exasperated little sigh. "Do you realize how ingenuous you sound? It simply won't do. Lord

Blidderphenk must think of you as his equal in maturity and gravitas, not as some young person filled with juvenile enthusiasms. You must remember your dignity at all times, Ptolemy. People won't take you seriously if you don't.

"And, no, I wouldn't like to come, too. Don't be offended. I would, of course, do whatever was necessary to aid in the writing of your monograph, but tramping about the world isn't required. Let other, less gifted men potter about the world collecting data. It is up to brilliant scholars like you to find the meaning in the data provided by others, as did Sir Fraser when writing his seminal work, *The Golden Bough.*"

"But I *like* pottering about collecting data."

"It is not the sort of work that will be expected of the Blidderphenk professor."

"No, I suppose not. But I shall miss field research," he said a little wistfully.

"Only those who are willing to sacrifice the bourgeois pleasures of the ordinary man can hope to achieve true greatness."

He supposed she was right. She almost always was, but he wondered if perhaps Cornelia wasn't giving bourgeois pleasures short shrift . . .

"Here we are," she said as the chauffer pulled to the curb in front of his grandfather's townhouse.

Ptolemy opened the door and climbed out, dipping down to look at her. "Are you sure you wouldn't like to accompany me?"

"*Very* sure, thank you," she said, leaving him to close the door with a vast sense of relief.

———

"His lordship will be down shortly, sir. Would you care for some refreshment while you wait?"

"No, thank you," Ptolemy said, moving past the butler into his grandfather's library.

"Very well, sir." The butler backed out of the room, shutting the doors as he retreated.

Ptolemy had always loved this room, with its wall of windows spilling the southern light across a patchwork of Persian and Oriental rugs, the scarred and blistered bookshelves, and the desk and tabletops stained by decades' worth of idly placed teacups and water glasses. A haphazard conglomeration of books, maps, and magazines lay propped against lamps and stacked randomly on the floor. It was dusty, grubby, cluttered, and uncatalogued. In other words, an unexplored Aladdin's cave of wonders for an adolescent boy.

He supposed his love of ferreting things out had been born here. It certainly hadn't been in his parents' well-ordered home. He spied his favorite paperweight on his grandfather's desk and, with a grin, picked it up and held it up to the window, squinting into its bright interior.

A little shepherdess had abandoned her charges for a swing strung from the boughs of an apple tree in full blossom. Her head was thrown back, her feet pointed skyward, her porcelain petticoats billowing around her knees. The artist had painted eyes pressed closed in the ecstasy of movement as a single plait of hair streamed out behind her in her flight. On the miniature mountainside behind her, her wooly charges turned from the far side of a fence to watch their inattentive guardian in befuddled fascination. He shook the globe and hundreds of tiny glittering pink shards swirled around in a faux shower of apple blossoms.

It had always instilled a curious conflict in him. On the one hand, he was jealous the girl could so easily forget her responsibilities and enjoy that swing; on the other, he worried about those damn sheep. What if they got lost or some wolf found them or they plunged off a cliff?

He shook it again, watching the petals swirl on the facsimile of a gentle breeze, catching on the shepherdess's carved skirts. He bet if she opened her eyes they'd be hazel . . .

"What's that you're whistling?"

He turned to see his grandfather being wheeled in by a robust-looking footman. His gout had flared up last week, making it excruciating for him to put any weight on his foot. "Was I whistling?"

"Yes. And it wasn't Handel, either."

At seventy-three, his grandfather still posed an arresting figure: tall and straight-backed—when he was standing—with an aristocratic nose, a thick, unkempt head of silvery curls, and the same cleft chin he'd bequeathed Ptolemy. His character was even more distinctive. His ungoverned wit and blunt observations had made him a glaring exception in a family noted for their serious-mindedness.

Not that he'd always been impolitic and outspoken. He wouldn't have successfully won the hand of Ptolemy's formal, perpetually unsmiling grandmother otherwise.

"In fact, that tune sounded suspiciously like *popular* music," he said.

"Really?" Puzzling. Ptolemy hadn't thought he knew any popular music. Not that he had anything against popular music; he just never had occasion to hear it, his work leaving little opportunity for that sort of thing.

Perhaps if Cornelia had shown an interest . . . but Cornelia considered theatre frivolous and believed popular music caused brain decay. But it really was a catchy tune.

"Good heavens, my boy! And where did you get that black eye? Did you walk into a door?" his grandfather asked in increasingly amazed tones as he nodded a dismissal to the footman.

Heat rose in Ptolemy's face.

"You . . . you haven't been in a *brawl*?" His grandfather's dark eyes gleamed with approval. Not surprising: his grandfather had always enjoyed being the black sheep of the family, a role Ptolemy's grandmother had claimed he'd come to rather late in life.

Apparently the dignity that once had been the hallmark of his lordship's character had eroded with time, eventually making him nearly unrecognizable as the somber, respectable young man to whom she'd been betrothed. At the time of her death last year, Ptolemy's grandparents had not shared the same address in over two decades.

"No. Of course not. I was involved in a minor incident at the Savoy. A misunderstanding."

The thick white shelf of his lordship's brows climbed toward his hairline. "At the *Savoy*? You interest me greatly. I didn't think you ever left the classroom. Or the mud huts. Or wherever it is you do your research."

"I was there with Cornelia and a fellow instructor, Lionel Underwood."

"Well, bully for Mr. Underwood for dragging you off that campus. You're a young man, Ptolemy. It won't kill you to act like one occasionally."

He smiled at his grandfather's misinterpretation of the situation. Lionel Underwood, a bon vivant? Hardly. Lionel was a consummate teetotaler. He'd only come along because Ptolemy had asked him, being as he was the only person both Cornelia and he liked.

Though, Ptolemy allowed with a twinge of guilt, he didn't like self-effacing, hardworking and, well, frankly, dull Lionel so much as found him useful. Lionel always made himself available to escort Cornelia to the seemingly endless and—Ptolemy admitted—endlessly boring functions associated with the college where both Lionel and he were employed as dons.

"*I* arranged the evening. It was to be a celebration."

"A celebration?" His grandfather tipped his head inquiringly.

"Yes." He took a deep breath. "I had planned on asking Cornelia to marry me—"

"Please, say it's not so!" His grandfather clamped his hand to his chest. "Not Cornelia!"

"I resent that, Grandfather. Miss Litchfield is a remarkable young lady. She's a highly organized and thorough researcher, with a true gift for management—"

"I can well believe that."

"Don't mutter. It makes me think you are saying nasty things."

"I am."

"Grandfather."

"I'm sorry—no, I'm not, I'm horrified. What on earth possessed you to ask Miss Litchfield to marry you?" He glanced sharply at Ptolemy. "You weren't sozzled, were you?"

"No!" He never got drunk. Drunk people lost their inhibitions and he had been trained from the cradle to believe that inhibitions provided civilization its best bulwark against anarchy. "And I haven't asked her yet."

There hadn't been any opportunity. Before coming to the Savoy, he'd planned to meet her at the British Library and propose somewhere in the stacks. But he'd missed his train and so had rung up Lionel and asked him to pick up the ring at the jeweler's and then escort Cornelia to the Savoy to meet him. It had worked out as smoothly as clockwork but there hadn't been a moment when they'd been alone so that he could propose.

In fact, now that he thought of it, he realized Lionel still had the ring. He supposed it was as well. Lionel never lost things. Dependable as a rock, old Lionel.

"Thank God for that."

"But I will."

"Do you think that wise, m'lad? I don't think you have any idea of what life with Miss Litchfield will be like. You have always been utterly oblivious where females are concerned. I blame my daughter."

"That was hardly her fault."

His grandfather ignored him. "She was not a natural mother. Sending you and your brothers off to school so young. Did you even know what a girl was before you were ten?"

"There were a few references in books."

"You make light of it, but it's true. You are absolutely a babe in the woods where women are concerned. Especially a woman like Miss Litchfield." He shook his head.

"I know you think her a tad dry—"

"A tad?"

"Cornelia has more in her head than the pursuit of pleasure." Unlike that strange girl at the Savoy. She had all the earmarks of a—what did the students call them? Oh, yes, a crackerjack.

"There's an understatement," his lordship said. "I dare-say Miss Litchfield has never taken a step in pleasure's direction, let alone actively pursued it."

Ptolemy blew out a deep breath. "Grandfather . . ."

His grandfather forestalled him. "I have nothing against Miss Litchfield other than that she is a managing sort of woman. The sort who inspires laziness in a man."

"Laziness?"

"Yes. You've always been a little obsessive when it came to your work, my lad. You can't deny it. It has made you—and yes, I know this is harsh, but it is said with affection—neglect other areas of life. Miss Litchfield has encouraged this neglect. Perhaps fostered the mistaken belief that nothing else matters aside from . . . What is it that you do?"

"I am an anthropologist. A cultural—"

"Yes. Well, other things *do* matter."

Ptolemy gave this a fair consideration. He did tend to become a tad obsessive about things he found fascinating, but he'd never found anything nearly as fascinating as people and cultures.

"Are you in love with her?"

His grandfather's abrupt question caught him off guard. "I . . . I . . . Of course. Yes."

His grandfather steepled his hands together and peered at him over the tips of his fingers. "I believe, Ptolemy, I *truly* believe, that the men in our family only love once. So choose your mate wisely, my boy."

He shifted uneasily. Cornelia expected him to ask for her hand in marriage. At least, he assumed she did. It was a natural progression in a relationship between an unmarried man and woman after a number of years, and he had given her no reason to expect otherwise.

"We'll make a brilliant team," he said. "She has only my best interests at heart and she'll help me achieve . . . er, those things that I want to achieve."

"Wonderful," his grandfather said. "Why don't you hire her rather than propose to her?"

"Grandfather."

"You sound like you're choosing a teammate, not a bedmate."

"Grandfather."

"Fine." He held up his hand. "I shan't say another word. Today. I'm sorry. I really won't. I mean if you want to marry a woman who—no, no, no! Sit back down. I promise. Don't leave. Tell me how you got that bruise?"

He'd forgotten about it. "Some college boy reeking of bay rum thought I was importuning a young lady at the bar."

"What were you doing in the bar? I didn't think you drank."

"Of course I do. I just don't overindulge."

"God, that you would."

"What's that?"

"Nothing. And what did Miss Litchfield think of you importuning this young lady?"

"Oh, for—I *didn't* importune her. I don't even know the girl."

Once again, his grandfather's brows mounted his noble forehead. "Then what happened?"

"What happened?" Ptolemy frowned. What *had* happened?

Before he quite realized it the words were spilling out, his forehead furrowed in an effort to sort out the events that had led to his black eye.

"—and I took a step after her, the girl, and in doing so stepped on her hem and it *ripped*, the whole back of her gown ripped open to the waist—a shoddy bit of workmanship if you ask me—leaving her in a state of immodesty."

He regarded his grandfather earnestly. "Do you realize young ladies wear practically *nothing* beneath these new gowns?" He didn't wait for an answer.

"She said, 'Do something!' So, naturally, I obliged. I threw my coat over her shoulders and it was then that this boy decided I'd intentionally insulted her and hit me. And he wouldn't have landed the blow except I was caught off guard. One doesn't expect to be knocked out in a restaurant." Ptolemy threw out his hands in an invitation to commiserate. "And that's what happened."

"I see."

"Do you?" Ptolemy asked, abruptly sitting down on the edge of the wingback chair opposite his grandfather. "Because I'm not sure I do."

"And when you came to she'd vanished, hadn't she?" his lordship said. "They usually do."

Ptolemy could think of no retort to this bizarre non sequitur and so made none. "No. She stayed there, all right, yelling in my ear and shaking me and insisting on helping me up even though she's about as tall as that wood nymph statue in your garden, and with similar features, too . . ." He paused, considering, then shook his head. "But not really. She actually looks a lot more like that shepherdess."

"Shepherdess?"

"Yes. In your glass globe," he explained distractedly. "Not physically, but there's a quality of careless . . . I don't know." He shook his head, defeated by his inability to properly describe the girl.

"As soon as I was on my feet she started in about the pen again, only her male friend had arrived by now—the one I mentioned who supposedly gave it to her—and he finally explained that he'd borrowed the pen off my table when I'd gone after Cornelia."

"Where was Cornelia going?"

"Cornelia? Oh, she had a ticket to some lecture and it turned out Lionel did too, so they went off together. Anyway, she said—"

"*Who* said?"

"The girl, Grandfather. Please try to attend."

"Believe it or not, I am."

"Anyway, she said, and I quote, Grandfather, 'Why didn't you say so?' and smiled with a sort of regal forbearance, like a queen forced to deal with a simpleminded peasant. Then she handed me my pen and *then* she vanished."

His grandfather clapped his knee. "I *knew* she would eventually vanish!"

"*And* she took my jacket."

His grandfather nodded.

"Why would she *do* that?"

"Take your jacket?"

"No, all the rest of it." He felt like he was twelve again, trying to sort out the mystery of why the cook's daughter had taken an inexplicable aversion to him when he'd returned from boarding school on one of his infrequent visits home, tossing her head and flouncing off whenever he said, "Hello."

"I haven't the faintest notion," his grandfather said with a broad grin. Why he should find the situation in the least amusing was beyond Ptolemy. "What's her name?"

"Name? Why . . . I don't know." An odd feeling of disquiet seized him at this realization.

Ptolemy stood up, annoyed and exasperated. He'd already wasted enough time wondering about the girl. "Anyway, that's how I came to have a black eye. Now that I've satisfied your curiosity perhaps you can satisfy mine and tell me why you sent for me."

His grandfather studied him for a long moment before replying. "I have an errand I need you to do for me."

"Of course. What is it?"

CHAPTER
8

Ptolemy stopped in front of the wrought iron gate and tipped his dripping black umbrella back to better peer at the manor house. He wasn't certain he had the right address. He pulled the folded paper from his mackintosh pocket and checked it against the placard embedded in the brick hitching post next to the gate; this was it, all right.

Once it might have been a prime example of Georgian architecture. No longer. It looked like pensioners' apartments. Or a not-particularly-well-funded charity hospital. A pea gravel drive sprouting tufts of grass arced in front of a slightly skewed front portico. From roof to base, dark streaks defaced the stone façade, marking places where the drain spouts had long ago come undone. A few of the upper windows were shuttered and, as evinced by the ivy growing across the planks, had been for some time. On the gabled eastern end, a pile of branches adorned the chimney top, home to a stork.

And yet, despite all that, the warm light glowing in the tall, front-facing windows and the incongruous pot of brilliant red geraniums sitting at the bottom of the steps leading up to the porch made it seem somehow inviting.

He pushed open the gate and closed it behind him, stepping over the water-filled ruts in the drive on his way up to the house. At the front door, he looked for a doorbell and, finding none, lifted the heavy knocker, letting it fall just as a wet, tailless cat slipped by him and shot through the four-inch opening under the front window.

From the other side of the door he heard the muffled sound of voices, one raised in question, another answering. The edge of the lace curtain covering the window moved, fell back into place, the door in front of him opened, and there *she* stood.

He gaped at her. She looked entirely respectable today, having traded the low-cut blue dress for a serviceable white blouse and dark gray skirt, a plain linen apron stretched taut around slender hips, her gleaming brown hair tied in a soft knot at the nape of her neck. A few curls trailed down to caress a rosy cheek. Behind her, the tailless cat sat on a threadbare Oriental carpet in a central hall and eyed him unblinkingly.

She tipped her head, her gaze traveling deliberately up and down his length. She didn't look at all surprised. In fact, she looked quite sanguine, as though she'd expected to open the door and find him dripping on her doorstep. She smiled, a roguish curve of her lips, one brow arching above her shining hazel eyes. Humor. He'd *known* she couldn't hold a serious thought.

"Don't tell me," she finally said. "It was the wrong pen."

"What? No."

She set a hand on her hip. "No? Then you've come for your jacket. I'll just—"

"Jacket? No. No, I didn't even know you were here."

She laughed, a pretty, infectious sound. "Now, that's just plain silly. Why else would you be here?"

The question struck him as bizarrely apt. He stared at her,

confused, a condition into which this young lady seemed to all-too-easily reduce him. "What are you doing here?"

"I live here."

"That's impossible. You can't be—"

"*Tch-tch-tch.*" She silenced him, making a metronome of her index finger. "It is and I can. The question better asked is why are you following me?"

"I tell you, I had no idea you lived here." The idea that she thought him capable of imposing himself on her in such a manner took him aback. "I wasn't following you."

She gave an unladylike snort. "Oh, aye. You just happened to show up here, twenty miles from London, the day after you ripped the seam of my dress open. Tell me another."

"Tell you another what?" With each passing second he felt more and more discombobulated. "And that was an accident."

If he'd believed in sorcery, he would have thought someone had put a spell on him, one that had caused his placid, well-ordered, and well-arranged life to tumble into pandemonium. And the sorceress would probably be her. No, he thought, *undoubtedly* it would be her.

He tried gathering his dignity. "I assure you, er, miss, er . . ."

"Eastlake," she supplied. "Lucy Eastlake."

"I assure you, Miss Eastlake, I would never insult a young woman in such a manner."

The warmth faded from her extraordinary eyes. He had the distinct impression that until this moment she hadn't realized such behavior would be considered offensive.

"Oh. Well, then, why are you here?" An unpleasant idea seemed to occur to her for she suddenly frowned. "You're not from the phone company, are you?"

"Phone company? No. I have come to see—"

"Lucy?" A genteel female voice called from deeper within the house a second before an elderly woman in an oilcloth coat appeared in the hallway, stomping mud off her rubberized boots. She was rail thin, with a long, sharp-featured face and deep-set blue eyes, soft white hair floating in a nimbus about her head. "Who is that you're talking to, dear? We saw a man coming up the drive and so I came directly. It isn't fair you always have to—"

She stopped abruptly and stared.

He took a chance. "Miss Litton?"

Her eyes went round, her head snapping up on her slender, crepe-hung neck like a startled grouse, setting the wattle swinging. "Oh," she said, then, "Oh," and then what sounded like, "Tom," and then her eyelids fluttered shut.

He caught her before she hit the ground.

CHAPTER

9

"In here." The girl, Lucy, pushed open the hall door and stood back, ushering Ptolemy into a front parlor. Once inside, he gently laid the old woman on a divan that had seen better days while Lucy jerked a bouquet of fall asters from the vase standing on a nearby table and dunked the end of her apron into the water. He stepped back as she knelt down beside the unconscious woman and gently dabbed at her brow.

The elderly lady stirred. Her eyelids fluttered open. "What happened?"

"It's all right, dear," Lucy said, relaxing back on her heels. "You just had a bit of a start."

"I thought I'd seen—"

"Is someone here?" another female voice demanded from somewhere deeper in the interior of the house. "Lavinia thought a man was at the front door." An elderly dumpling of a woman, her retroussé nose turned up from her double chin, appeared in the doorway. She stopped short upon seeing him. "You're not from the phone company, are you?"

"No," Lucy answered. She waved a hand in his direction. "This is the fellow I was telling you about, the one whose pen I nipped the other night."

"Good heavens!" The plump woman puffed out her cheeks like a disgruntled bull terrier and started into the room. "I realize that you young people follow a different set of standards today, but still! To stalk a young lady to her home—" She stopped abruptly, having spied the reclining figure of the other old lady. "What's wrong with Livie?"

"I had a bit of a startle, is all. Quite silly," the woman on the divan replied. "I'm quite all right now."

"She fainted," Lucy explained. "She took one look at this fellow, called out 'Tom!' and fainted dead away." She turned her green-gold eyes on him. "Your name isn't Tom, is it?"

"No, it's Ptolemy Archibald Grant."

"Truly?" she sounded unconvinced. "Well, you don't look like a Ptolemy. Does anyone actually call you that?"

"Yes. But most people call me *Mister* Grant," he said quellingly.

She was not to be quelled. "Grant?" She laughed. "I should say not. People will mistake you for some sort of endowment. Maybe Archibald? No . . ." She snapped her fingers. "I have it: *Archie*."

"No one calls me—"

"Anyway, Aunt Lavinia spotted Archie here and fell into a swoon. Quite elegantly done, too," she said approvingly.

"Thank you. I thought I'd seen a ghost but, of course, now that I really look at this young man, whoever he is . . ." A sudden, unwelcome thought occurred to her and she motioned Lucy closer. "We've paid the phone bill this month, haven't we?"

"Yes, dear. It's quite all right. I'm not sure what Archie is doing here but doubtless given adequate time he will inform us." She turned her head and gazed at him encouragingly.

"I have been *trying* to do so."

She didn't seem to take offense at his tone. She looked quite entertained, her hazel eyes sparkling and a smile threatening.

"No one told me as we was expecting company this afternoon." A red-haired, teenaged girl with magnificently protruding ears had at some point joined their number. "Unless . . . You from the phone company?"

"*No.*"

"Oh. Well, whoever you be, you're dripping all over the carpet which means I'll be on me knees sponging it all up, doesn't it?"

"Oh. I'm sorry."

"Sorry don't—"

"Polly," Bernice admonished. "Mr. Grant is our guest."

"Guest? Should I make some sandwiches?" The prospect appeared to delight her.

"Well, dear," Bernice said. "I'm not sure that would—"

"That would be lovely," Lavinia announced, struggling into an upright position.

"And I'll bring tea, too. Back in a jiff," the girl promised and bustled back out of the room.

"What is a 'jiff'?" he asked, intrigued. He'd picked up a bit of slang here and there from his students, and found their variations on what was often ancient argot fascinating. Sometimes he wondered why he studied civilizations in far-off countries when there was such a vast wealth of cultural curiosities amongst his own countrymen.

"Jiff," Lucy repeated as though doing so would stir his knowledge of the word. It didn't. "You know, make it snappy, shake a leg, get cracking." She grinned at his befuddlement. "*Hurry.*"

"Ah!" Enlightenment dawned. "*Hurry.*"

"Exactly."

"Enough is enough. Who are you, young man? And what are you doing here?" Bernice, who did not share their interest in this linguistic curiosity, demanded.

"Yes, what are you doing here, Archie?" Lucy asked.

"I have come," he said very carefully, very patiently, "at the behest of my grandfather, Lord Barton. He has asked me to—"

"Your *grandfather*! Of course!" the woman named Lavinia exclaimed. "How could you be anyone else? You look the very image of him."

The girl's face lit with comprehension. "Aha! You said 'John' not 'Tom.'"

"So *you* are what John Barton looked like," the dumpling-like lady exclaimed. "Well, small wonder Lavini—"

"*Bernice*." At Lavinia's mortified utterance, the other woman fell silent.

Lavinia cleared her throat. "You were saying, young man?"

Based on admittedly short experience, he figured he had between five and eight seconds before something else siderailed the gathered company's attention. Taking the metaphorical bull by the horns, he stepped forward and handed Lavinia the letter of introduction his grandfather had sent with him.

"This will explain."

Lavinia looked about. "Do we have a letter opener around somewhere?"

"Yes," Lucy said and, taking the envelope, ripped off the top of it, blew into the pocket, and withdrew the folded sheets from inside along with an additional smaller envelope addressed to Bernard DuPaul, Junior. "Here."

Lavinia took the sheet and opened it, quickly reading over his grandfather's cribbed scrawl. Emotions rippled across her countenance: anticipation, tenderness, surprise, disappointment, and finally uncertainty.

"What does it say?" the girl prompted.

"He says he is unable to make the trip to France." She looked up, her eyes shadowed with worry. "Is he very ill?"

"Not in the least," Ptolemy reassured her. "He has had a recurrence of gout in his foot and cannot tolerate any weight on it."

"That's all?" Lucy said, clearly surprised, and not in a good way.

"Lucy!"

"I'm sorry. But you have to admit it's rather disappointing. After fifty years he writes to tell you he has *gout?* I should write back and tell him to go—"

"No, of course, that's not all he said," Lavinia broke in, her gaze still on the letter. "He writes that he is relinquishing his portion of the rubies. He says he hasn't any need of them and instead wants me to have his share."

"He does?" Lucy exclaimed, her face clearing. "Well, I call that awfully spiffing of the old boy!"

"Lucy!" Lavinia scolded, but in a way that told Ptolemy she had uttered the girl's name in just such a tone many, many times before and anticipated having to do so many, many more times in the future.

"I'm sorry, Aunt Lavinia." She didn't look in the least sorry. She looked unrepentantly winsome.

But Lavinia was not attending. "I'm not sure we ought to accept such generosity."

"Oh, yes, you ought," Lucy said without hesitation. "And at once, before he changes his mind." She swung toward Ptolemy. "*Is* he likely to change his mind, do you think? I mean, is there any chance of his forgetting he made the offer? He isn't gone off batty or something, is he?"

"*Lucy,*" Bernice said severely. "I am sure I do not know what that term means but I do know that I have repeatedly asked you not to use street argot."

"Sorry," she said yet again and then turned to him. "He isn't, is he?"

"Not at all. He is in complete possession of his faculties. And finances."

She turned to her aunt. "Well, there you have it. He doesn't need it, he wants you to have it, and I am sure it would be selfish to disappoint the old darling by refusing."

He started. *The old darling?* To his knowledge no one had ever been moved to call his grandfather an "old darling."

"*That* is facile reasoning," Lavinia said.

"So it is," Lucy admitted. "But true, nonetheless."

"I'm not convinced."

"I think Lucy is right," Bernice suddenly announced.

Lucy's head snapped around, apparently unused to support from this particular corner. "You do?"

"Yes. It only makes sense. If Lord Barton doesn't want the rubies, there's no reason why we shouldn't have them. Better us than . . . who all is left of those who were at Patnimba did you say, Lucy?"

"Bento Oliveria and Luis Silva, the Portuguese lads."

"Just so. If Lord Barton had wanted his share split up evenly, he needn't have written otherwise. I'm sure he has his reasons."

"All right," Lavinia allowed after a long moment's consideration, during which both Bernice and Lucy appeared to be holding their breath. They released it in unison. "But at least we won't accept the offer of his grandson."

"Lord Barton is offering us his grandson?" Lucy exclaimed, mischief sparking in her eyes. "Well, that *is* too generous. Because however will we afford to feed him? I mean, look at him! He has to be at least six feet tall. Not to mention how much keeping him decently clad is likely to set us back—"

"Lucy."

"Sorry."

He was beginning to develop an unexpected, and unwanted, *and*, he was sure, completely unnecessary sympathy for the girl. She only meant to have a spot of fun. Though highly inappropriate at the moment, he was certain she didn't mean any harm by it.

"What I meant," Lavinia said in crushing tones, "is that Lord Barton has sent his grandson to escort us to Saint-Girons. While thoughtful, such a gesture is quite unnecessary."

"It is?" Ptolemy asked in spite of himself.

He'd never considered his grandfather's offer might be refused. He'd assumed the elderly woman would gratefully accept his escort and had reconciled himself to shepherding his grandfather's old siege-mate, if one could call her that, across France. He had even convinced Cornelia that the closeted environs of a train car would be the perfect place to prepare for his interview with Lord Blidderphenk.

He hadn't bothered to mention that he also figured that while the authorities cleared up whatever paper was necessary to divide up the rubies he could hie himself off the short distance to Les Eyzies and have a look-in on some recently discovered cave paintings there. Then he'd escort Lavinia Litton back. All of which was to be completed within the course of a week or so. Possibly less.

He'd planned it all very neatly. Except now it appeared all his planning had been unnecessary and he found himself unaccountably disappointed.

"Yes," Lavinia said. "Our niece has everything well in hand. She has already made the necessary travel arrangements."

He was still trying to work through why he wasn't pleased, or at least mildly relieved. Now he'd be able to attend Vice-Chancellor Litchfield's yearly reception for the incoming professors.

His reaction suddenly made sense.

He'd spent nearly his entire professional career in the field, far preferring it to the classroom and far, *far* preferring it to the drawing room. Once again, the prospect of spending a whole evening amongst insecure academics jockeying for position while Cornelia introduced him to "important men" loomed before him. Small wonder he was disappointed. It had nothing to do with not being able to provide a service for his grandfather or these elderly ladies.

Or the girl.

"Are you sure?" he asked.

"Oh, yes," Lavinia said. "Lucy is quite extraordinarily capable."

He looked at the admirably capable Lucy. She avoided his eye, remaining mute. Even on such a short acquaintance, he recognized this as an inauspicious sign.

"You've traveled extensively, have you, Miss Eastlake?"

"Some. Yes."

"And doubtless you speak French?"

"Doubtless."

"Fluently."

"Hmm."

"She had French lessons in town twice weekly from the age of eleven until she was fifteen," Bernice said proudly. "She made the arrangements with the local tailor's French wife, Madame de Barge, herself. As I said, she's quite competent. Always has been."

Something was amiss but he couldn't quite say what it was. Something about Lucy, er, Miss Eastlake's expression was shouting at him as loudly as if she'd spoken. He just couldn't make out what it was saying . . . And then he had it: *she didn't speak French*. He would have staked his reputation on it.

But he could hardly make such an accusation. Besides which for some reason this minor deception regarding the quite possibly fictional Madame de Barge was important to her—that, too, was clear to him in the same mysterious but indisputable way. He couldn't expose her.

Lucy cleared her throat. "Ahem. You know, perhaps we should consider accepting Lord Barton's offer. I mean, if he felt strongly that Archie here ought to accompany us—"

"Absolutely not," Lavinia declared proudly, her chin high and her color higher. "We have gotten along very well without Lord Barton's help until now and we shall continue to do so. I am sure

Mr. Grant has better ways to spend his time than escorting three strangers across France."

Of course he did. "Not at all. It would be my pleasure."

"Such nice manners. But no. Thank your grandfather and"— Lavinia glanced away and the pink bloomed even brighter in her sunken cheeks,—"and give him my regards."

It was a clearly a dismissal. So why did he hesitate? He glanced at Lucy. She was looking away from him. *Forcefully* away.

He couldn't very well foist himself on them. With a murmured "good day," he took his leave, exiting the house with the distinct sensation that he was doing someone a monumental disservice—and the very odd notion that that someone was very possibly himself.

CHAPTER
10

"I tried. I swear it. But they were resolved." Ptolemy raked his hand through his hair and muttered something under his breath as Lord Barton watched in amazement—and no small amount of relief—as his favorite grandson continued to wear a path in his Oriental rug.

Amongst the entire dismal, earnest, and pedantic brood of Grants, of which his daughter was not only the matriarch but chief pedant, Ptolemy—and why in the name of all that was holy would his daughter have clamped such a ridiculous moniker on the poor boy? Why not Jim? Or Tom?—was the only interesting one.

In Ptolemy, Lord Barton saw vestiges of his younger self, someone wary of passion and impulsiveness, having been indoctrinated into the belief that both inevitably led to a man's ruin. Yet, despite Ptolemy's dutiful efforts to eradicate these undesirable traits, he kept evincing disturbing symptoms of both. Disturbing to his parents, that is. For example, early on Ptolemy had politely but categorically disregarded their insistence that he pursue a purely academic career and instead followed his passion for obscure cultures out into the world.

Though he didn't pretend to understand his grandson's predilection, Lord Barton was happy he had one, and equally pleased that Ptolemy had often disappeared for months on end doing research in far-off corners of the globe, often without informing anyone of his whereabouts. Lord Barton wasn't sure this was the result of absentmindedness or simply a brilliant strategy. Certainly he'd have liked his well-intentioned, humorless, and obstinately dutiful daughter to lose his own address from time to time.

Yes, he'd had high hopes for Ptolemy.

Had.

But then Cornelia Litchfield had come along.

Ptolemy had introduced them a year ago. Within five minutes Lord Barton had taken Miss Litchfield's measure: a natural-born manager. Within ten, he'd learned everything else he needed to know to realize the danger she represented to his grandson.

She'd spent her youth burnishing her illustrious widowed father's reputation and at the same time polishing her own skills as hostess and adviser. Then, upon reaching her midtwenties, perhaps out of some vague reaction to society's assumption that all women ought to have families but more likely because she realized her current project had reached its zenith, she'd decided to cast her nets into new water. And it was there that she'd landed Ptolemy.

In Lord Barton's handsome, brilliant, oblivious grandson, she'd detected someone worthy of her gifts, someone whose career she could bolster, whose star she could lift higher.

Lord Barton did not doubt Miss Litchfield was a worthy young woman and that she sincerely wanted the best for Ptolemy. The problem was she had no imagination and therefore could not conceive of anything being best for Ptolemy that wasn't best for her.

But Lord Barton could. Rather a lot, actually.

Even then, had Lord Barton divined any real attachment between Ptolemy and Cornelia he could have been satisfied. He was not so narrow-minded as to believe that everyone loved with the same depth of passion and faithfulness as he had. But he could not glean any bit of tenderness or pleasure or delight in their feelings for one another.

Indeed, Lord Barton had the distinct impression that Ptolemy had not so much fallen in love with Cornelia Eastlake as fallen into the habit of her. And now, unless he missed his guess, his grandson wasn't exactly sure how, or even if, he should extract himself from the situation. Ptolemy could be excruciatingly and wrongheadedly honorable.

Much like he'd been at that age.

And there was nothing Lord Barton could do except despair.

Yet now, watching Ptolemy dishevel his hair with another careless, exasperated gesture, he felt the distinct stirring of hope. Lord Barton wasn't sure how, but his simple request that Ptolemy escort Lavinia Litton through France had stirred a fire in the lad that had been lying dormant far too long.

"And she doesn't speak French. I'd stake my reputation on it," Ptolemy suddenly said.

"Miss Litton? I should think she has some gentrified schoolroom French. True, she might be a bit rusty but—"

"Not Miss Litton," Ptolemy said in a tone that suggested Lord Barton hadn't been listening. "*Her.* The niece. Miss Eastlake."

Lord Barton folded his hands in his lap. "Pray, excuse my dullwittedness. Age, I suspect, has robbed me of my ability to read minds."

This comment brokered nary a glance, confounding Lord Barton even more. Generally speaking Ptolemy was quick to pick up on his grandfather's sarcasm. Instead, he stood scowling out the window.

Lord Barton tried again. "Let me see if I have this right. The Litton sisters have a niece, a Miss Eastlake, who does not speak French."

"Not *a* girl. *The* girl. Didn't I tell you this?"

"*The* girl?"

"Yes, yes." Ptolemy crossed the room and sank down on his haunches in front of Lord Barton's chair. "*The girl*, Grandfather. The girl from the Savoy. The one who stole my pen. She's Lavinia Litton's great-niece."

All the pieces slipped into place as neatly as tumblers turning in a well-oiled lock. Somehow Lord Barton managed not to grin. "Oh. *That* girl."

"Yes." Ptolemy leapt to his feet and began pacing again. "Exactly. That girl. And she does not speak French and yet her two elderly relatives are trusting this girl, this inexperienced, impetuous, green *girl*, to see them safely across France."

"Preposterous."

Ptolemy swung around, snapping his fingers and pointing at Lord Barton as if he were a student in his classroom who'd just given the right answer to a difficult question. "That's it! It's preposterous. Absurd."

Of course, it wasn't really. France was hardly the wilds of Borneo. And as Miss Eastlake had enough savvy to turn his brilliant grandson's world upside down in the course of one short evening, she might not be as inexperienced or green as Ptolemy believed. Indeed, the fact that she'd been singing from a perch atop the Savoy's bar strongly suggested otherwise. But far be it from Lord Barton to point this out.

"I should never have left without persuading them to let me escort them. I can't think where my head was."

"Neither can I."

"It is my guess that she has never even been out of the country. She'll be taken advantage of at every turn." He clucked his tongue like a disapproving old uncle before his gaze lit on Lord Barton. "Not to mention putting *your* ladies in heaven knows what sort of predicaments. I shan't wonder that they all end up marooned in some disreputable little hovel having to wire back for funds."

"Good God." Lord Barton allowed himself the indignity of a small gasp. "Do you really think so?"

"I *assume* so. Why, there's every chance that left to their own devices and owing entirely to Lucy's lack of experience, they might not make it to the rendezvous point *at all.*"

"Lucy?"

"Miss Eastlake." He tossed this off as if he were already well accustomed to calling her "Lucy."

How very, very interesting.

"Well," Lord Barton said mildly, "what can you do about it?"

CHAPTER

11

"'Tis a good thing yer traveling this morning, miss," the ferry office's elderly ticket agent said, printing out a receipt and sliding three tickets beneath the little caged window.

"Why's that?" Lucy asked, taking the tickets and tucking them into her purse.

"The late crossing looks to be coming on particular rough and like to stay that way for a few days unless I miss my guess—and after forty years staring at that sea and that sky, I'm seldom wrong."

She followed his gaze. Overhead, the sun shone in a clear blue sky, but farther out a dark cobalt smudge bled into the ocean's western horizon. "Hate to think of them old ladies being tossed around like a cork in one of them new wash machines. Channel can get considerable tempestuous this time of year."

She thanked him and headed back across the wharf to the wrought iron bench where she'd deposited her great-aunts, relieved they would beat the bad weather to the French coast. Lavinia in particular seemed to consider the journey a necessary evil, and though clearly a little worried, seemed resolved to endure it with as much dignity as possible. She'd spent yesterday on the train from London gazing out the windows at the landscape tearing by.

"I can't imagine what Mama would have thought of speeding along," Lavinia had said more than once.

"Would she have disapproved?" Lucy had asked.

"I'm not sure," she replied. "It's just so different. Remember when travel was an art?"

"No." She'd never been out of Great Britain.

She found the whole thing a grand adventure. Just the idea of walking the streets of a real French city sent ripples of excitement dancing along her skin. It would be marvelous! Though it would have been even more marvelous had Archie Grant been with them to make arrangements, look deliciously piratical—or even more deliciously confounded by something she'd said—and, well, speaking French.

She had never met anyone more in need of a good time than the proper, and properly gorgeous, Professor Grant. But for all his naiveté where women were concerned—and it hadn't taken her ten minutes of watching him at Robin's Hall to figure that out—he was no chump. For example, she'd had the uncomfortable suspicion he'd tumbled to her little deception about Madame de Barge, one she'd managed to keep from the old dears for years. And how likely was that? She'd made a career of acting, and had easily convinced her great-aunts that she'd taken French lessons.

She'd never out-and-out lied to them, of course. She really had received lessons from the tailor's temperamental wife. Three lessons, to be exact. But when she'd realized that her great-aunts were paying for those lessons by foregoing their favorite blend of tea, one of their very few remaining indulgences, well, why would a girl like her need to know French?

Occasionally, she'd swept out the tailor's workroom for a few pence, eavesdropping on the de Barges to add a few phrases to her repertoire so that on those occasions when her aunts requested an example of her progress, she could dutifully trot them out, having a vague idea of their meaning based on the context in which she'd heard them. Being a natural mimic and even more natural story-teller, she managed to keep her secret.

She figured she'd do well enough in France as long as the conversation did not extend much beyond, "How much does that cost?" "I would like milk with my tea," and "You would look very handsome in a new jacket."

Besides, surely one could always find someone who spoke both French and English? She just wished that someone were Archie Grant. He'd looked so delectably nonplussed when she'd teased him about hunting her up. She simply hadn't been able to resist. Not that she'd tried.

How coincidental that her pirate should be the grandson of the same man Aunt Lavinia had fallen in love with all those years ago. Why, if this were a popular musical, and a girl were a starry-eyed romantic, one would say they'd been destined to meet, the past having found its echo in the present. And in the next act, Archie Grant would be waiting for her on the ferry, his dark hair rumpled, the cleft in his chin accenting the manly cut of his jaw . . .

But she wasn't, this wasn't, and he wouldn't be.

Drat.

Aware she was frowning, she fixed a smile on her face as she approached her great-aunts.

"What are you two talking about?" she asked, taking a seat at the end of the bench. "You look positively guilty."

"Nonsense!" Bernice sputtered. "We were simply discussing Lord Barton's grandson."

Lucy started, wondering if the old ladies had added telepathy to their talents.

"Actually," Lavinia said, far more tranquilly than her sister, "we were discussing the dimple in his chin."

Mind readers, for sure.

"It is a cleft," Bernice said, her former embarrassment forgotten.

"A cleft is a notch. He had a dimple."

"What do you say, Lucy?"

"I should call it a cleft," Lucy replied in a similarly serious tone, and Bernice shot a triumphant glance at Lavinia. "But that doesn't mean someone else calling it a dimple would be wrong."

Lavinia gave her younger sister an equally smug smile.

"Cleft or dimple, Professor Grant is a most well-composed young man," Bernice said, willing to let the matter rest now that she'd been vindicated. "With much to recommend him."

"He seems a mite solemn," said Lavinia thoughtfully. "His grandfather was just such a somber young man. Very highly principled. Very honorable."

It seemed strange for her great-aunt to look so unhappy about this assessment, especially as Lavinia generally admired those qualities. "But then, I could be accused of the same." A touch of melancholy shadowed her face.

"Accused?" An odd choice of words.

Lavinia released the softest of sighs. "Believe it or not, I was accounted quite a modern woman for my day. I rode to the hunt, I wore the latest fashions, I read the daily newspapers." She spoke with undeniable pride. "I was no beauty—no, Bernice, you needn't protest. We are both well beyond the need to be complimented on our looks either through kindness or charity. I was no beauty, but I had character."

"Of course," Lucy said.

"But I was also a lady."

Lucy tipped her head inquiringly.

"Though I have never said as much, I think it time to acknowledge that what I felt for Lord Barton was more than simple friendship."

Her great-aunt had spent nearly fifty years guarding her privacy and her secrets, or so she'd believed. Lucy wondered why she'd suddenly decided to confess.

"I assumed he shared a similar attachment, though I will not belabor you with the reasons why I thought this—"

"I don't feel belabored," Lucy piped up. "Not in the least."

At this, a twinkle appeared in Lavinia's eye. "I won't belabor you," she repeated. "Suffice to say, I was hopeful that when the siege ended, our relationship would not. After we were rescued, John escorted me to Bombay, but with each mile that we drew nearer to our destination the young man on whose friendship I had grown to rely, who had been my bastion against fear and despair, seemed to fade. He became distant. Uncommunicative. Never sullen, but sober."

Though she did not turn her head, Bernice's hand crept over and clasped her sister's tightly in her lap.

"I suppose I imagined a great deal of it. Under the circumstances, it wouldn't be unusual." She smiled a little sadly. "At first I harbored a tender hope that had it not been for certain factors beyond his control John would have declared himself, or at least informed me that there were commitments or obligations that required his attention before he spoke."

"At first?" Lucy prodded gently. Lavinia had never been so forthcoming before. Her tale had always been told couched in allegories and allusions.

"Yes. At first. But with the passage of time I realized how foolish I had been."

"Never!" Bernice muttered under her breath, her lower lip quivering with indignation.

Lavinia gave her hand a squeeze. "Yes. It is not entirely John's fault that I never knew his feelings; I never asked. I bid good-bye to him in Bombay without saying a word about my own attachment. I told myself I was being honorable as well, stiff-lipped and silent as he. And now I will never know."

"But you do," Lucy said. "He would not have given you his share of the rubies otherwise."

Lavinia shot her a wry look, releasing her sister's hand with a comforting pat. "Knowing I had feelings for him that he either could not or would not reciprocate would have been a lifelong burden for such an honorable fellow as John. He may feel he owes me this." And then, amazingly, she smiled. "And so he does."

Then she amazed Lucy even further by laughing. "My dear, don't look so stricken. Not on my account. It was fifty years ago. I would be pathetic indeed, if after all these years I was still moping over some lost love I'm not even sure was mine to lose in the first place. I have had a happy life. Not exciting, but filled with the pleasures of home and family. Including you.

"Truth be told, I don't suppose I could have choked the words out had I tried. I was eighteen and though intrepid, still a product of my time. No, I just wonder sometimes, is all. About what would have happened had I said something."

Impulsively, Lucy bent over and pressed her cheek against Lavinia's. It felt delicate and powdery, like rose petals pressed in a book. Not unexpectedly Lavinia, who was, as she had just acknowledged, a product of a much less demonstrative generation, blushed. But, Lucy noted, she looked mildly gratified.

Bernice gave a small gasp.

"Don't be so puritanical, Bernice," Lavinia chided. "I know it is a public place but Lucy—"

"It's not that!" Bernice lumbered to her feet, her little straw boater bobbling atop her head, her face red with emotion. "Oh, Lucy. I am so very, very sorry!"

"What ever is wrong?"

"I have left our jewelry case back at the hotel!"

CHAPTER
12

Lucy's shoulders drooped with relief. The Litton "jewels" consisted of a few not-particularly-good paste replicas of her great-grandmother's parure. They'd been sold and replaced with copies a decade before Lucy had arrived at Robin's Hall. Even at eleven Lucy had recognized them as cheap imitations, though she'd never been so impolite as to point out that fact, of course.

"No, you haven't, dear," she said. "I very carefully combed both hotel rooms before we checked out and I am sure we did not leave so much as a hairpin behind."

"It wasn't *in* the hotel room. I was worried about something untoward happening and so I entrusted the case to the manager to put in the hotel safe."

Lucy sympathized, but there was nothing to be done for it. There simply wasn't time to return to the hotel before they were due to board and she doubted the ferry company would hold the boat while she fetched a few pounds of worthless glass.

"It's all right, Aunt Bernice," she reassured her. "I will telephone the hotel at once. They will keep the case safe as houses until our return."

"It's not the jewels, Lucy." Bernice wrung her hands fretfully. "Lord Barton's letter was in the case, too."

This was an entirely different matter. Even with the letter Lucy worried whether Lavinia would be allowed to claim Lord Barton's portion of the rubies. Without it there wasn't a chance the bank would release the rubies to her.

She glanced up at the clock set in the pediment above the ticket office. They were due to sail in thirty minutes. If she managed to hail a taxi, *and* if traffic was light, *and* if she found the hotel manager the minute she entered the premises, *and* if he obliged with all haste in opening the safe, she *might* make it back. She might also dance a fandango at the Palace tonight. But the distance between possibility and probability stretched a long way.

The only other option was to take the later ferry.

Her worried gaze slipped to the western horizon where the cobalt smudge had thickened. A couple of *days* of bad weather, the ticket attendant had said.

She would just have to risk it.

"I am so sorry, Lucy." Bernice's pug face tightened with misery. "I thought only to be cautious and didn't want to ask you to have to do it—you've already done so much—but I forgot to retrieve it! I never would have forgotten five years ago."

Lucy patted her hand distractedly, her thoughts racing. If she *didn't* make it back in time, who would shepherd her great-aunts to France? She didn't want to expose them to rough seas . . . but she didn't want to take the chance that they would be late arriving in Saint-Girons and that all-important anniversary. If Lavinia missed being present at the bank on the anniversary date, she might very well face being eliminated from securing a share altogether.

Lavinia placed a consoling hand on her sister's arm. "Oh, darling, that's not true. You would have likely forgotten ten years ago, too."

Perhaps they ought to forfeit Lord Barton's portion and be content with Lavinia's?

Bernice frowned, distracted from guilt by affront. "I am sure *not*, Lavinia. Ten years ago my memory was as clear as—"

What in blazes was she thinking? Of course, she wasn't going to just give up a fortune! Not without a fight, she wasn't.

"It's all right, dears. I'll just go fetch it now. Wait here."

"But—"

"If I'm not back before the boarding we'll figure something else out. But I'll be back," she promised with a great deal more conviction than she felt. "Wait here for me."

And with that she picked up her skirts and fled down the wharf toward the street, hoping against hope that a hansom cab would be standing there with fresh horses dancing in their traces.

A hansom cab *was* there. It stood at the curb while an enormous load of luggage was being handed down piece by piece from the top racks, the driver working at a snail's pace. Lucy looked around. There was no other conveyance in sight. She peered closer at the cab and made out the silhouette of the man still inside. Perhaps if she appealed to the luggage's owner?

She went to the side and rapped on the window. "Look here, my good fellow, could you ask the driver to hurry up? I have an emergency—"

"Don't we all?" drawled a silky, familiar voice as the door swung open and a well-polished boot appeared.

"Margery!"

"In the flesh and ready to embark upon my triumphant tour of France's many quaint but sadly entertainment-deprived towns."

He emerged from the carriage, swinging an ebony-handled cane and beaming with avuncular affection.

"I thought you were going to Paris?"

"My darling girl. One does not *start* a tour in Paris, one concludes it triumphantly there. I start in . . ." He frowned, pulled a face, and shook his head. "Oh, who can remember French towns? I'll look it up when I arrive.

"Now, what is this emergency? I do hope it doesn't involve money. You know I never carry cash upon my person; it only encourages people in the misguided assumption that I intend to pay for something."

She shook her head, miserably regarding Margery's luggage. The driver hadn't even unloaded a third of it. Drat. Drat, drat, drat! The sense of urgency left her like air seeping from a punctured balloon. It was too late.

Reading the disappointment in her expression, Margery took her elbow and propelled her across the street and beneath the awning of a café. "Tell me," he said.

The words spilled out in a brief, succinct flurry. When she was finished, Margery tipped his head and smiled with preening self-satisfaction.

"What?" she asked.

"But, my darling one, it is so simple. *I* shall accompany the dear old tabbies on the ferry crossing."

Lord, she adored the man. He had an enormous, trusting, and egalitarian heart.

If only her aunts had been cut from the same cloth. But they weren't. They would *never* allow themselves to become obligated to a strange man.

"If only you could." She smiled regretfully.

"But why could I not?"

"My great-aunts would never agree to being under a debt of gratitude to you."

Margery's ginger brows flew up.

"It just isn't done amongst their generation. A gentleman simply does not impose upon a lady by placing her in a position of indebtedness."

"That is *so* odd," Margery muttered, unoffended but mystified. His own antecedents were far from genteel. Though he'd polished a bright veneer of refinement about himself, it was only a veneer and he, at least, never mistook it for something more.

"Ain't it, though?" Lucy agreed disconsolately.

"Truly? They won't accept me as an escort even though you will vouch for my character?"

She shook her head. It was ridiculous and narrow-minded that a letter of introduction from a man Lavinia had known more than fifty years ago endorsing a grandson they had never set eyes on could make that grandson acceptable, while Margery, whom Lucy had known as a friend for years, was relegated to the ranks of "suspicious" due to his working-class roots. But there would be no arguing with them.

"The only men with whom I could possibly be acquainted and whom they do not also know could only be a fellow performer. I strongly suspect Bernice would actually prefer to die rather than be escorted anywhere by a male entertainer."

Margery didn't argue. He puzzled a moment, his perfectly manicured nails tapping the head of his ebony walking stick. His face cleared. "I know what to do."

"You do?"

"Yes. Now, you return to your aunties and I shall be with you anon. Say not a word until I join you."

"But—"

"Never fear, my dear. All is in hand." And with that, he strode back to where the carriage driver was still unloading his trunks and started gesticulating urgently.

Lucy did as he instructed, retracing her route back along the wharf. She didn't see that she had anything to lose.

Her great-aunts greeted her with surprised consternation. "You couldn't have made it to the hotel and back already?"

"Ah . . . no, but everything is taken care of. Don't worry."

She sat down between the pair of them, contriving to look confident. They peered at her in concern. Lucy remained mute, crippled by ignorance and worried that whatever she said would somehow prove detrimental to Margery's plan. But her uncharacteristic silence only made them more fretful.

"Now, Lucy . . ." Lavinia finally began.

"Don't harass Lucy, Livie," Bernice hushed her. "If she says everything is taken care of then I am sure that everything is taken care of. She has never failed us yet."

She looked expectantly at Lucy. *Very* expectantly. "Of course, one might wonder what evolved during Lucy's brief absence that has allowed her to state so confidently that everything has been attended to. It would be unnatural not to be curious."

The expectant look became an insistent one. Lucy felt her resolve to remain silent begin to crumble.

"Because whatever she has decided not only affects her but intimately involves us."

Ah. *Guilt.* Lucy had been wondering when that bit of ammunition would be brought to bear.

"Which I am sure she is well aware of—"

"Luuuucccy!"

Startled by the rich contralto voice trilling Lucy's name, the three women swiveled on the bench. A female figure swept toward them, awash in a sea of billowing pink feathers, trailing a raft of fuchsia-colored lace. A huge Merry Widow hat dripping with cabbage roses and lilac sprays perched atop her a blancmange of pale gold curls.

She bore down on them like an ambulatory wedding cake, arriving to grab Lucy by the shoulders, haul her to her feet, clasp her to her bosom, and bus her smartly on the cheek before pushing her back down onto the bench. She beamed at Lavinia and Bernice.

"And are these the darlings whose company I am to be privileged to share on the crossing?" asked Margery, the World's Premiere Impersonator of Female Characterizations.

CHAPTER

13

Lucy studied "Mrs. Marjorie Martin" with frank admiration. Fully immersed in his female persona, Margery was charm incarnate, cooing about how he'd known "darling Lucy ever since her triumphant debut on the same musical stage as I." He then revealed his surprise at spying "dear Lucy" whilst disembarking from his carriage and subsequent distress over finding the girl in abject misery over some possession or other left behind at some hotel, unable to reconcile herself to risking her aunts' discomfort by taking a later ferry crossing, yet equally unhappy at the prospect of having them go on without her.

"So, of course," Margery said, "at once I thought how wonderful it would be if *I* might join you. I realize that a strange woman," here he had the temerity to actually wink at her, "of a certain age is a poor substitute for a beloved niece, but I would be so grateful if you would allow me the pleasure of your company. These European tours can be so lonely."

The adroit manner in which he set the bait proved irresistible.

"Tours?" Bernice asked.

"Yes. Didn't Lucy tell you? Naughty girl." He dimpled at her. "I am touring the French countryside, bringing a bit of culture to the smaller cities before proceeding on to Paris where I will perform at the . . . Grand Opera House."

Liar.

Lavinia gnawed her lip, wavering between being impressed or scandalized. Bernice had no such a quandary.

"You are someone famous!" she said, wide-eyed. "Are you Collectible? Lucy is a Collectible, you know."

Happily, Margery, who adorned many cards, all of which took salacious pleasure in revealing his true gender, sidestepped the one question by answering the other. "I did know! And a lovely thing it is, too. Not as lovely as the original, of course."

Bernice beamed.

"*Do* say I might join your little party," Margery implored. "I am convinced we shall get on splendidly."

The sisters convened a quick confabulation a discreet distance away from the charming Mrs. Marjorie Martin. As might have been expected, Lavinia initially balked: Mrs. Martin's ensemble was simply too flamboyant for a gentlewoman's.

But then Bernice pointed out that though somewhat ostentatious in dress, Mrs. Martin's superior breeding and good taste was clear in her admiration of Lucy. Besides, the Litton sisters hadn't been in society for decades. What did they know about what ladies wore these days? Except for Lucy, of course, and she was a *young* lady.

Mrs. Martin could hardly be expected to wear the same sort of gowns as a girl. Not that she was old, but she was definitely mature and, as with many beautiful women who spy the advance of age before they expect it, had discreetly remedied a few of time's little indignities with the judicious use of cosmetic fixatives. One could not argue with the results, and if her gowns were a tad closefitting, well, Bernice generously opined, it would be unnatural not to want to show off so well-maintained a figure.

Loath to be thought stodgy compared to her sister—especially as everyone had always considered Bernice the more conservative one—Lavinia reversed direction and was soon championing their would-be fellow traveler as if she'd never looked askance at her boas and lace. Though she could not entirely approve of Mrs. Martin's use of powder and paint, at least she was honest enough to concede that if powder and paint could do as much for her own features as they did for Mrs. Martin's she might be tempted to employ them, too.

And so within five minutes the matter was settled.

"We'll take all the luggage with us, Lucy, so you won't have to deal with it," Margery said after thanks and reassurances and courtesies and compliments had been traded. "Then your great-aunts and I shall find a nice cozy corner in which to tuck ourselves for a spot of tea and a chat, shall we?" She leaned toward the sisters and twinkled. "I always carry my own special mixture in a thermos when I travel. Along with a few sundry delicacies of which I am eager to see if you approve."

The sisters nodded in pleased unison.

Margery turned to Lucy, a three-pointed cat's smile on his face. "We shall see you in Saint-Malo this evening." He turned toward the ladies, one arm open in an encompassing gesture. "Come along, my dears. We will want a good seat."

Hurriedly, her great-aunts bid Lucy adieu and then, without a hint of reluctance, followed their new friend across the gangway and onto the ferry like ducklings after their mother. And why not? Mrs. Martin had the air of a seasoned traveler and was clearly a woman of the world and, while they would never question Lucy's abilities, they were all well aware that she had never been out of Great Britain.

"Be off with you, Lucy!" Margery called, taking a position next to the rail and making a shooing gesture with his lace-gloved hands. "We will be fine."

And then the sailors hauled the gangway up onto the boat and threw off the heavy cables. Margery linked arms with her great-aunts and led them toward the first-class salon as the ferry churned slowly out to sea.

The hansom cab Margery had used was long gone by the time she returned to the street so Lucy ended up walking to the hotel. There it took seemingly forever before the desk clerk was able to locate the manager, who held the only key to the hotel's safe. He was finally found taking a nap in one of the hotel's unreserved rooms.

By the time Lucy had the jewelry case *and* Lord Barton's all-important letter in her possession, ate a leisurely lunch at the hotel restaurant (because there wasn't much else to do while she waited for the next packet) and walked back to the wharf, nearly three hours had passed.

She didn't worry too much about Margery and her great-aunts. Margery would be reveling in his role. No, as long as her great-aunts didn't tumble to Margery's true gender, Lucy had no doubt that they would all enjoy themselves immensely.

She smiled at the ancient ticket agent still ensconced behind his grated office window as she approached. "Passage for one, please."

"Missed your boat, eh? That's too bad." He started writing on his ticket stub. "When?"

"The next available."

He put his pen down. "You're not thinking of taking this afternoon's crossing?"

"I'm not thinking of it. I'm intent on it."

"Well, I hope you have more to wear than that, miss. 'Cause that coat ain't gonna keep you dry in a squall."

She followed the ticket agent's pointed glance, looking over her shoulder at where her few fellow passengers were already boarding the ferry. Behind them a huge anvil-shaped cloud loomed up from the horizon. The sight gave her momentary pause. All her clothing was in the luggage accompanying her great-aunts.

"I shall stay inside if it rains." She pushed her stack of bills under the small space beneath the little grate.

He pushed them back. "No *if* aboot it, miss. It's gonna rain. Pitchforks. You sure you want to go?"

She pushed the bills forward. "I'm sure."

He ignored her money. "You ever been on a ferry, miss? It ain't no punt. Great, unwieldy creatures ferries are, slopping about with every pitch of the channel."

She tamped down her impatience, telling herself that he only had her best interest at heart. He couldn't appreciate that she was no shrinking society miss, but a stout-hearted adventurer. A little water wasn't enough to put her off her pace because, really, how bad could it be?

Besides, she *loved* storms: the sharp, pungent scent of an oncoming tempest, the electrical prickling across her bare flesh, the wind whipping her hair and clothing about. It was invigorating and exciting and, truth be told, she was actually looking forward to experiencing a storm at sea.

"Indeed, I have, sir," she said, smiling. "I truly appreciate your concern, but I was actually *born* on a ship. My father was a merchant vessel captain and my mother traveled with him. I learned to walk on a"—oh, dear what was it called? Oh, yes—"*quarterdeck* in the Indian Ocean." She smiled brightly.

His eyes widened in surprise that quickly segued to admiration. "Thought you had a bit of the sea in your gait."

She dimpled modestly. Of course he'd bought what she was selling. She'd expected no less. She'd fashioned a career out of telling people what they wanted to hear. Or needed to hear. She wouldn't say she was a *liar* but sometimes she forged a more palatable truth.

He took her name, printed it on the ship's manifest, and passed a ticket to her. "Safe passage, miss."

She thanked him then made her way toward where the ferry was boarding its final few passengers. The wind had picked up. A freshening breeze tugged at her hat, threatening to lift it from her head. She clamped a hand atop her head, quashing down her hat's crown. But the wicked wind found its way beneath her coat, sending it flapping about her calves.

Smiling into the coming storm, filled with the cheek and optimism that had been her companions since the day she was born, she flew across the gangway and onboard then up a short flight of stairs to the observation deck that perched atop the salon. There, she fell breathless against the rail, exhilarated, as, on the wharf below, workers hurried to untie the lines, worried eyes darting to the oncoming storm front. Beside her a smattering of her fellow intrepid passengers nodded a greeting, buoying Lucy with a shared feeling of anticipation.

She smiled back brightly, for the first time in months unencumbered by worry over Lavinia's health or fear over the fate of Robin's Hall. She felt free, bohemian, and adventurous. All she needed to complete her delight was a companion on her adventure . . .

At once an image sprang to mind, an image of a man with thick, blue-black hair and dark brows above lushly lashed black eyes, a wide, sensually shaped mouth, and a square jaw with a cleft in his chin. But what if Lavinia was right and Archie Grant was too staid to go adventuring? Perhaps he wasn't a pirate after all. Perhaps he was just a stuffy professor, a stickler for rules and conformity.

No, not with that chin, he wasn't. He might try to be, but The Chin would have out. *That* was the chin of an undomesticated ne'er-do-well, a scoundrel and a scallywag. A pirate.

She propped an elbow on the rail and cupped her chin in her hand, idly watching the last stragglers hurry aboard as her inner speculation grew increasingly more dramatic—and more gratifying. A pirate took what he wanted without a by-your-leave, through charm or by force, whichever best served his purpose. He would sneer at adversity and race headlong into the teeth of any storm . . . Like that fellow racing down the wharf.

A man was running pell-mell toward the ferry, his hand clamping his hat to his head, obscuring his features. In the other he clutched the handle of a leather valise. His unbuttoned mackintosh flew behind like him dark wings and the wind plastered his shirt to a hard, muscular chest—

Archie?

It *was* Archie. She snapped upright. Though closing fast, Archie was still eighty yards away. The gangway had already been pulled on board and the lines untied from the wharf cleats. The ferry was slowly pulling away, water churning between the pier and the boat's port side.

"Don't shut the gate!" she yelled at the pair of deckhands about to swing the metal arm shut at the top of the gangway. They squinted up at her through the salt spray.

Having spotted Archie, too, other passengers were adding their voices to hers. "Wait! There's a man coming!"

"There!" Frantically, she pointed at Archie as she flew down the steps to the main deck. "You've got to open the gate!"

The sailors followed the direction of her finger to see the madman running down the wharf, clearly having no plan to stop when he reached the end. Feverishly, they hauled the gate back open and leapt to the side, waving him in.

His sprint had taken on the feel of a sporting event. The passengers on the deck above cheered him on as the sailors gesticulated wildly. Twenty feet from the end of the wharf he swung the valise up and around, sending it twirling through the air. It landed dead center of the gateway and skidded across the polished deck.

"Come on!" the sailors shouted encouragingly. Six feet separated the wharf and ferry.

"You can do it!"

Eight feet.

Ten feet.

"Jump, Archie! *Now!*"

He never paused, never broke stride. One minute he was on the wharf, the next he was sailing through the air, his arms pinwheeling as he landed, his momentum pitching him straight toward her.

CHAPTER
14

Archie's eyes widened with horror as Lucy set herself squarely in his path, her arms outstretched as if—good God! She was going to try to *catch* him!

Before he could react, he catapulted into her. A whoosh of air exploded from Lucy's lungs as she flung her arms around his waist. Terrified he might fall on her he grabbed her around her waist and at the last second wheeled around. His back crashed against the salon wall. "Ow."

A smattering of applause broke out around them. From the corner of his eye he saw one sailor glumly peel off a bill from the wad in his hand and pass it to another. They swung the gate closed. The show over, people scurried out of the elements and into the enclosed salon.

He barely noted them, too intent on running his hands over Lucy to see if she was broken. Quickly and forcibly he discovered she was not only whole, but wholly female.

Her slender form flattened against him, her unexpectedly strong arms holding tight around his torso. A potent surge of physical awareness drilled through him. He took a deep, steadying breath, but that only made things worse since he inhaled her scent, a thought-disrupting combination of electricity and verdant earth and . . . and orange blossoms? Why would she smell like orange blossoms?

What was he thinking? He wasn't even sure he knew what orange blossoms smelled like; he only knew they ought to smell like her.

She made a sound.

He released her at once, only to take hold of her shoulders and anxiously search her face. "Are you all right?"

He needn't have asked. She'd let go of his waist, too, and now clasped his lapels, trapping him a foot away as she tipped her head back, laughing. Her rich brown hair had come undone and rippled in the wind, skimming across the backs of his hands, silky and cool.

"That was spectacular, Archie!" she exclaimed, green-gold-brown eyes sparkling with admiration. "Where did you learn to do something like that?"

He probably should release her. "Public school."

She smiled. "I didn't realize jumping was a standard part of a public school curriculum."

Yes, he really should let her go, but . . . "I was an unruly student. The headmaster concluded that a physical outlet for my energy would aid my attention in the classroom." Why had he said that? What could she possibly care?

"Oh." She nodded wisely. "They thought to wear the unruliness right out of you, did they?"

"Something like that." He could not imagine why they were having such a conversation on the deck of a ferry while a storm brewed all around. Yet here she stood, regarding him with as much fascination as if he'd just discovered a Neanderthal skull. And a good deal more approval. It was a little unnerving. A little heady.

"You must have liked it."

"Yes," he allowed, more interested in watching her fingers slowly uncurl from around his lapels than his twenty-year-old memories.

She stepped back. It was just as well. He found having his arms empty of her much more conducive to clear thinking.

For instance, until now he hadn't realized that she hadn't asked him what he was doing here or why. In fact, just like the morning he'd come to Robin's Hall, she didn't appear particularly surprised to see him. She was either the sort of come-what-may, come-what-will type of person who simply followed whatever path showed up under her foot or she considered his presence predestined. Neither possibility was reassuring.

The steam ferry had left the wharf behind, its engines churning mightily as it headed toward the white-capped water beyond the harbor. It was bound to be an uncomfortable crossing. Particularly for the older ladies . . . He'd forgotten all about them. Damn!

"Are your aunts inside?"

"Hm?" Lucy was industriously putting to rights his abused coat, smoothing the crumpled material.

"Your aunts." Whether she required a reason for his presence or not, he felt compelled to explain himself. "I came because I thought you might . . . they might . . . I couldn't just let you . . . them . . ."

"Of course not, Archie." She agreed with his unfinished statement as if she knew perfectly well what he meant—which was impossible because he wasn't sure that *he* knew what he meant.

"I assume you've already tucked your great-aunts into a safe corner in the salon? I hope so because it's going to be a nasty crossing." He frowned. "Frankly, I'm surprised the agent even sold you tickets considering the ladies' advanced years."

She finally seemed satisfied with her ministrations, for she gave a short, approving nod. "Oh, he didn't. Lavinia and Bernice took the morning crossing. They should have docked in France hours ago."

"They did?"

"Yes. Honestly, Archie, what are you thinking? I would never expose them to unnecessary discomfort."

"Why aren't you with them?"

"Aunt Lavinia left your grandfather's letter back at the hotel and discovered it was missing just before the ferry was to leave. There wasn't time to fetch it and still make the earlier crossing. So I sent them on ahead and went back for the letter myself. Good thing I did, too," she confided. "Because otherwise you wouldn't have found me. How *did* you know where to find me, Archie?" She beamed at him.

He stared. She was twisting things around again. She had a positive talent for it. "I didn't find *you*, Luc—Miss Eastlake."

"Of course you did." Her confidence was absolute.

"I meant I wasn't *looking* for you. I was looking for your great-aunts."

"But you found me," she said brightly. "How did you know where to look?"

"Because the girl at your house, Polly, told me your plans."

"And so you followed me here."

"I did not follow—" He should just give up. She meant to be deliberately obtuse. "Do you think it was wise to let your great-aunts cross unaccompanied? Of course I trust your judgment, but—"

"You do?" Her eyes widened with gratification.

She really did have extraordinarily pretty eyes. But he would not be distracted by them *or* her pleasure in something as simple as his vote of confidence in her. Which might have been bending the truth since he didn't actually trust her judgment. In fact, his complete lack of trust in her judgment was the primary reason he was here right now.

"Ah. Yes." He might as well add lying to the list of sins he'd already committed since meeting this woman, a list that included wriggling out of a party given by his future father-in-law, foisting Cornelia off on Lionel for the same occasion, and stowing away on this ferry—because he hadn't actually had time to pay the ticket agent before making his mad dash down the wharf. He must remember to do so when they disembarked.

"How sweet!" Her smile was meltingly lovely.

No one had ever called him sweet before and had he been told that someday someone would do so *and* that he would not take exception to the label, he would have laughed in their face. He cleared his throat. "Ahem. Still, I don't know that I would be as confident as you in their capabilities to deal with unforeseen difficulties, and unforeseen difficulties *always* arise on journeys abroad." He fixed her with a long, penetrating look. "But as a seasoned traveler, I'm sure you already know this."

"Of course." She stared him dead in the eye. "Which is why I was so pleased to discover a friend of mine who just happened to be on the same ferry. He generously offered his escort to them."

Well, that was a relief—"*He?*"

Her bright gaze slipped to a spot beyond his shoulder. He wasn't sure what to make of that. He could easily read the not-so-subtle changes in her demeanor that telegraphed she was about to tell a hummer or had just told a hummer: her face cleared like the sun arriving after a cloudy day, her brow smoothed, and her eyes shone with innocent candor. It was as telling as if she wrote on her forehead, "I am having you on." But this shifting, her slight but unmistakable discomfort, was something else. Something more suspicious.

"An old family friend?"

"Not exactly." She let the words play out slowly, clearly racking her brain over how to answer. "I met him when I sang at a music hall my first season on stage. Before I started singing light opera."

Had she sent her great-aunts off with one of her admirers? Something in his chest flinched. He decided it was disapproval.

Which was absurd. He had studied without judgment societies whose members shared varied and multiple understandings of moral situations, including sexual interactions. She was a performer, a songstress; undoubtedly she had many admirers. Some of them even apparently importuned her in public bars and asked her to dine. He would do well to remember it. Though why he ought to do so was an open question, because what she did or with whom was no concern of his and . . . And? Oh yes. And he was planning to marry Cornelia. "I see."

"I assure you he'll take very good care of them." She slid by him, heading toward the rail. He followed.

They were in open water now, the stinging spray anointing her head while the gusting wind sculpted her billowing coat and skirts against her body.

She was going to get soaked.

"You should come into the salon," he said.

She pivoted, leaning back on her elbows against the rail. Her hair flew about her face like Medusa's snakes, though it was a great deal prettier, and the dark sea climbed behind her in growing swells. "Isn't this exhilarating?" she called over the tearing wind.

"You're getting wet!" he shouted back.

She spun around again, eyes shut as she speared her face into the wind and flung her arms wide. "I'm queen of the sea!"

"You're going to be *in* the sea any second!" he yelled, just as the ferry dipped into the trough of a huge roller. She grabbed at the rails as the stern tucked into the wave's shoulder, pitching the boat sharply up, the deck canting ominously. Her laughter tattered on the blistering wind, filled with both fear and exhilaration.

"Come inside!" He wrapped one arm around the column beneath the upper deck, waving her toward him. "Please!"

She nodded. Then, gauging the next swell that would tip the deck toward him, she let go of the railing and skittered in a run-slide straight into his arms where some deep part of him regretfully acknowledged he'd missed the feel of her ever since he'd relinquished her.

Four hours later

"I'm going to die." A sepulchral whisper issued from the form Archie cradled in his arms. And just as he'd done in answer to the previous twenty such lamentations, he ignored it. One of Lucy's hands curled limply against the base of his neck, her fingers chill against his warm skin. The other was tucked between them, over his heart.

He stood next to the ferry's boarding gate, his legs spread wide, braced against the pitch and roll of the ferry as it limped painfully into Sark's small harbor, shuddering as it scraped against the rocks below. It was well into the night, hours since they'd left Weymouth. Bad weather and worse seas had finally forced the captain to sound the emergency horns, alerting the island's residents to their arrival.

On shore was a scene from some medieval tribunal. A black sky loomed overhead, the stars blotted out by thick cloud cover. Along the beach scores of torches held aloft by unseen figures flickered luridly.

Archie shifted his arm beneath Lucy's knees, moving her higher against his chest. He had never actually carried a woman in his arms before—as a rule, the females of his acquaintance generally didn't require transporting—and the sensation was unique. Yet it also felt oddly *un*remarkable. Her warm head dovetailed neatly beneath his chin. Her arm snugged between them as neatly as pieces of a jigsaw puzzle.

If he believed in reincarnation he would have said he spent a great deal of a former life carrying women—he glanced down, frowned—no, carrying *this* woman, or whoever Lucy might have been in a former life that had never occurred. Because, of course, reincarnation was nonsense. But, God help him, that's what it felt like . . .

The ferry's engines reversed with a jolt and he clutched her tighter as deckhands jumped into action, preparing to moor. Many of them shared Lucy's bilious look.

Lucky for him, he had a cast-iron gut.

Something Lucy Eastlake did not.

His gaze lingered on her. She was an altogether unappealing package. Too weak to aid in her own comfort, her legs dangled over his forearm, her head lolled against his chest, and her twisted, tangled tresses of hair dripped in witchy locks down to her breasts. Her sweat-damp skin had taken on the most astonishing greenish hue and her clothing was twisted and crumpled around her small, malodorous person.

Another wave rolled the ferry and she groaned, turning her face into his shirt and shivering. He might have been more concerned for his clothing if he'd believed she'd anything left to cast up. She didn't and he ought to know; he'd held her forehead as she bent over a bucket throughout the entire trip.

She'd made the transition from exuberant joie de vivre to abject misery more slowly than many of the other passengers. It had taken a full twenty minutes on rough seas before her delight had fallen victim to her stomach. But when it had succumbed it had done so with a vengeance.

"I'm going to die," the muffled voice reiterated.

"No, you are not," he reassured her, watching impatiently as crewmen released the anchor with splash then hurried to tie off the aft lines.

"You say that as if it's a good thing," she said, eyes pressed tightly closed.

He smiled at the drama. "We'll be on land in a minute. You'll start feeling better almost at once."

"How do you know?" she asked, cracking open a bleary eye to peer at him accusingly. "You've never been seasick, have you?"

"I've seen innumerable men recover from seasickness as soon as they made solid ground. There's no reason to believe you will be any different."

The island's inhabitants, used to the occasional unplanned arrival of boats that for one reason or another could not reach the isle of Guernsey, let alone France, and anticipating the windfall of revenue that came with paying guests, crowded the small jetty. A score of small boats awaiting passengers bobbed around the ferry like pilot fish around a whale. The ferry's draft was too deep to moor at the wharf, making it necessary to transport the passengers via fishing boats.

"One more short trip and you'll be on dry land," he said handing her down to the men below. She barely had it in her to protest as she was passed from hand to hand. He jumped down into the boat and immediately Lucy was thrust back in his arms as the men turned to assist more passengers.

True to his expectation, within a short time the fishermen were hauling the boats onto the beach. At once the island's women surged forward as their men stood back, holding the heads of horses and ponies hitched to any available conveyance. Clucking sympathetically, the women met each stumbling passenger by wrapping a blanket around their slumping shoulders before whisking them off to a waiting wagon. From there they headed to crofts, taverns, houses, and farms, anywhere there was a spare bed to be let.

"Ach, the poor dear." A grim-faced woman of indeterminate age in a heavy shawl appeared beside them as soon as he set Lucy down. She doffed her broad-brimmed hat and held it over Lucy's face.

"A biscuit and bit of broth will put the color back in yer darlin's cheeks." She darted a quick, assessing gaze at him. "Two quid for bed and board for the pair of you."

He hesitated. Two quid was an obscene amount of money for what might well be nothing more than a pair of straw pallets in a barn. He'd slept rough enough times to know.

She seemed to read his mind. "Beds in the house. Ye'll not find another sech offer on the island."

Already, the beach was clearing. Those either unwilling or unable to pay the exorbitant prices the islanders were demanding for their hospitality were opting instead to find a place back on the ship to bed down. He had a notion Lucy would pay fifty times over what the woman asked not to go back to the ferry.

"Done," he said. The woman nodded then led the way to where a small, expressionless man with skin like shoe leather huddled on the hard plank seat of a small dogcart, rain dripping from the brim of his hat. The woman climbed up beside him while Archie gingerly leaned Lucy into the corner of the cart then leapt up and sat down alongside her.

"Are you all right?" he asked.

"Yes. I feel better already." She gave him a tentative smile, as much to bolster his spirits, he decided, as her own.

But then the driver snapped his whip above his horse's rump and the cart lurched forward, bumping over a rut in the road. Every bit of the reclaimed color vanished from Lucy's cheeks. Her hand flew to cover her mouth. She twisted, grabbing the side of the cart and leaning over it.

Apparently her stomach had something left to give after all.

CHAPTER
15

Bernice set her dessert fork beside her empty plate, until recently occupied by a chocolate bombe, and waited for the others to finish their desserts before broaching the subject foremost in her mind.

"Do you think something terrible has happened?"

Drat. Lavinia had beaten her to the mark. Bernice dolefully studied her sister. There was something different about her this evening. She could not quite think what . . . Good heavens, Lavinia was wearing *rouge*.

She stared. The rouge made Lavinia look . . . pretty. Or as pretty as Lavinia—who even a very fond and very loving sister, which Bernice most assuredly was, had never called a beauty—could be. And her dress? There was something different about it, too. It looked somehow more stylish.

"I am sure not, Lavinia," said their new friend, the fascinatingly worldly Mrs. Martin, who was doubtless the author of Lavinia's painted cheeks.

"Then where is Lucy?" Bernice said. "She ought to have arrived by now."

Mrs. Martin pursed her lips. "You may be right, Bernie. I may call you, Bernie, mightn't I? Bernice is simply far too old-fashioned a name for someone as young in spirit as you."

Bernice, distracted by this utterly transparent, but nonetheless flattering, appeal to her vanity, sat straighter. "Well, if you don't think it's too . . . what is the word Lucy uses? *Zippy*? You don't think it *zippy*, do you? I should hate anyone to think I was attempting to appear younger than my years. I do so dislike a poser."

"No one would ever take you for a poser, Bernie," Mrs. Martin assured her. "As for something having happened to Lucy, you must not think it. I am confident the ferry agents would apprise us if such were the case. But just to put our minds at ease, let me send one of the hotel pages to the ferry's office and see what he can discover. I'll be right back."

She rose to her feet, the glitter from the gems around her throat and wrist vying with the jetty beads adorning her elaborate black gown. The sisters watched her go, then, as soon as she'd disappeared, turned and regarded one another with similar expressions of guilt.

"I feel quite wicked," Lavinia whispered sotto voce.

"I know," Bernice agreed in equally dolorous tones.

"If anything has happened to Lucy I will never forgive myself for . . . for . . ."

"For enjoying yourself so much," Bernice finished.

"Exactly!" Lavinia breathed, relieved to have her could-be transgression out in the open.

Bernice nodded. "I know. I admit I was not altogether in favor of leaving Robin's Hall but now that we have embarked on our adventure, and with so convivial and knowledgeable a guide, I find it quite invigorating."

"And we only left England this morning!"

"Exactly so. Who knows what agreeableness the next days will bring?"

"Who knows?" Lavinia echoed.

"And all the while, poor Lucy may be in mortal danger."

"Never say so." Lavinia reached across the table and patted her hand. "I believe, dear sister, that our fear for Lucy is in actuality guilt over not missing her company more."

Bernice narrowed her eyes. "You have been reading progressive literature again haven't you?"

"Some," Lavinia admitted.

Bernice opted not to criticize. "Well, you and your books may be right. I do feel awful admitting it, but I don't believe I would be nearly as, well, relaxed if Lucy were with us. I would worry about exposing her to some of Mrs. Martin's more sophisticated conversation."

Lavinia leaned across the table. Bernice did likewise. Lavinia glanced right and left and lowered her voice. "Such as her story about the 'jolly little trout' in the chorus?"

"Precisely."

"You don't think Mrs. Martin ever told Lucy that story?"

"Good heavens, no! I am sure she has every respect for Lucy's youth and unmarried state."

"I think so, too. But if Lucy were here we would have had to quash that interesting chat."

"Just so."

"I have news, comrades!"

At the sound of Mrs. Martin's voice the sisters sprang apart.

"I had no sooner reached the lobby when I spotted an emissary from the ferry company speaking to another guest awaiting the boat. First the good news," Mrs. Martin said. "Dear Lucy is fine. Safe and on dry land."

"Oh, good!" the sisters breathed in relief.

"Unfortunately, that land is not France." She waved the air impatiently. "What I mean to say is Lucy is on an island. Sark. The seas were so rough that the ferry was forced to seek safe harbor there."

"Oh, poor Lucy!"

"The agent assured me that everyone is fine. Apparently the situation is not without precedence."

"So she will arrive in the morning?"

Mrs. Martin's lovely face crumpled. "I am afraid not, ducks."

"What do you mean?"

"The ferry was damaged on some rocks coming into the island and they need to make repairs before it is once again seaworthy. They'll be stuck there for another day at the least."

"Then we must wait here for her? What am I thinking? Of course, we must." Though Lavinia tried to sound hearty, Bernice was not fooled. Tension threaded through her voice and pulled at the corners of her eyes. The last time Lavinia had left home had been fifty years ago and look what had happened then. It would be a small wonder if she did not feel some trepidation, for it was one thing to go on an adventure with competent companions, quite another to be marooned in a foreign land without friends or resources. She might not recall how to say "good morning" in French, let alone how to order a meal, though she supposed she could pantomime.

What interested Bernice was her own *lack* of trepidation. She had always been the cautious one in their family, the one least likely to take chances, run risks, or do anything interesting for that matter; yet the prospect of being alone in France didn't overset her at all. Her concern was all for Lavinia.

Mrs. Martin lifted her hands. "I would stay with you if only I could. But I have prior commitments. I am expected in Châtellerault tomorrow night for a performance. I know this—"

"Oh, my. Of course. We would not think of imposing on you!" Lavinia exclaimed in an agony of embarrassment, reaching for her water glass and in doing so upsetting her wineglass. She stumbled to her feet as it spilled across the table, drenching the linen cloth. At once, a waiter appeared to mop up the mess, contempt implicit in his silent efficiency. Lavinia's eyes shimmered with unshed tears.

Feeling her sister's mortification keenly but uncertain how to help, Bernice stared at the red wine pooling beneath her dessert dish.

"*Ça ne fait rien!*" Mrs. Martin snapped at the waiter, rising majestically from her seat and pulling out a chair while ignoring the surreptitious gazes of the other diners. "Please be seated, Lavinia. We might as well enjoy this fellow's little one act play. I saw a similar piece in London once. *How to Avoid Being Tipped*, I believe it was called."

At this, the waiter, who hitherto had evinced no knowledge of English, became all gracious consolation, smilingly bidding "*les madams*" to forgive him for placing the wineglass so unforgivably near the edge of the table.

Lavinia sank down in the proffered seat, her color high. Bernice made no effort to restrain an unladylike smirk of satisfaction.

"I didn't mean to be so clumsy."

"You weren't," Mrs. Martin said. "Now, where were we? Oh, yes. About my tour. I was about to say that though I understand what I am about to ask is an imposition, but I would count it a great favor if you would consider coming with me rather than staying here and waiting for Lucy. Châtellerault is practically on the way to Saint-Girons."

Bernice stared. Whatever Mrs. Martin had been about to say, she would bet the deacon's life it hadn't been that. And from the look on Lavinia's face, she thought as much, too.

Mrs. Martin, however, continued on in the same slightly apologetic tone. "As silly as it may seem to you ladies, I always perform so much better knowing there are familiar faces waiting to greet me afterwards. I am afraid I cannot ask you to attend my little performance—I am in the envious position of playing to sold-out venues," here she lowered her eyes modestly, "but I can guarantee you will not be disappointed in the town or the hotel.

"And we can leave word for Lucy, telling her where we have gone. Or rather where I have absconded with you." She chuckled lightly, her gaze darting from face to face. "That is *if* you would be so kind as to let me abscond with you? Just for a day or so?"

Bernice knew little about people outside her own small sphere. She knew still less about theatre people and other artistes. But she understood innate kindness and recognized generosity of spirit and in Marjorie Martin she saw both.

"Why, thank you," she said before Lavinia could demure. "It would be our pleasure."

CHAPTER
16

Lucy awoke with a start and bolted upright, dazed and disoriented in the thick darkness. Her narrow bed felt lumpy and unfamiliar. And the *smell*—dear Lord. Was that *her*?—was definitely unfamiliar. Where . . . ? How . . . ? *Archie.*

"Archie? Archie!"

A loud bang greeted her frantic call, followed by a muffled curse. Then the door at the foot of the bed swung open and the figure of a tall, strapping man was silhouetted against the doorway. He held one hand to his forehead.

"What is it?" He sounded terse. "Lucy, are you all right?"

At the sound of his voice, her tension dissolved. He hadn't abandoned her. "Yes, Archie. I'm all right."

Broad shoulders slumped with relief then tensed again; this time, she suspected, not with anxiety. "Then why did you shout like that? You scared the hell—the daylights out of me. I banged my head jumping up."

She didn't take offense. She liked that he'd leapt to her aid. It made her feel like a damsel in distress. And he played knight-errant so naturally . . . a tad crabbily, true, but naturally nonetheless, as though he'd rescued slews of damsels . . .

Her smile faded. In point of fact, he would probably come running to any old damsel's aid. She wasn't sure whether this was a good thing or a bad one.

"Well? What happened? Mouse? Bug?" She couldn't see his expression, backlit as he was, but his tone was long-suffering. Apparently the females he'd known were not keen on wildlife. Weak sisters, the lot of them. "Bat?"

"As if a cute little bat would rattle me." She gave a sniff. "I woke up and I didn't know where I was and the only thing I could remember was you but you weren't here so I . . . I called for you."

It was all coming back to her now. The horrific sea voyage, the nearly-as-horrific cart ride, the frequent stops for her to . . . the frequent stops, and finally, gloriously, Archie lifting her from the cart and carrying her against his warm, solid chest for far too short a distance before laying her down on a lumpy mattress. Then a woman with a nose as thin and hooked as an oyster knife had stripped her clothing from her before giving her face and hands a cursory wiping, and *then* had come blessed sleep.

"Oh." He didn't sound displeased, just mildly bemused. As if he didn't really know how to feel about her admission.

"Where are we?" she asked.

"We're in the Beaufort house on the island of Sark, about twenty-five miles from the French coast. You're occupying their recently married daughter's room." He turned and started to close the door.

"Wait!"

He stopped. "What?"

"Where are you sleeping?"

"In the next room."

"There's another bedroom next to this?"

"No. It's a sort of parlor. I am making use of what passes for Madame Beaufort's settee."

She was asking questions just to keep him there. He'd already half turned to go, allowing the light from the parlor to wash over his features. The top two buttons of his white shirt had come undone, presumably while he slept, and she could see a dark whorl of hair just below the notch at the base of his neck.

She'd never seen a grown man without his shirt on, only a couple male cousins in their early adolescence with whom she'd once snuck out to go swimming when she was ten. They'd been as pale and smooth and narrow as worms, only the jut of shoulders hinting that something more prepossessing might await in their future.

She wondered just how hairy Archie's chest was under his shirt. The thought made her hug her knees tight to her chest. "Why not a bed?"

"Because there is no other bed." His tone implied she ought to have realized this without being told.

"But I distinctly recall the woman offering bed and board for the both of us."

Even in the dim light, she could detect color rising in his face. "That is because she thought we were married."

"Oh."

Once more he started to pull the door shut and once more she stopped him. "Is it hideously uncomfortable?"

"I've slept in worse."

Now, that was intriguing.

"Why didn't you go find a real bed in another house?"

"Because I didn't want you to wake up and think I'd left you." This time, he did close the door.

Lucy flopped on her back in the bed, listening to the sound of the surf pounding against the rocky shoreline. She strained her ears to hear if she could detect Archie moving about, but other than a single scrape of chair legs against bare floorboards it was silent.

First he had come after her—well, he had actually come after her great-aunts, but she wasn't going to quibble over trivialities—and then he'd stayed with her when he might have left to find a warm bed of his own in some other house. Why?

In Lucy's short life all the people who had ever concerned themselves with her well-being had done so out of a sense of duty. Even the great-aunts, whose love she did not doubt, had originally accepted her into their home because they had felt obliged to do so. It was probably true of Archie as well. He was just that sort of an inherently decent type. A gentleman born and bred. But deep within, she found herself hoping something more than simple decency accounted for his concern.

She snuggled down beneath the blankets, thinking about how it had felt to be in his arms—at least when she hadn't been worried she was going to get sick all over his shirt—how strong and capable and warm he'd been. She thought about the spark of amusement he tried to douse whenever it ignited in his coal-black pirate's eyes, and the utterly endearing perplexity he evinced when he looked at her.

Something about her upset and confounded and attracted him. Poor darling. He really did need someone to teach him how to enjoy life.

And she was just the person to do it.

CHAPTER

17

Tap! Tap! Tap!

Once more, Lucy came awake with a start. Something, or someone, was rapping somewhere. Loudly. She pulled the blanket up and struggled to a sitting position. Pale, early morning light drifted in from the bedchamber's single window.

Tap! Tap!

Where . . . ? She frowned and peered out of the clouded glass. Over a hundred years of the house settling had raised the landscape to the point where the ground outside was just under the window sill. Consequently all she saw was a pair of trouser-clad legs above feet encased in serviceable-looking rubber Wellies and a tanned, strong hand curved over the top of a stout-looking stick. The stick rose to rap on her window again.

"Miss Eastlake? Are you awake?" asked a voice muffled by the thickness of the cottage walls. The man bent at the waist and squinted, trying to look inside.

Archie! She scooted out of bed, flinging the blanket over her shoulders and pushing back the latch on the cottage window, throwing it wide open and in doing so nearly hitting him in the shins.

He jumped back, startled.

She peered up, giving him a saucy grin. "Just what are you doing peeping into a lady's bedchamber, Professor Grant?"

Bright red color flashed up his neck and filled his face, and Lucy decided right there and then that nothing could be more appealing than a blushing pirate. And he did look piratical this morning. Deliciously so. The wind had invested a bronzy hue to his face and tousled the loose black curls back from his forehead. He hadn't shaved and his hard angled jaw looked blue-black with a nascent beard, making the cleft in his chin even more apparent.

"I didn't mean to . . . that is, I . . ."

She waited patiently, charmed, wrapping the blanket closer as she sat down on the open sill. She wondered how long it would be before he was accustomed enough to her teasing that he could complete a full sentence in response.

His mouth flattened, but more from exasperation with himself than her, she'd wager. "A messenger brought news of the ferry a short while ago. I wasn't going to wake you but then, when I started out on a walk, I realized you might want to know."

"Know what?" The wind whipped a strand of her hair across her face.

"The ferry was damaged on some rocks coming in last night. They're working on repairs now but it will take at least a day before they anticipate we can leave here."

She stared at him, torn between offering a prayer of thanks for this small delay and ingratitude that it was only a day. But then, he had said "at *least* a day." The important thing was to take every advantage of whatever Providence offered and in this Lucy knew herself to be expert.

"I'm sorry, Miss Eastlake."

Apparently, he'd mistaken her silence for dismay. "That's all right." She released a small, brave sigh. "We'll muddle through."

"That's the spirit." His tone suggested he thought she was being uncommonly gracious by not putting up a fuss.

"Thanks. And *please*, call me Lucy. After yesterday, I am sure we know each other well enough for you to use my Christian name."

"I suppose you're right." Without seeming to think about it, he reached down and tucked a loose strand of hair behind her ear. "Well then, Lucy, there you have it. We won't be leaving any time soon."

He smiled brightly. Indeed, he looked quite pleased.

"Mrs. Beaufort will make you something to eat when you're ready. And don't let her convince you that you'll need to pay extra; she specifically said room *and* board."

"Won't you be joining me?'

"No. I've already eaten. I'm going to take a walk along the cliffs and stop at any crofts I find. Mrs. Beaufort tells me there are at least a dozen on this side of the island alone."

The prospect seemed to make him positively giddy. He beamed with enthusiasm. Hmm. Perhaps he had some sort of mania for crofts? Not that it mattered—she knew scads of odd people. Some might even point at her family for examples.

"How delightful. I love a good croft. So crofty. I should think there are some wonderful examples throughout the island."

"Really? I've never noticed that one croft was substantially different from the next."

No mania for crofts, then. Maybe cliffs? "They probably aren't, I just like them. But not as much as I like a good bracing walk along a cliff. One never feels so alive as when one is staring down a two-hundred-foot precipice."

"Oh?" He was regarding her with some concern. "You don't feel compelled to do anything other than *stare* down them do you?"

"Heavens no. Why would I?"

"I don't know. You seem peculiarly ardent."

"*I* seem peculiarly ardent? What about you? You were practically giggling as your recited your plan to go lurking about the cliffs and sneaking up on a dozen unsuspecting crofts."

At this he actually laughed, a deep-throat rumble of mirth that seemed to surprise him. "It's not the crofts I'm interested in, it's their tenants."

"Their tenants?" she repeated blankly.

"Yes. Do you realize this island has been inhabited for over a thousand years?"

She shook her head.

"It has. The inhabitants here are the only known people to speak an ancient Norman dialect called Sercquiais. Mrs. Beaufort claims her family has been on this island since the fourteenth century. The *fourteenth*. She told me that the oatcakes she served me this morning came from a recipe handed down since that time."

Lucy, whose vague recollection of Mrs. Beaufort's biscuits last night could in no way account for Archie's enthusiasm, continued to regard him blankly.

"This is a microcosm, Lucy. I could travel to islands in the middle of the Pacific Ocean or to the Arctic sea and not find a genetic pool as concentrated as this one. It's magnificent!

"The oral traditions and customs that have been kept alive here may well predate the Roman occupation. I would not be surprised to find reference to Taranis in some form or other."

She had no idea who Taranis was but contrived to look astonished.

"You haven't a clue who Taranis is, do you?"

She frowned. Had she lost her acting skills along with her dinner last night? *Somehow* he'd known she was pretending to be impressed, just like she suspected he'd known she was lying about knowing French. It was an ability she found both off-putting and mysterious.

"I realize it might not sound impressive to a layman but to someone in my field the chance of adding to the canon on British Iron Age culture is too good to pass up."

"Your field?"

"Yes. Cultural anthropology."

"*Golden Bough* sorts of things?" she asked, naming the recently published book on comparative religions that had London society in an uproar.

If he was surprised she knew about *The Golden Bough*, he didn't show it. That pleased her. "Some. Basically it's studying the relative development of people. I'm sure you'd find it dull. Most folks do."

"I think I'd find it plenty interesting. You're trying to figure out how people got the way they are, right?"

He slowly nodded.

"How a bloke speaks and moves and acts would not only tell you a lot about him but the people and place he came from, too, right?"

He was studying her closely. "Yes."

"Well then, how could I find it dull? It's what *I* do, Archie. I read a libretto and decide how a song ought to be sung by first figuring out who the character singing it is. That includes where she came from and *who* she came from. A person doesn't just burst into song for no reason, you know. She comes from some place. Some place that has fashioned her and which she has to some degree fashioned."

"I had no idea your craft involved such sorts of analysis."

She rather liked his calling what she did "her craft" and gave him a nonchalant smile. "Now you do. So, how do you mean to go about finding this Taranis."

"Oh, I don't expect to *find* him. That would be asking a bit much. But I might uncover some hint of his presence, like footprints in the dust. In some cultures the best metaphorical footprints a previous culture leaves can be found in the stories handed down from one generation to the next. I intend to interview the islanders, get them talking. "

"Then we best get going."

"We?"

"Yes. I'll go with you."

He hesitated. "I'm not sure that's such a good idea."

"It's a wonderful idea. I'll help you."

He was looking decidedly uncomfortable. "It's a generous offer, but really, I can't accept."

"Yes, you can. I'll be dressed and ready to go in two shakes." She hopped up and started to close the window. He caught it halfway. "Lucy. I don't know how to say this. I know you mean to help but I'm afraid you'll . . ."

"What?"

"Not help," he finished lamely.

She burst out in a little trill of laughter. "Of course I will, Archie. You'll see. I have a positive knack for putting people at ease."

He groaned. She ignored it.

"You stay there. I'll be ready in five minutes." Without waiting for a real invitation, as she was fairly certain none would be forthcoming, she pulled the window shut and dragged the curtains over it.

She dropped the blanket from her shoulder and looked around, realizing that she didn't have any clothes. All of her things were waiting for her in Saint-Malo. The things she'd had on yesterday were unwearable.

She opened the bedroom door and peeped out. The main room had been separated into two areas, one for cooking and the other, a sort of parlor, for everything else. Mrs. Beaufort stood at a stove against the wall, hands on her hips, glaring at something popping and sizzling in a cast-iron frying pan.

At the sound of the door, Mrs. Beaufort glanced over at her shoulder.

"I kin clean yer dress fer two bob."

Lucy's eyebrows flew up. "Two bob? That's ridiculous."

Mrs. Beaufort shrugged and turned back to the stove. "Suit yerself."

"I shall clean it myself."

"And what will you wear in the meantime?"

Lucy scowled. She hadn't thought of that.

Mrs. Beaufort looked over her shoulder at her. "Lucky fer you, my Kate's aboot the same size as you. Ye'll find sometink in the chest at the foot of the bed."

"Thank you."

"Five bob for the brown one and—"

"Five bob! But that's outrageous! I could buy a brand-new skirt and petticoat for that price in London."

Mrs. Beaufort regarded her stonily. "But we ain't in London, are we? Six bob if ye fancy the green skirt and blouse." She turned her back on Lucy. "Breakfast is on the table. Only three pence—"

"Mr. Grant informed me it was already paid for."

The woman muttered something about "pinch penny Londoners" under her breath and went back to glaring at her skillet.

Lucy didn't make it out the door in the promised five minutes. A sniff of her person made it obvious that she couldn't go anywhere without a quick sponge bath. In the process of that she realized that her hair was the worst offender and . . . well, she hoped Archie could appreciate that twenty minutes to bathe, wash and comb out one's hair, and brush one's teeth was an amazing accomplishment. Especially since she'd spent five of them haggling with Mrs. Beaufort over the price of soap.

She flew out of the door in her newly purchased green skirt and moth-eaten jumper. If Mrs. Beaufort estimated her Kate was the same size as Lucy, the woman needed stronger spectacles than were currently available, because the Beaufort's daughter was at least four inches taller and ten wider than she was. She'd been forced to use the curtain tieback for a belt and a shoelace she pilfered off a boot in the closet to tie back her hair, but at least now she was ready to follow Archie to, well, anywhere.

CHAPTER
18

Archie sat on the ancient stone fence that followed the lane leading to the Beaufort farmhouse, one leg dangling, whittling away on the stick he carried. The wind nickered and fussed, the promise of rain hanging in the nickel-plated sheet of sky. He felt more than heard Lucy's approach. Not surprising, as she seemed as much an element of nature as the wind or the surf, just as capricious and unpredictable, following some odd inner logic of her own.

He stood up and turned. She came trotting toward him, her unbuttoned coat flashing open to reveal the disastrous outfit beneath. Compliments of Mrs. Beaufort, he'd guess, though, upon closer consideration, there'd probably been no compliments about it. She looked like a beggar.

"Right then," she said a little breathlessly upon gaining his side. "We're off."

This was not a good idea. Interviewing indigenous people was an art. Under optimum circumstances one would beg an introduction from an intermediary; spend time establishing first rapport and then, hopefully, trust; and finally, carefully, ask a few precisely calibrated questions. There wasn't time for any of that here. Even a trained interviewer such as himself could only hope for a few bits and pieces and only if he asked the right questions in a circumspect manner.

"Do you understand the meaning of the word *circumspect*?"

"Yes. Why?"

"What does it mean?"

She set her hands on her hips. She looked ridiculous, her skirt all bunched at the waist and held in place by some sort of rope, her hair bound by a bit of cord, and a soft hat pulled low on her brow. At least her coat fit.

"It means to stash it and keep a glim eye."

He didn't understand a word she said and she knew it. She was having him on, teaching him a lesson for patronizing her. He probably deserved it.

"English, please."

"You don't want me to muck up your pow-wow with the locals."

Pow-wow he understood. "Exactly."

"I won't. I promise. You won't even notice me."

Which was patently impossible, but he didn't see what he could do about it so he started walking. She fell easily into step at his side, reaching into her coat pocket and producing one of Mrs. Beaufort's oatcakes wrapped up in a bit of brown paper.

"I didn't have time to sit down to breakfast," she explained, taking a bite. She grimaced and swallowed with evident difficulty. "Good Lord, that's awful."

"It's an ancient recipe."

She gave a little snort. "The Beaufort family tree would have been better served if they'd buried it along with the malicious ancestress who thought it up. No wonder Mrs. Beaufort looks so constipated. Did you actually eat those things?" She tossed the cake to the side of the road.

He shrugged. "It's an interesting relic."

"I'm all for relics as long as one is not obliged to eat them."

He hadn't thought that much about it at the time, as he was far more interested in its history than its flavor, but now that she'd pointed it out he noticed a rather unpleasant aftertaste in his mouth.

Lucy nodded. "I'll bet she used sheep tallow. And curdled milk."

He was saved from having to think further about the ingredients in Mrs. Beaufort's oatcakes by the appearance of a middling-sized black-and-white dog that slunk from under a patch of low-growing junipers and darted across to where Lucy had pitched the cake. With a toss of his head, he gobbled up the snack and then began following behind them, hoping, no doubt, for another treat.

"I shall feel dreadful if that dog falls over dead," Lucy said.

The dog's head drooped between his shoulder blades, ears flattening to his head. He lifted his lips in a silent snarl.

"From his demeanor, I'd say he's no stranger to Mrs. Beaufort's cooking."

Lucy laughed, looking thoroughly entertained. Cornelia found humor vulgar. But why was he comparing the two women anyway?

"I bet our friend here belongs there." She pointed at a squat, irregularly shaped croft hard against a rocky knoll. Grass carpeted the roof and a tin chimney protruded from the corner, burping little commas of white smoke into the air.

Archie's steps quickened with familiar anticipation, the thrill of possible discovery, of finding something unexpected and unique. Lucy trotted to keep up with his longer stride. "How are we going to talk our way in?"

"*We* aren't going to. I am. You are going to remain circumspectly quiet, remember?"

"I promised to be circumspect. I didn't say anything about being quiet."

"Lucy . . ."

"Fine. I'll be quiet." Her voice dropped. "Ish."

"I mean it," he said severely. "You can't just blurt out questions. It makes people wary. You have to make them comfortable first so they become loquacious."

"In my experience the only thing most people need to become loquacious is an opening."

"Please. Just let me handle things."

They'd arrived at the croft. Archie knocked on the door, then stepped back.

A moment later, the door opened to reveal a small, humpbacked, and very old man. He was the color of teak, his face craggy, his nose migrating toward a collapsing adit of a mouth. Tufts of white hair sprouted from a knotted, jutting chin and from beneath a foul knit cap. Milky blue eyes scraped over Archie and landed on Lucy.

"What ye want?"

"Good day to you, sir. I was hoping for a cup of water for my . . . for . . ." He stopped, confounded by his inability to catalogue just what Lucy was in reference to him. She stood demurely a few feet back and to his side, her hands folded neatly at her waist, looking absurdly young in her oversized clothing, a long pennant of hair dancing behind her.

"What's that?"

He turned back around with a start. "Oh. Yes. What I was saying is that we were walking and have grown quite thirsty." Lucy swallowed audibly, doing her part to add verisimilitude to the claim. "If you could oblige us we would be most grateful."

"Well's out back. Dipper in the bucket." The old man's clouded eyes narrowed. "Sixpence." He held out a hand every bit as gnarled as his face.

Lucy gasped. Immediately Archie recognized the danger implicit in that gasp. He stepped in front of her, blocking her from view of the old man and digging in his pocket for some coins.

He didn't have any.

"Do you have any money on you?" he said to Lucy.

"Not to buy water, I don't," she said furiously, standing on her tiptoes to glare over his shoulder at the old man studiously ignoring her.

"Please, Lucy," Archie said in a low voice. At this rate, he was never going to talk his way into the house, let alone get the old man to start spinning yarns. "The islanders clearly have developed something of a cottage industry that centers around tending to the needs of marooned ferry passengers."

"By soaking every penny out of them that they can get their hands on?" She made no effort to keep her voice down.

He fervently hoped the old man was hard of hearing.

He wasn't. "What's that yer wife said about soaking? Tain't rained yet today."

"She's not my wife," he answered.

"She ain't?" The man's face knotted like a fist. "Then what were ye doin' carryin' her into Marie Beaufort's house and then setting outside her bedroom all night like a dog guarding a bone?"

Apparently, the island's communication network had been operating overtime. But how? They'd arrived after dark and he'd risen before dawn. Fascinating. He'd experienced something similar in other small enclaves where each member was uniquely dependent on others for information and aid. There'd been a tribe in Angola—

"We're eloping."

He spun around, mouth agape.

Lucy stepped briskly to his side and hooked her arm possessively through his. The wind played with the hem of her skirt and teased color into her cheeks. She looked fresh and young and bold as brass, eyes bright, head cocked.

"What do you mean 'elope?' Do yer folks know?" the old man demanded.

"You know *exactly* what I mean," Lucy said in a bizarre accent, a

weird amalgamation of precise diction and broad Devonshire conso-
nants. She gave her head an imperious toss. "For weeks Archie here
has been hounding me, saying as how he'll die if he doesn't make me
his. So *I* says, 'I'll be yours all right, as soon as I'm wearing your ring.'"

She paused here and actually had the nerve to wink at the old
man. Amazingly, he chuckled and then cleared his throat, abashed
at having been lulled into amusement at such improper goings-on.

"Problem is, *his* father don't think I'm good enough for him."
Lucy jerked her chin in his direction. "I don't know about you,
Granddad—I can call you 'Granddad,' can't I? You put me in mind
of my own dear paw-paw. He had just such a canny look to him as
you. Anyway, as I was saying, I don't know about you, Granddad,
but *I* come from a long line of"—her gaze flicked through the open
door into the room behind—"fishermen, who taught me that
whilst I wasn't ever to think I was better than anyone else, I should
always keep in mind that I was just as good."

"And so you are," the old man said, his glare accusing Archie
of rank elitism.

Archie stared, riveted by equal parts awe and horror that Lucy
actually thought she could pass him off as lecherous womanizer
and herself as—well, he wasn't exactly sure what role she was writing for herself but it seemed to have found favor with the old man.

"I need not tell you, Granddad, that I wouldn't budge an inch."
She sniffed. "Nor unbutton a button."

Archie choked back a groan.

"No, sir, I know my value." She was embracing the role of
innocence triumphant in the face of debauchery to the fullest.
She'd set her fists on her hips and now angled her chin to the sky,
her eyes flashing with moral righteousness.

"Well, *finally*, Archie here says we'll have to elope to France.
Which is fine by me. I always fancied seeing France. But then the
ferry ended up here and we at Mrs. Beaufort's who, by the way, will

swear on a stack of Bibles that I kept the door barred against him all night long." *Dear God.* "And if she doesn't, she'll be condemned for eternity as a liar."

"She won't be the only one," Archie muttered. She pretended not to hear.

"But now with day come and everyone going about their business and it looking like it'll be nightfall at least before the ferry can be under way again, we're left to our own devices. Archie thought we might take a peek in at some abandoned crofts." She gave a snort of derision. "Like I'm so green I don't know where he thinks *that* will lead."

He didn't even attempt to protest. He stood silently by and wondered if it were possible to simply drop dead from incredulity before he glumly concluded it wasn't.

"So *I* suggested we go for a walk. A nice *long* walk. *Vigorous,* if you catch my drift. The kind to wear a bloke out," she confided in a tone rife with outrageous self-satisfaction. "But we've been tromping since sunrise now and my feet are near to failing me. I reckon it would be best to park them in a place where there's other people to keep us company because, well, Archie's getting a mite impatient and"—her gaze dropped, her lashes fluttered, and he didn't know how she did it but she actually seemed to blush—"he can be very persuasive." She glanced up. "If you take my meaning."

For what seemed an eternity but was in fact probably no more than ten seconds, the old man stared at Lucy while Archie waited for him to sic the dog on them. She couldn't really expect to talk them into the old man's home by pretending she was a runaway bride who was trying to keep her would-be lover's overly ardent advances at bay by basically asking the old man to act as her chaperone? It was the most ludicrous, transparent, obviously fallacious bit of tripe ever—

"Come in, then." The old man opened the door wider and beckoned them inside.

CHAPTER
19

"And then the Moon Boy took the axe that had been sunk deep into his own forehead and wrenched it out and fell upon his brother, chopping off first his arms and then his legs and finally cleaving his head from his trunk." The old fellow stopped, taking particular relish in the gruesome story.

It was their second day in his company, the first having extended long into the evening, during which time Michel Bolay, their host, had put together a surprisingly appetizing soup of salt cod, potatoes, and cream. After feeding them he had insisted on escorting them—or rather, Lucy—back to the Beaufort place.

There, he'd informed Archie that he intended to stand outside until he saw a light in "Kate Beaufort's old room" and a single— with a pronounced emphasis on the word "single"—silhouette on the curtain before leaving. Archie had been preparing to refute the old man's veiled indictment when Lucy had jumped into the breech, sniffing virtuously and saying, "He'll not spend another moment with me this night!" before sailing into the house.

Though he'd followed close on her heels, true to her word, he hadn't seen her for the rest of the night. But early that morning, she'd been waiting for him by the stile, announcing that she'd already washed her clothes, hung them to dry, eaten breakfast and was asking whether he always slept in late. The dimple in her right cheek teased him as much as the light in her eyes, drawing him like a moth to a flame.

The light had stayed all through the morning, during which they'd once more been privileged to share Michel Bolay's table. The man could cook as well as spin a tale.

"And then what happened?" Lucy now prompted, evincing an unnerving predilection for the more bloodthirsty tales.

"Why he drug out his brains and—"

"Hoy! Hoy the house!" A voice from outside interrupted the old man just as he'd reached the climax of his gruesome tale.

Archie glanced at where Lucy sat curled on the bed, the sheepdog's head in her lap. She winked at him.

Perhaps humor was some sort of aphrodisiac because whenever she laughed or teased him, rather than be affronted, he felt the most intense and visceral attraction as well as the most compelling desire to *kiss* her. Someone should look into this. But who? Was the reaction physically induced or culturally? Or maybe it was to Lucy. Or maybe a combination of Lucy and him . . .

The old man took the interruption with a great deal less grace than Lucy. With a sour look on his face, he heaved himself up from his chair to answer the door. "What are you doin', come screamin' at a feller in his house like that, Jonny Dearborn? What do you want?"

A pimply-faced youth with a mop of dusty curls springing from beneath a knit cap appeared in the doorway. His gaze touched Archie then moved past him to Lucy. His eyes widened.

"Her." His attention wandered reluctantly back to Archie. "Them."

"What fer?"

"The ferry's fixed and set to take off in a half hour."

"Half an hour?" Archie leapt to his feet. "Why didn't you come sooner, lad? It will take all that and some to return to the Beaufort's, collect our belongings, and make it down to the harbor. Come on, Lucy. We've no time to waste."

"Been lookin' fer you for near on two hours," the boy said defensively. "You didn't say as to where you were heading when you left Mrs. Beaufort's and she says she weren't watching."

"The only reason she wasn't watching was because she didn't realize we'd left," Lucy said drily, standing up and donning her coat.

"Ain't gonna argue there," the boy said. "Anyway I went north; you gone south. Otherwise I woulda found you earlier."

Lucy leaned forward and touched the boy's arm in a companionable manner. "He didn't mean it as a criticism."

At her touch the boy's pugnacious air evaporated. He snatched his cap from his head, spurred to manners by what was obviously an instant case of puppy love.

"Archie, you didn't mean to sound so crabbed, did you?"

"What? Of course, I—" He broke off. She was regarding him with unblinking faith, making it impossible to purposefully disappoint her. He had the oddest feeling. Like he was in a boat on a river that was moving much faster than he'd realized. "No," he said. "I didn't."

She smiled warmly at him. The sort of smile one should be happy to receive from a pretty young lady. He wasn't. Instead it made him feel something akin to panic.

She took a step forward, stopping when the boy didn't move to vacate the doorway. The kid didn't catch on but just stood there with a barmy expression on his face, twisting his cap in his hands. Finally, with a muttered oath, Archie took him by the shoulders, picked him bodily up, and set him to the side. Then he pumped the old man's hand gratefully. The notes he'd taken would make a small but significant contribution to the canon on Iron Age Britons. He had Lucy to thank for that. The thought multiplied his sense of internal alarm.

Yesterday, as soon as they'd been seated, Lucy had grabbed the dog—who after a cursory and unconvincing display of temper had curled up on her lap—and asked the old man if he knew any good stories because, apparently, she "collected stories like other girls collect magazine clippings."

Archie had been certain the old man would call her out on that patent lie. What girl collects folk stories?

But instead the old man had launched into a tale as though he'd spent the last ten years just waiting to be asked. And he may well have. By the time Jonny here had arrived, Archie had surreptitiously jotted down the outlines of a dozen stories, again at Lucy's behest because, as she'd confided to their host, "I want to remember your stories just as you tell them and I have no head for details so we'll have Archie scribble them down."

"Thank you for your hospitality, Mr. Bolay," Archie now said. "Come on, Lucy. If we hurry we might just make it." He started out the door but the old man snagged his arm as Lucy sailed outside ahead of him.

"Here now, son," he said, lowering his voice. "Truth is, you don't seem near as bad a feller as I worrit you might be—you scribbled like the very devil to keep up with me blathering, just cause the young miss there wanted you to, so you must have some decent feelings toward her after all. And she is a fair bright little lolly. I can see how a young man might be hard pressed to keep his—"

"Yes! Just so." He didn't want to think of Lucy as a lolly, bright or otherwise. It would be far too easy to do so and he wasn't sure why that would be a bad thing—a man can appreciate a lovely, lively girl without it meaning anything, couldn't he?—but he was certain it was. "Thank you again. Good-bye."

"Good-bye, Granddad!" Lucy put in. "Thanks ever so much for the jolly stories. I shall remember them always. And on my wedding night I—"

Archie grabbed hold of her elbow to hustle her before him. She waved happily. "Good-bye!"

As soon as they were out of earshot she asked, "Whatever did the old dear say? You're as red as beet juice and keen as mustard to get me out of there."

"Nothing. We are just in a hurry, is all."

"You're a terrible liar."

"You'll have to excuse me. I haven't as much practice as you," he said meaningfully.

This brought her up short.

"What are you doing?" he asked. "Why are you stopping? We're in a hurry."

She scowled instead of moving. "What do you mean by that? Are you saying that you didn't find my portrayal of a savvy shopgirl eloping with her gentrified beau convincing?"

"Not in the least. I'm stunned Mr. Bolay did. One can only assume poor sight and poorer hearing accounts for it. What *was* that accent supposed to be?"

"I wasn't *supposed* to be anything. It *was* Guernsey Island. Ish. And you're being unfairly critical. I am a very good actress. In fact, I am a Collectible." She said this last with a proud lift of her chin.

Since he had no idea what a "collectible" was he didn't respond directly. "Tell me, have you ever considered that the simple truth might serve you just as well as concocting some fantastic story to get what you want?"

"No," she said.

"Well, you might."

"It is my experience that people seldom find 'the simple truth' as appealing as fantasy. That's why they go to plays and read fiction and poetry, listen to music and look at art: to experience something they don't encounter in their everyday life. A little excitement, something out of the ordinary, a different interpretation to make something painful less unpleasant." A dark note touched her voice.

"For instance, my great-aunt Lavinia might have led a far different and happier life if your grandfather had fabricated some excuse, no matter how poor, for abandoning her rather than letting her spend fifty years wondering what she might have done to engage his heart after he'd engaged hers. It would certainly have been kinder than simply leaving without a word."

He'd been in the process of trying to propel her forward but her words stopped him short. "What did you say?"

Her dry expression slowly turned into an incredulous one. "Don't you know? Didn't he tell you?"

"Tell me what? What are you talking about?"

"Your grandfather. My great-aunt. At Patnimba, during the siege, there developed what Aunt Lavinia called 'a sympathy' between them—though I suspect it was a great deal more than that. In short, Lavinia fell for him like a ton of bricks. She *thought* the feeling was mutual and believe me, Lavinia is not the sort of woman who imagines men are just waiting in line to court her.

"But *apparently* she was wrong because as soon as the siege ended, your grandfather decamped without a word. She never heard from him directly again. Until you showed up at our door."

He was dumbfounded. The behavior Lucy outlined in no way described the man Archie knew. Lord Barton was the very byword for integrity. He was the last person in the world Archie could imagine trifling with a young lady's feelings.

But then, there *was* something "off" about this whole situation: the sudden revelation of a cache of rubies of which Lord Barton held a share, his summons to Archie, and the subsequent request that Archie escort a woman he had never heard his grandfather mention to a town in the middle of the French Pyrenees. Perhaps Lord Barton *had* bequeathed his share of the rubies to assuage fifty years of guilt he'd felt over securing a young woman's regard that he could not return. It made an unpalatable sort of sense.

"Didn't he ever say anything to you about Lavinia? About Patnimba?" Lucy asked.

"No." He shook his head distractedly, trying to make her story match the image he'd always held of his grandfather. He couldn't.

"I'm sorry, Archie," she said, her voice softening. "It must be hard to find out your grandfather is a bit of a bounder."

"That's just it, Lucy. He's not. I'm sure there's more to it than appearances suggest."

"Sure there is," she agreed in patently disbelieving tones.

He didn't begrudge her her low opinion of Lord Barton. How could he? On the surface it appeared that at the very least Lord Barton had acted caddishly. And Lucy didn't know Sir John like he did. But what proof could he offer her except his own certainty—which was no proof at all? A scientist relied on documentation, not "feelings." Feelings always landed a bloke in trouble.

Hadn't he learned that lesson often enough and forcefully enough during his childhood? He'd been a passionate lad and all it had garnered him were broken bones and reprimands.

"Mr. Grant, stop daydreaming. What would your father say?"

"Mr. Grant, perhaps another hour of sitting in silent contemplation will cure you of interrupting your teachers."

"Mr. Grant, I do not care what Mr. Donnet did, there is no excuse for brawling. I shall have to inform your parents."

"Mr. Grant, you have only yourself to blame for your current suffering. You should never have tried to climb that wall, that tree, that hill, that ladder . . ."

"We'd better hurry," he said.

"You're mad at me."

"No, I'm not."

"Yes, you are. I can see it in the way you're holding yourself. All braced up and prickly."

He took her elbow, pulling her along with him. "I'm not angry with you. Now, please, hurry."

"I wouldn't have said anything, except I thought you knew."

Again, he urged her forward. "I'm Lord Barton's grandson, not his confidant."

"*I've* always known the story. I was practically raised on it. Which is telling in and of itself, wouldn't you say?"

"What do you mean?"

"It only makes sense that Aunt Lavinia would have told *her* family and friends." She was working it out, speaking aloud to herself, trotting along at his side. "I mean, the siege of Patnimba colored everything that happened to her for the rest of her life. But what to her was the most monumental, life-altering chapter in her life was just a side note in your grandfather's. Which is rather lousy when you think of it . . ."

He didn't say a word.

Because if what she said was true, she was right.

They made good time returning to the Beaufort place. Archie tore about the room stuffing his belongings into his valise and pausing only long enough to make frantic motions for Lucy to do likewise.

Obediently, she headed toward the sink where the garments she'd washed this morning hung. Mrs. Beaufort stepped in front of her and crossed her arms over her flat chest. "Do ye think to wear damp clothing then, miss? Skirt's not yet dry."

"No," Lucy replied shortly. She'd had enough of Mrs. Beaufort's hospitality. "I think to *pack* damp clothing. Now, if you'll kindly move aside. Or do you charge for that, too?"

Things went poorly after that. Rather than move, Mrs. Beaufort calmly announced that if Lucy wished to keep "dear Kate's pretty things," she would need to purchase them. Stunned, Lucy replied that she'd already bought "fat Kate's nasty clothing."

What Lucy had paid for, replied Mrs. Beaufort, had only been the lease on the clothing. The price of taking permanent possession of the skirt, blouse, and moth-eaten jumper would be two crowns.

Lucy's sense of justice howled at such blatant extortion. She'd spent years squeezing every drop of value from every ha'penny that came into her possession. She had bought Kate's wretched clothing, not rented it, and she had no intention of buying it anew. She assured Mrs. Beaufort of this in extremely colorful London street language that, though unfamiliar with it, Mrs. Beaufort nonetheless understood perfectly well. In response, she raised the price of the garments by three shillings.

Archie, recognizing that the situation was fast approaching crisis level, dug into his valise for his wallet.

Lucy barely noticed. She was too busy dropping her coat from her shoulders, ripping the curtain tie from around her waist, and letting the disputed skirt fall into a pile on the floor. She set her hands on her hips, taking savage pleasure in the red color that swept up Mrs. Beaufort's wattled neck and into her hatchet-shaped face.

The perpetually silent Mr. Beaufort gaped delightedly.

"I am not paying for these rags twice."

Before Mrs. Beaufort's scandalized gaze, she peeled off the scratchy sweater and started in on the blouse's buttons. "I would rather leave here in my combinations for all your neighbors to see than pay you another penny, let alone two crowns. What do you say to that, you miserly old crone?"

For thirty seconds the two women's eyes locked in silent combat until finally Mrs. Beaufort spoke. "Did I say two crowns, three shillings? Meant three crowns."

Lucy gasped.

Frantically, Archie pulled some bills from his wallet.

"Don't you *dare pay that creature so much as a farthing*," she breathed in tones that he dared not ignore.

He stuffed the bills back in his wallet and snatched Lucy's blouse off the line, grabbed one of her arms, and shoved it through the sleeve, then treated the other to the same before clumsily buttoning the back up and spinning her around.

"Not a word, Lucy. Not. A. Word," he muttered between clenched teeth. He dropped her damp skirt on the ground, bent down, picked her up and set her down inside the waist opening, and then jerked the skirt back up over her hips. Lucy had unfortunately washed it in water that was too hot, for it had shrunk, the hem four inches above her ankles and the waistband pinching her middle. And the lye she'd used had left bleached spots on the material.

He tossed Lucy's coat over her shoulders then edged her past Mrs. Beaufort, opened the door, and shoved her outside.

She wheeled on him. "I cannot believe you were thinking of paying that *sea hag*!"

"Ahem."

The expression of Mr. Beaufort, who'd followed them out, was as wooden as ever. "I kin drive ye." It was the first time she'd heard the man speak.

She sniffed, collecting what she could of her tattered dignity. At least the poor, downtrodden fellow had a sense of decency. "Thank you, Mr. Beaufort."

"For a bob."

"*What*? Why, you miserable old bloodsucker. I would not get on that carriage to save my—"

Archie grabbed her round the waist and tossed her over his shoulder. He nodded to Beaufort. "Thank you."

"Round back," Mr. Beaufort said, leading the way around the house.

Lucy bounced on Archie's shoulder with every step. "Put me down! At once. I would rather crawl on my knees all the way to town rather than pay these . . . these *people* a single sou."

"*You're* not paying anyone anything."

The pony was already hitched to the cart and waiting. Archie dumped her in the back.

"There's another half-crown in it for you if we make it to the ferry in time," he told Beaufort.

CHAPTER

20

A quarter hour later they arrived in the small harbor. The last of their fellow passengers stood on the pier, waiting to be handed into dories that would transport them to deeper water where the newly repaired ferry waited. The carts and wagons that had brought them were already disbanding.

Archie leapt from the dogcart, pressed some coins into Beaufort's hand, and came round the back to take custody of his valise.

"Well done, Lucy! We made it."

She stared at the sea, her anger vanishing. "Oh, dear."

The muttered "oh, dear," should have alerted him. But Archie was so pleased that they'd actually made it in time he didn't pay it much heed. He hefted the valise to his shoulder and held out his hand to help Lucy hop down from the back of the cart.

She didn't hop. She just stared at his hand as if it were a snake about to strike.

"What's wrong?"

"I can't."

"Can't what?" A lone dory awaited them, bobbing up and down in the rolling surf alongside the rickety pier. The fishermen who would row them out—no doubt for a pretty remuneration—stood in their rubberized wading boots thigh deep in the surf. Inside the boat sat a half dozen people, their expressions displaying various degrees of impatience.

"Get on that." Lucy nodded toward the ferry.

"Of course you can," he assured her in his heartiest voice.

She shook her head. "I'll become ill again. Horribly ill. The sort of ill where death doesn't seem such a bad alternative."

"No, you won't." He hoped he sounded more confident than he felt because all his assurance was based on anecdotal information, which he now kindly shared. "I'm told the trick is to keep yourself distracted and your eye on the horizon."

"You're *told*?" she echoed. "I'm afraid that's not enough to persuade me."

"Don't be unreasonable."

Rather than encourage reasonableness, his words seemed to have the reverse effect. Her lips tightened. "You're right. I probably could get in that boat."

He released a gusty sigh of relief. "I knew you'd—"

"But I won't."

"Hoy! You there!" one of the fishermen bellowed. "You staying or coming?"

"Coming!"

"Staying!"

"Look, Lucy," Archie said. "I understand your concern, but there really is no choice."

"I'm getting queasy just looking at it. I'm sorry, Archie."

"It's only twenty-some miles to France, Lucy. We'll be on dry land in an hour. Or so."

She looked away, shaking her head.

"What do you intend to do? Stay here forever?" He threw up his free hand in exasperation.

"Just until the seas are calmer." She peeked up at him worriedly. "They do get calmer, don't they? I mean, eventually?"

"I don't know and I'm not staying to find out."

She looked sharply at that, her eyes widening with hurt. He fought down the nearly overwhelming urge to reassure her. "You're not?"

"No. And neither are you. How can you? Where will you stay? Are you going to appeal to Mrs. Beaufort's sense of charity? Because I don't think you'll have much luck finding it and I daresay the other islanders aren't going to be any more sympathetic once you run out of funds which, at the going rate, won't be long.

"And before you ask, I'm nearly tapped out. I left England in a hurry, without stopping at a bank, assuming I would wire for money once in France, so don't look to me for a loan." This flawlessly practical argument had no visible effect. If anything the set of her chin grew more stubborn.

"I know." He snapped his fingers. "Maybe you can find work with the Beauforts? I'm sure Mrs. Beaufort could find something for you to do. Maybe she'll teach you to make oatcakes."

Her eyes narrowed. "Oh, that was *low*, Archie."

"Low it might be, but true. You have no money to spare, no place to stay, and no *reason* to stay."

The sailor beside the dory waved his arm. "Hoy! Ferry's fetching to leave!"

The stubborn line of her jaw softened. Her expression became pleading. "I know this must seem fantastically impractical to you but—"

"Oh, hell." He grabbed her wrist, pulled her to her feet, and then dipped down and chucked her over his shoulder again. He had no choice. He wasn't about to be marooned here.

"Put me down!"

He ignored her screech, picking up his valise in his free hand.
"What *is* it with you? Is it only me you feel compelled to treat
like a sack of potatoes or is it every girl?"

"Just you."

He strode down the pier to where the dory waited, tossed his
bag down atop the plank seat, and in one economical motion
swung Lucy off his shoulder and into the waiting arms of the
grizzled old seaman. Then he jumped in after her.

"Get going! Before she dives over the side and swims to shore,"
he advised.

One look at Lucy's belligerent, desperate face and the fishermen on either side of the dory clambered in, shedding water like
drenched spaniels as they scrambled into place and heaved back on
their oars, sending the boat shooting out over the waves and toward
where the ferry waited.

"Ohhh!" A low whimper escaped Lucy's lips. Archie patted her
hand. She snatched it back and glared at him.

"Won't be long," a fisherman assured her.

She squeezed her eyes shut and clutched the gunnel. It only
took a short while before they pulled up next to the ferry. Archie
stood up and, leaving her no chance to object, plucked Lucy from
her seat, lifting her above his head. "Take her!" A pair of sailors
leaned over the side of the ferry and, each clasping an arm, pulled
her up and over the edge as she squealed in protest.

A seaman on deck threw down a rope ladder. One of the dory's
other passengers, a fat man in a tight checkered coat, heaved his
portmanteau over his head and into the crewmembers' waiting
hands before ponderously struggling onto the first rung. He'd made
it to the second when a comely female leg appeared over the gunnel
followed by an even shapelier female posterior draped in a dingy
skirt. The foot began groping for a toehold.

By God, she was trying to jump ship.

"Don't let her get on the ladder!" Archie shouted. If she got back into the dory, they'd never get her out. She'd burrow in like a tick and the captain of the ferry wouldn't wait for him to dislodge her.

He grabbed the side of the ladder and started up the outside of it one-handed, fettered by his valise as he tried to climb past the fat man staring in frank appreciation at Lucy's flailing leg.

"Catch my bag!" he shouted up to a red-haired lad.

"Lemme go!" he heard Lucy squeal from above.

"Don't let her go!" he yelled. "Here! Catch my valise!" With a grunt, he swung the heavy bag out and heaved it upward, sending it sailing through the air and into the lad's outstretched arms . . .

. . . and out again.

The valise bobbled against the gunnel as the boy's eyes grew round in his face and his mouth formed a silent "o" of surprise that turned into a gasped, "Oops."

Archie arched back, nearly dislodging the fat man from his perch as he grabbed at the bag plummeting inches past his outstretched fingertips.

It hit the water and sank like a dead weight.

For a second everyone froze. Then, in quick succession, the fat man dropped back into the dory, the red-haired lad disappeared, and Lucy's posterior and leg withdrew from sight with politic swiftness.

"You go ahead of me," the fat man said, edging away from the fury in Archie's expression.

"Thank you."

He was up the ladder and on the deck in seconds. The deckhand was nowhere in sight. But Lucy was. She'd backed away from the side of the ferry and was smiling nervously, her hands twisting together at her waist.

"I suppose all your things were in there," she said.

"Um-hm."

"I suppose you somehow hold me to blame."

"Um-hm."

"You shouldn't. You mustn't. Not in all fairness. Because really, you have only yourself to blame. If you hadn't manhandled me . . ." At this point some deep-buried scintilla of prudence wiggled to life and she trailed off. "I daresay you will be able to replace your things once we are in France."

"Oh. So, you've decided to go to France now, have you?"

"Why, yes." She smiled with noble fortitude then, realizing he wasn't going to commend her, her smile faltered. "You don't seem too happy about it."

"Don't I?" he asked, his voice deceptively mild. "Perhaps that's because I was thinking how nice it would have been had you made the same decision, say, oh, five minutes ago. Before every article of clothing I'd brought with me had sunk to the bottom of the English Channel.

"Selfish of me, no doubt, to be dwelling on something so banal when you have so graciously decided to do what you really had no option but to do in the first place."

She stared. Swallowed. Stared some more as her eyes welled up with tears. Real tears. He could tell they were real because her nose was going pink and she was sniffing in a truly off-putting manner and her lower lip was wobbling treacherously. For the first time since he'd clapped eyes on her, Lucy looked massively unappealing and yet, conversely, every fiber in his body yearned to take her in his arms and—

Good Lord! What was he thinking? He going to ask—to ask—why couldn't he recall her name? Not that it mattered, he was going to get engaged!

She sniffed again, blinked, and now the tears overran her lower lids and spilled down her cheeks. He watched in horror, rising panic obliterating every ounce of his former anger. He'd never made a woman cry before. He'd never even *seen* a woman cry before. It was terrible! It filled him with the most awful sensation, one he would do anything to rid himself of.

"Stop. Please. Stop," he said, taking a step toward her.

"I . . . I . . . I can't!" she blubbered. Her eyes had turned red and puffy and her nose was dripping.

He reached out and gave her shoulder an awkward pat. "Of course you can. Just stop." He patted her shoulder again. "Now."

She shook her head, snuffling miserably. He reached into his jacket pocket and pulled out his handkerchief, snapped it open, and handed it to her.

She took it and loudly blew her nose. "Thank you," she sniffled.

"There, see? Isn't that better?" he asked, relieved that she'd gotten hold of herself.

Apparently it was the wrong thing to say for as soon as he'd uttered the word *better* the tears welled up again in her gold-green eyes. "No!"

"Oh." He looked around desperately for help, but every man in the vicinity was pointedly looking elsewhere and the only woman in the area glared at him as though he were craven. He turned back to Lucy. She was weeping with a closed mouth now, her face screwed up and her chest moving in spasms with each stifled sob.

With a weird sense of inevitability he put his arm around her shoulders and led her to one of the benches lining the exterior wall of the salon. He sat, pulling her down alongside him. She came without resistance, turning at once and burrowing her face into his shoulder.

"There, there. Everything will be all right." An easy enough promise since he had no idea what was wrong. Not really. True, he'd been somewhat acerbic in his comments, but she didn't strike him as the sort to be overly sensitive to a little verbal scrimmage. In fact, he would have guessed she'd enjoy it. "You'll see."

"No, it won't."

"Now, why would you say that?"

"Because I *am* responsible for you losing your valise—"

"Strictly speaking, I didn't lose it. It was—"

"Semantics," she cut in, lifting her head from his shoulder to gaze earnestly up at him. "The point is, Archie, if I hadn't tried to escape—"

"*Escape?*" he echoed. "Don't you think that a rather dramatic misrepresentation of the situation?"

"Not at all, but that's irrelevant. What is relevant, Archie"—her fingers curled around the edges of his lapels in her effort to impress him with her sincerity—"is that if I hadn't tried to escape, you never would have thrown your valise into the ocean and—please don't interrupt me again, Archie, I am trying to accept culpability here—and lost all your lovely things, though I am being generous here because you don't really dress all that spiffily except when you were at the Savoy in your tuxedo. You really were most strikingly turned out that evening."

"Thank you," he murmured. He remembered one of the only fantasy novels he'd read as a child, *Alice's Adventures in Wonderland*. This must have been how Alice had felt when she'd tumbled down the rabbit hole. He regarded Lucy in mild bewilderment; he was getting unaccountably used to being bewildered and it no longer disconcerted him as it had when . . . was it only a few days ago that they'd met?

"You're welcome. Anyways. Now, Archie, it is quite clear that you regret having agreed to your grandfather's request to accompany my great-aunts because that has stuck you with me. And now . . . and now . . ."

A fresh lot of tears fell from her eyes and coursed down her cheeks. He reached up and swept them away with his thumb. Her skin was like satin. "And now?"

"You don't like me!"

"What?" he asked, taken completely off guard. "What are you talking about?"

"You don't like me!"

"Yes, I do," he said in desperation.

She shook her head violently. "No, you don't. You're just saying that because you're . . you're . . . you're being . . . *kind*!" The last word erupted from her lips as if it were the worst possible condemnation she could utter.

"No, I'm not."

"Yes, you are."

"I'm not! I'm not! Truly." He grabbed her by the shoulders. "See? I'm smiling at you, aren't I? I wouldn't smile at you if I didn't like you, would I?"

"Yes, you would."

"No, I wouldn't!" He'd pulled her closer to him, trying to make her see that he was telling the simple truth. "I wouldn't know how. I don't have those skills."

She regarded him doubtfully. "You don't?"

"No." He pulled back just far enough to cross his heart.

"And you do like me?" she asked hopefully.

"Yes. I do. In fact, under normal circumstances, I would find you oddly engaging."

"You would?" Her face lit up and she leaned closer, peering up at him intently, but smiling now. She had a deuced pretty smile.

"Yes," he admitted. "Not that there is likely to be any normal circumstances where you are concerned."

As soon as he said it, he realized this might not have been the best line to take. But she didn't bat an eye . . . well, actually, she did.

Her eyelashes, unexpectedly long and curly, fluttered. A pink stain washed up into her face, turning her cheeks apricot beneath their light dusting of freckles. This close to her he realized the gold flecks in her hazel eyes were actually more copper and what he'd thought simple green was actually a deeper, mossier hue.

"Pshaw." She scoffed softly. "What would you want with normal circumstances, Archie?"

"I don't know, " he murmured, distracted by the way the light caught on the curve of her sharp cheekbones and molded itself to the soft, warm line of her lower lip.

"That's what I thought." She looked very wise and very young and very serious, staring up at him.

With a sense of something akin to despair, he realized that no woman had ever looked at him like Lucy Eastlake was looking at him now and he strongly, very strongly, feared he'd never looked at any woman before the way he was looking back.

"Oh, Archie," she whispered, tipping her head back just enough that he could feel the soft heat of her breath against his mouth.

He bent his head—just in order to catch her words, only because she was speaking so softly—and his lips brushed within a feather's width of touching hers . . .

An electric current danced and arced between their mouths. Oh, maybe it wasn't actual electricity, but it was something just as potent, lightning hovering in the air on the flashpoint of striking, just as imminent, just as dangerous, and every nerve in his lips shivered, agitated by her proximity.

He jerked back. *What the hell was he thinking?* He wasn't thinking. He was reacting. To her. She was like some sort of experimental drug, a clearly dangerous one.

Startled by his abrupt retreat, her eyes widened.

He cleared his throat, scowling as he pulled away and hastily doffed his jacket.

"Here." He put it over her shoulders, taking too-elaborate care in settling it there so he wouldn't have to meet her eyes again. He was very much afraid of what would happen if he did.

She didn't say a word, for which he was profoundly grateful. By the time he'd finished, he felt more himself again, or as near as he could remember what "himself" felt like. Nothing seemed familiar these past few days and yet, conversely, everything felt natural.

He eased away from her, hoping against hope that she would continue to be quiet. Somehow he had to put things back in order, though in his deepest core he realized things had already moved far beyond a place where he could easily turn back. He needed to think. He needed to keep a cool head, not a hot—he needed to keep a cool head and above all, he needed Lucy not to distract him.

"Archie?"

He supposed he might as well have wished for the tides to stay put.

Reluctantly, he turned to her. "Please, Lucy. I need to think and I can't do that when you're talking. Or looking at me. So, *please* be quiet."

"Oh," she said, a mournful little sound.

My God, what a bungle he'd made of things—he shot a sideways glance at Lucy's profile—not that it wasn't a fair ways mucked up already.

He couldn't be late returning to London, where he'd promised to attend a small dinner Cornelia's father was hosting. What Cornelia called "influential people," including Lord Blidderphenk, were also on the guest list. It was a chance to impress the man. Desperately, he reminded himself how important such a position as the Blidderphenk professorship could be to his career. He'd be able to pretty much write his own check for infrequent future expeditions.

Infrequent.

He was never happier than when he was working in the field, interviewing people, learning their stories, their traditions, their histories, connecting the dots through time and distance. It had been too long since he'd been on a research expedition. The hours he and Lucy had spent with Michel Bolay had reminded him of how much he loved it.

But Cornelia was right. One couldn't go gallivanting about the world if one was the Blidderphenk professor. It was too bad he'd never been comfortable with all the glad-handing that went along with an academic career. It was an objection Cornelia dismissed as dangerously naïve and sentimental. He supposed she was right.

He closed his eyes.

Cornelia. What did she look like? Taller than Lucy. Eyes . . . Eyes? He only knew they were not hazel.

"You were correct, you know."

"Was I?" He opened his eyes. "About what?" He had to get off this boat, get to a telegraph office, and wire Cornelia.

"About the distraction."

"Oh? That's good." There was bound to be an office near the docks.

"Was." She rose to her feet, swallowing hard.

"What's that?"

"*Was* good. You're not distracting me anymore," she said and promptly lunged for the rail.

CHAPTER

21

At least she was able to walk off the ferry under her own steam. She ought to get credit for that, Lucy thought, stealing a glance at Archie's profile as they headed down the gangway. The late afternoon sun glinted off the inky curls falling down over his brow, making him look particularly roguish. He didn't glance back, let alone admire her brave stoicism. In fact, he wasn't paying her any attention at all. Nor had he been for the past half hour.

She gnawed at her lip, worried that her sea-unworthiness had proved too unpalatable for Archie. He'd stopped noticing her, which was most confusing. Especially since Lucy could have sworn that on the ferry he'd been about to kiss her.

She'd been kissed a few times and she'd avoided being kissed *plenty* of times. She was well versed in reading the signs that a fellow was about to kiss a girl and Archie had definitely been displaying them all. His breath had laced with hers, warm and sweet, his irises had gone all jetty and focused, like she was all that he was seeing or wanted to see, and his body seemed to hum with purpose . . .

She'd wanted him to kiss her, she realized with a thrill of long-ing. She'd leaned forward, closing her eyes and offering her lips only to be suddenly pushed away, as he flung his coat jacket over her shoulders and then told her not to talk. Normally she would have ignored such a stricture but she was confused and a little offended so she'd done as bid and shortly thereafter, well, she'd spent another hour leaning over the rail.

Hardly the sort of position that casts one in the best light. Or a kissable one.

When they reached the bottom of the gangway, Archie took her elbow and steered her through the crowd gathered to meet the weary travelers. Hawkers offered pastries, hot lemonade, roasted nuts, and newspapers as street urchins—*French* street urchins, Lucy noted with a thrill—darted amongst the throng, pantomim-ing offers to carry bags or clear a path. Scrawny, fleet-footed, and avid, their cheery demeanor masked sharp-eyed opportunism. Lucy knew them well; their English counterparts loitered about theatre back entrances, flitting amongst the swells waiting for the actresses to appear and relieving them of their watches, fobs, and handkerchiefs.

"Best keep a hand on your wallet in this crowd," she advised Archie as she intercepted a lad of no more than six about to "acci-dentally" back into him. She'd seen this ploy before: as soon as the boy bumped into a mark, he'd fling himself to the ground as though he'd been hurt and while his intended victim was busy picking him up and dusting him off, one of his cohorts would be emptying their target's back pocket. It was one of the first dodges she'd witnessed when she'd started working in London.

"What?" Archie hadn't even noted the boy. She wasn't sur-prised. Archie lived in an ivory tower. She spun the kid around and gave him a shove, launching him back into the crowd. He turned his head to stick his tongue out at her before darting away.

"The kids around here," she explained. "You have to watch out. They're so light-fingered you'll never know their hands are in your pockets until you reach for something and find it missing."

"I assure you, I would have known had that little boy tried to pick my pocket."

"It's not him I'm advising you against. It's his older brother. The one you won't see standing behind you."

He regarded her sadly. "Couldn't the kid simply be trying to earn a few honest pennies?"

She rolled her eyes. "Fine. But don't blame me when you discover your knickers have gone missing."

He suddenly smiled, making her forget her earlier grievance. "I won't. Now, come along before all the cabs are taken and we find ourselves afoot." He took hold of her hand and pulled her through the crowd to the end of the wharf where cabs had queued up, waiting for fares. He waved to the first cabbie in the line.

"Here." He yanked open the door and helped her inside as he held a brief conversation in French with the driver.

"Apparently there is only one really decent hotel in town," explained Archie, "a place called Hotel Ligure, but it's very expensive."

"Then that's where they'll be," said Lucy, thinking of Margery's propensity for staying at the finest establishments when someone else was footing the bill.

"*L'emmener*," Archie told the driver, shutting the carriage door behind her.

"What are you sa—doing?" Lucy asked through the window.

"I need to find a telegraph office. I'll meet you in the Hotel Ligure's lobby. If your great-aunts aren't there, we'll ask around."

"But—"

"I won't be long."

Oh dear.

"No need to look distressed. Just ask to speak to the manager."

But in what language?

He hesitated. "Is there a problem?"

She sat back and tittered as though the idea were nonsensical. "Of course not." She racked her brain for a reason she would have looked nonplussed and came up with a perfectly valid one. "I'm short of funds, is all. I didn't realize the expense of things and I'd like to wear something other than this." She lifted her rough, shrunken skirt.

"Don't worry about it. I'll be happy to lend you whatever you require. I just need to get to a bank first. I'll see you later." He said something to the driver, handed him some money, and stepped back to let the carriage roll past into the street.

Lucy sat forward on the seat and watched until his figure disappeared, torn between wishing he'd come with her and relief that his introduction to "Mrs. Martin" had been postponed, however briefly. She didn't doubt that Margery had managed to keep his gender secret from her great-aunts; he was a professional. He'd managed to fool some very famous men to very comical effect when he'd first appeared on stage—though just how comical he never did reveal to her, saying she was too gently bred to appreciate the joke. But she had a feeling Professor Grant would be an entirely different kettle of fish; he seemed unerringly perceptive. He certainly had her on her toes.

Ah, well, it didn't do any good to fret. *Things would turn out.* She'd adopted that credo early on and lived by it ever since. As a seven-year-old orphan she'd been shuttled from place to place, person to person, without any control over where she went or with whom or for how long. Anticipating a good end had kept the worst fears at bay: that tomorrow's guardian would be cruel, or that she'd be sent to an orphanage, or abandoned altogether. Far better to cleave to the belief that everything would turn out for the best.

So now, rather than brood, she leaned out the carriage window, putting thoughts of Archie—well, as many as she was able—from her mind as she drank in her first taste of France.

At first blush Saint-Malo seemed very like any English port city but upon closer scrutiny she noted a certain, indefinable élan that was missing from its English counterparts. It revealed itself in the bright blue flowers spilling from the sun-drenched sill of an open window and in a slender gray cat delicately cleaning its paws in the doorway of a patisserie while a swarthy shopgirl reviewed her reflection in the shop window and smiled confidently at what she saw.

A quarter hour later, she arrived at the Hotel Ligure, a two-story brick building, discreet and unadorned, only the plaque suspended above the main door acknowledging the structure's purpose. Instead of a grand entrance there was just a painted door at the top of a pristinely clean stairway, at the bottom of which a languid-eyed porter in a blue jacket leaned against the exterior wall and smoked a cigarette.

The carriage pulled to a halt and the doorman reluctantly straightened, flicking the still-burning gasper away as he pulled open the door. *"Bienvenue,* mademoiselle."

He muttered something in an aside to the driver, who shook his head in reply. She supposed the porter had asked after her non-existent luggage. She felt a blush rise to her cheeks. She knew the sort of women who arrived at hotels with no luggage. The man gave her a broad smile and a wink as he hustled past her to open the front door, but he did so with such good-natured charm she couldn't find it in her to be offended.

The lobby was furnished in the art nouveau style, tricked out with carved blond wood panels and imitations of Mr. Tiffany's stained-glass lamps. Slender whiplash curves defined the elegant staircase's iron balustrade and handmade carpets lay scattered about the highly polished floorboards. A middle-aged man with a thick, bushy moustache emerged from behind the front desk, hastening toward her with outstretched hands.

"You can only be Mademoiselle Eastlake," he exclaimed in English.

"Yes, how did you know?"

"Your great-aunt told me to expect you. I am Leon Navarre, manager of the Ligure. I am so pleased to see you are finally arrived after your most difficult journey." His gaze traveled discreetly over her ramshackle appearance. He lowered his voice sympathetically. "You were marooned on Sark?"

"Yes."

"*Quel dommage!*" He shook his head, clucking his tongue. Then he straightened, brightening perceptibly. "But you are here now and we will make you forget the discomforts you have suffered."

"*Please*," she said feelingly. "Though first I would like to see my great-aunts."

"Charming ladies. Absolutely charming. And Miss Lavinia . . ." He kissed his fingertips. "There must be French blood somewhere in your lineage."

Lucy regarded him in confusion. "Excuse me?"

"Your aunt. She is so . . ." He screwed up his face, his English failing him. "So . . . *recherché.*" He lifted his hands. "You understand."

She didn't, but she wasn't about to tell him that. One of the many life lessons she'd learned performing in the West End was never to advertise one's deficiencies.

She smiled demurely. "Of course." And then, lest her French be further tested, "If you could direct me to their rooms?"

"Alas, I cannot." Monsieur Navarre's face crumpled. "They are gone."

"*Gone?* Where? When?"

"With their companion, the most gracious Mrs. Martin."

Good heavens. Margery had kidnapped her aunts.

"'Twas she who told me to expect you and," he lowered his voice to a discreet level, "that you would be paying the older ladies' outstanding bill."

"But where are they?"

"First, the bill." Like a burlesque magician producing a rabbit from his hat, a chit appeared in the manager's hand. He bowed as he presented it to Lucy.

She glanced down and her eyes went wide. "But this is almost seventy pounds!" It was more than she earned in two weeks and nearly everything she had left in her purse. She'd have to see about wiring Monsieur DuPaul for an advance.

"*Exactement*," the manager said cheerfully. "Under Madame Martin's guidance, your aunts have developed unexpectedly sophisticated palates. They have enjoyed some truly magnificent wines."

"Mrs. Martin's guidance?"

"*Oui.* She says to add the fee to your great-aunts' bill and that you would pay it as soon as you arrive. Normally I would not agree to such an arrangement. This is a hotel, not a bank. But for your great-aunts, I make the exception. So."

"But where are they?"

"Ah! I almost forget." The manager reached into his jacket's inside pocket and produced a thin envelope. "They have left you this letter. I am certain you will find an answer within it."

Handing it to her, he discreetly removed himself a short distance, allowing her to read undisturbed. Like its author, Bernice, the note was short and to the point.

Dear Lucy,

Your arrival having been delayed for an indefinite period, and Lavinia feeling uneasy without friends or language to safeguard us, we have accepted Mrs. Martin's kind offer to accompany her to Châtelle-rault where we shall meet you at the Hotel St. Georges.

In spite of the inconvenience you have experienced, I do hope your trip proves as pleasant as ours has been. Mrs. Martin is such an inspiration! By the simple virtue of her own intrepid spirit, she persuades one that a woman of a certain age needn't be overly wary of venturing out into the world. And the world, I am learning, is a very interesting place.

Lucy nearly dropped the letter in surprise.

Frankly, I feel quite confident we would have fared just fine staying in Saint-Malo, but Lavinia is not. Besides which there doesn't seem to be any reason to deny ourselves Mrs. Martin's splendid company.

I look forward to seeing you.
Affectionately, Bernice Litton

Post scriptus: At Mr. Navarre's insistence, we have taken your luggage with us. The ferry's delay has filled the town with people awaiting its arrival and he claims not to have the wherewithal to store luggage, nor does he feel able to guarantee its security. I know this will be another inconvenience for you, but Lavinia and Mrs. Martin found a very accommodating modiste a few streets away where you might purchase some garments should you need do so. A Madame Tuttle, though Tuttle hardly seems a French name to me, and why Lavinia is suddenly so interested in fashion is a mystery yet to be explained.

"Monsieur Navarre?"

The dapper Frenchman hurried to Lucy's side. "*Oui?*"

"How would one get to Châtellerault?"

"Châtellerault? I believe the train to Bordeaux stops there. But there are no more trains today."

"Drat. How far is it? Could I hire someone to drive us?"

His mouth twisted apologetically. "Not today. Today is Sunday."

"You're certain?" Lucy asked. She wasn't overly worried yet about making it to Saint-Girons in time for the anniversary since she'd allotted a week for sightseeing. But the misadventure with the ferry had already used up nearly three days and she wasn't sure how far out of their way Margery's detour had taken her aunts. And after paying the staggering sum of this bill, she would be short on funds.

"Very certain." The manager gave an apologetic shrug. "A driver might be arranged for tomorrow but it would be costly and it is at least an eight-hour trip. Better to have a ba—" He caught himself just in time, "to freshen up, have a good meal at our most exceptional restaurant, then sleep. Tomorrow you may leave bright and early on the train."

What he said made perfect sense. Which meant she and Archie would be traveling together, just the two of them, for a bit longer. She suddenly smiled.

"Do you know where Madame Tuttle has her shop?"

Monsieur Navarre nodded approvingly. "Just two streets down, off the main thoroughfare. I highly recommend it. She can be most nimble-fingered for a price. And speaking of price, would you care to see to your great-aunts' bill now?"

"Later. Thank you, Monsieur Navarre."

She glanced down at her attire. She was loath to spend any of the money she had left, but her current state was truly dreadful. She wanted to remind Archie that she was more than a troublesome, seasick songbird. She wanted him to see her in a more appealing light—she looked down at her stained and shrunken clothing— and dress.

After all, she was in France, the home of Worth and Fortuny and Poiret. How could she return home without at least one French gown?

Archie looked around the Hotel Ligure's lobby. With the exception of the over-moustached man behind the front desk poring over a newspaper, it was empty. He couldn't deny his disappointment at not finding Lucy—and her great-aunts—but neither was he surprised; he'd been delayed longer than he expected.

It hadn't taken long to find a telegraph office but on the way back he'd passed a dry goods store, the sight of which reminded him that he didn't have so much as a toothbrush to his name or a kit to carry it in, let alone any clothing fit to dine in. It would be . . . disrespectful to Lucy to appear at dinner in such shabby clothes. He didn't want her thinking he didn't consider that she deserved his best efforts. The same effort he would have made for any lady.

No, his inner, obnoxiously honest voice informed him. Not any lady. *Her. Just her.* He couldn't remember when he had given his personal appearance a second thought.

Fine. She brought out an unanticipated desire to look . . . acceptable.

Acceptable for what? The inner voice demanded. For kissing?

Fine. Yes. He'd wanted to kiss her. He wanted to take her in his arms and feel her body next to his. He *wanted.* More than he could remember wanting anything in a very long time. Wanted as in craved. With the same ardent desire that had led to so many unpleasant consequences in his youth. But he'd learned since then. By God he had. Wanting to do something did not mean one must do it. Ruthlessly he drowned that nobly honest inner voice, refusing to examine his motives further. He was going to find a toothbrush and that was all.

He'd found a toothbrush and small leather satchel easily enough, but when he'd asked the sales clerk where he could at least buy a fresh collar, he'd only been answered with a shrug and an impatient gesture for him to move along to make way for the next customer.

Outside the shop a teenaged lad had approached him, exuding pleasant sympathy. He'd overheard Archie's query and would gladly escort him to a nearby haberdasher, his uncle, who could supply him not only with collars and cuffs but a ready-made shirt.

Archie had gratefully accepted the offer and was now in possession of a pristine set of collar and cuffs, and a clean, well-fitted shirt. He hoped Lucy approved. And, of course, her great-aunts, too.

"Monsieur?" he asked, approaching the front desk.

"Oui?" The Frenchman didn't raise his gaze from the paper.

"I am looking for a girl."

The man turned the page. "Are not all young men?"

"No. You misunderstand."

The man gave up trying to read his newspaper and sighed. "I doubt that, monsieur. But this is not the sort of place in which to find one."

"Not that type of girl. I am looking for Miss Lucy Eastlake. She was supposed to meet me here. I was hoping to find her and her aunts."

This abruptly triggered the man's interest. He straightened, eyeing Archie closely. "You are a friend?"

"I am escorting her—them."

"You are?" The interest became more pointed.

"Yes. Well, I expect to be. I was planning to join them here."

"Well, you will have to wait longer. They are gone."

"What?" Why would she leave without him? Panic drilled through him. She mustn't. "Where did she go?"

"She?" The hotel manager regarded him in puzzlement before his expression cleared. "Non. I am speaking of the Misses Littons and their friend, Mrs. Martin. *Those* ladies have gone, having left a letter for Miss Eastlake. And a bill. A large bill. Of which, despite assurances, I have yet to see a *sou*."

"You'll get paid," Archie said impatiently. "Where is Miss Eastlake?"

The manager ignored his question. "But by *whom*?"

"Miss Eastlake, I suppose. Could you please tell me where—"

The manager's lips turned down. "I am not sanguine."

"Look. You'll get paid what is owed you. I personally will vouch for it."

The manager brightened perceptibly, his gaze raking over Archie's expensive if mud-spattered coat and shoes. "*You* will pay?"

"Yes. Certainly. As soon as the bank opens tomorrow. Now, please. Where can I find Miss Eastlake?"

"She is in her room. But, before you ask, since you are not interested in *that* type of girl and because I have three daughters who are not *that* type of girl, and I know what men who accept the responsibility for young lady's bills expect in return—no, do not bother looking indignant. I am a man; you are a man. We both know the truth of what I say—I will not tell you her room number," he said in grim paternal tones but then spoiled the effect by adding, "That is the lady's prerogative."

"I was not going to ask."

"Then you are either a fool or saint."

Archie suspected he knew which category he fell under, but didn't feel the need to share.

"Now, about a room."

"I am sorry. There is nothing available. See?" The manager reached across the counter and with an adroit flick of his wrist spun the open register so that it faced Archie. "Miss Eastlake was fortunate that the delightful Mrs. Martin reserved one for her. I could have rented her room for twice what I charge her."

Archie had his doubts. "Fortunate indeed. Where is the nearest hotel?"

"La Maison is a short distance, but it will be fully occupied, too, as, I am much afraid, will all the hotels in town."

"How about some place near the docks?" he asked, though he didn't like the idea of being so far away from Lucy. She might require him for some reason. Like asking anyone *anything* in French, he thought drily.

"Perhaps. But I should recommend you have a penchant for bed bugs if you stay down there."

"Could you let me bed down in a storeroom for the night?"

Navarre *tutted.* "This is not a home for itinerants. What would my staff think? They see you there and the next thing I know the cook will insist I let his drunken brother-in-law sleep off his debauch or the accountant will expect to have a bed there the next time his wife kicks him out. No."

"Would an additional twenty francs help you to explain my presence?"

"Ah, that is different. Then I am not providing charity. You may avail yourself of my office. Very cozy. I will add it to what is owed. And of course, you are welcome to dine at our very fine restaurant. Feel free to charge it to the room. Miss Eastlake's room."

The little swindler. He wouldn't offer him a cot in a back room gratis but he was pleased to let him spend his money in his restaurant. He'd be damned if he'd spend another penny here. "Thanks, but I'll—"

"Miss Eastlake has reserved a table for seven o'clock." The Frenchman tipped his head in the direction of an elaborately carved set of doors. "Should I have the table set for two?" he asked innocently.

Dinner for two. With Lucy.

"Thanks. Do that."

CHAPTER
22

". . . so I spent the night beneath the dugout and walked back to the town in the morning," Archie finished, realizing he'd been rather going on for a while. "I'm sorry. I'm afraid I tend to become overenthusiastic when I'm talking about my work."

"No. Please. It's fascinating," Lucy said.

He studied her, assuming she was simply being polite but finding no evidence of it in her rapt expression. She looked beautiful sitting across the dining table from him, her elbow next to an empty sherbet glass, her small, pointed chin nestled in her palm. Her hair had been pulled up in rippling brown waves secured by a black velvet ribbon, a few curls released to tease the long line of her neck and tickle her cheek.

She wore a subtle blue-green gown made from a softly lustrous, draping material that brought out the sea colors in her eyes. Shimmery, copper-colored lace, embroidered and beaded, covered a low-cut bodice that closely followed the natural curves of her body and exposed the soft, sweet swell of her breast, in any other woman a modest display, but with Lucy one he had to forcibly keep his eyes from straying toward. What the hell was wrong with him?

"I would love to see water the color you describe. And birds flying above the jungle canopy with tails like party streamers," she said wistfully.

An image of Lucy appeared in his mind, Lucy dressed in a chemise and a skirt, her feet bare on the warm sand, the sun glinting off her hair, her face tipped to the brilliant sky. Her expressive face would be alight with pleasure and interest. He'd never known anyone who took such joy in things, who found humor in the oddest places, pleasure in the most unusual things. But then, maybe he was imagining things. Maybe she wasn't as unique as she appeared to be. How could she be?

"Most people would find the experience more enjoyable viewed in a photograph than firsthand."

"I can't see how. A photograph might capture the look of a thing, but it can't re-create the feel of warm sand beneath your toes, the sound of birdcall in your ears, the scent of . . ." She trailed off with a laugh. "What does it smell like in Fiji?"

"On the beach? Salt air and brine, but as you move into the forests, there's a humid, earthy scent of growing things, a subtle sweetness, more spice than floral."

Her eyes drifted shut. "Mmm."

He couldn't look away from her. Her skin glowed in the romantic candlelight. A smile played about her lips as she imagined the scene he described. Who cared what Fiji smelled like; what did *she* smell like? His body tensed at the idea. He forced his gaze elsewhere.

He had to put an end to this purposeless speculation. In a few days they would be in Saint-Girons and, a few days after that, he would say good-bye to her in Weymouth. There was no reason they would ever meet again. She would return to the theatre and he would go back to St. Phillip's. Maybe someday he would get a ticket to one of her shows. She might recognize him if he stayed afterward to congratulate her. She would smile and perhaps he would remind her of . . . of what? That she had thrown up all over him? That he had hauled her over his shoulder like, what was it she'd said? A sack of potatoes? That he'd almost kissed her and spent the months in between wishing he had . . .

And what would she say to that? Would she be shocked? Amused? Would she touch his hand and say, "Well, you're hardly the first?"

He *hated* the idea.

"Yes. It smells good enough on the beaches. But the towns and villages aren't on the beach," he said, his tone reflecting his anger with himself. "The places I've stayed have all had hard beds, if there are any beds at all, a plague of biting insects, and as for hygiene, it's more a theory than a practice and ofttimes not even that. I guarantee you, the smells in the villages generally are not convivial."

But rather than look put off by this attempt to insert some much-needed realism into the fantasy her words had conjured, she laughed. "Oh, I've slept rough my share of times. I daresay I could tolerate a few jiggers and the smell of rotting fish."

She'd surprised him again but then he recalled her propensity for storytelling. "You? Where? Don't tell me your aunts kept you in the attic because I won't believe it."

She laughed again. She had a lovely laugh, one she used often. When was the last time he'd heard Cornelia laugh? Had he *ever* heard Cornelia laugh?

"Of course not. They spoiled me rotten."

"Aha!"

"But I didn't always live with them."

"Your parents were poor?" he asked sympathetically.

"No," she replied promptly. "Well. Perhaps. But if they were I didn't notice it. Of course, I don't know that I would have; I was only seven when they died."

"Accident?"

She nodded.

"I'm sorry."

She tipped her head, her smile unexpectedly poignant. "Thank you."

"It must have been difficult for your great-aunts, as well."

She gave an odd smile. "I don't think they even knew she'd died until I showed up. Mention of her name was strictly forbidden at Robin's Hall. You see, my great-grandmother disowned my mother when she was sixteen."

"What for?" He shook his head. "I'm sorry. That was unconscionably ill-mannered of me. Believe it or not, I really was raised properly. Not that you've had much evidence of that."

She didn't look offended; she looked amused. "Oh, I think I've seen a hint or two. And I don't mind, anyway. Secrets breed sorrows, as my dad used to say.

"As to what Mum did to earn being vanquished, she fell in love with a conductor." She leaned forward, her eyes sparking with mischief. "A foreign conductor. Hungarian. She met him at a party her grandparents were hosting in his honor. By all reports, it was love at first sight and, according to those same reports, my great-grandparents were apoplectic. It wasn't just that my future father was foreign, you understand; it was that he was foreign and with no aristocratic antecedents."

"What about your mother's parents? Did they object, too?" His mouth tightened in chagrin. "Again, I shouldn't have asked that."

"And again, I don't mind. My grandmother was the oldest of the Litton sisters. She died shortly after giving birth to my mum, whereupon my grandfather turned his newborn baby girl over to his in-laws to be raised. He remarried years later but his new wife did not want children, either her own or anyone else's, so my mother stayed with her grandparents.

"At any rate, thereafter the conductor was refused at the door. In response, my mother climbed out the window, an act for which her name was struck from the family Bible. They eloped, I was the result, and disowned in turn through association." Her brow furrowed. "Gads. I just realized how few children my immediate ancestors produced. Hm. Maybe they weren't as happily married as I assumed."

He supposed he should be shocked, but he wasn't. He was charmed. She simply said whatever popped into her head. At least when she wasn't spinning yarns, a process during which you could practically see the possible storylines unfurling. It wasn't politic, it probably wasn't polite, but it was certainly novel.

"You were an only child, too?"

"Yes. So perhaps the fault lies there. Maybe musicians just aren't fertile." Her eyes lightened. "That would explain the dearth of good composers, wouldn't it?"

He laughed. He couldn't help it.

She joined him. "Actually, Dad came from a line of not very successful but very creative types and there were scads of them. You know, musicians and actors and poets and playwrights. The only one of the lot who ever made a penny was my dad's cousin Eloisa and she wrote penny dreadfuls." Her gaze turned musing. "I always thought I'd pen a jolly good gothic romance . . ."

He nodded as things fell into place. "That's how you ended up sleeping rough. You were sent to live with your father's people."

"I was rather hoping you'd forgotten that. Rough may be doing it a bit brown. *Simple* is more like it. I never actually slept on the ground."

"Who had custody of you before the Littons?" The more he found out about her, the more he wanted to know.

She laughed again. "Who didn't? I spent time with seven different relatives in four years. It was hard right . . . right after. I was used to being the center of my parents' world and suddenly I wasn't the center of anyone's world. I was more like a meteor, crashing others' orbits before spinning off to the next planet."

She spoke lightly, but he heard the yearning behind the words, the slightest hint of confusion at how life could so substantially change from one moment to the next, from being well-loved to . . . not. "I'm sorry, Lucy."

She shrugged. "Things worked out. They always do." There wasn't a trace of irony in her voice. "Besides, no one ever claimed they could take care of me forever. Quite the contrary. I knew straight off they were not permanent situations.

"And I learned something new in every place I stayed, too. How to make a penny disappear, pick a lock, play the piano, swim like a fish, speak like a duchess, sew my own dresses—which reminds me, I'm afraid I'm going to have to ask you for that loan. I'm tapped out. In fact, I still owe the dressmaker a few quid."

"Of course," he said, impatient to hear the rest of her story. "Then what happened?"

"Then?" Her expression softened and her gaze slipped to somewhere far away. "Then I came to Robin's Hall."

The way she said it, tenderly, with the expression of someone remembering something wonderful, told its own tale. "As I said, things always have a way of working out."

She caught his eye and grinned. "So you see, I think I am quite within my rights to assume I could enjoy your island despite a few bugs and the straw pallet."

"I believe you might, at that. I wish you could." The words spilled out before he realized he'd spoken aloud. He felt the heat rise in his face.

She'd tipped her head to the side and was regarding him with a puzzled little wrinkle between her brows, as if she had just spotted something she hadn't been looking for but had misplaced long ago, and wasn't convinced it could be what she thought it was. But then, her brow smoothed, her eyes cleared, and she took a short, deep breath, her lips parting on the promise of a smile. He found himself recalling the nearly magnetic attraction of her mouth, as he had all night and most of the day, ever since, in fact, he'd held her on that damn ferry. He forced himself to remember he was about to become engaged, that Cornelia considered it a foregone conclusion, that only the worst, most dishonorable sort of cad would keep such information silent—

"I intend to marry." He blurted it out like a confession. Which it was.

She blinked, surprised. "Of course, you do. So do I." Her gaze dipped and she smiled shyly. He'd never seen her look shy. It made her seem extraordinarily normal. When she was only . . . extraordinary. "Someday."

"No. I mean . . . That is, there is a particular young lady. Miss Litchfield."

Lucy froze.

"This young lady expects—" God. What a dolt. Could he *be* any less chivalrous? "We've known each other a good long time and I believe an understanding has developed between she and I . . . and I mean to ask her to marry me."

He waited for her to reply. He didn't know what he expected her to say: *Congratulations? Why should I care? Am I invited to the reception?*

But in a thousand years he would never have expected her to respond as she did, with a scoffing little trill of laughter. "Really? What for?"

Hallo, rabbit hole. "What do you mean, what for?"

Her gaze was direct, challenging. "Just that. What for?"

He started to speak. Stopped. Started to speak again and clamped his mouth shut and knew that the moment when he should have said, "Because I love her," had slipped away. If he said it now, it would only sound facile. Cornelia deserved better than that.

"See?"

He couldn't think of a reply. No gentleman would discuss his future wife with another young lady. Especially one who had turned his world on end and who increasingly filled his thoughts, leaving no room for anyone else.

He waited in some trepidation, half expecting her to argue with him about his intention. She wouldn't mean anything vulgar by it. It was just that Lucy was impetuous, a little audacious, and frighteningly candid. Her conversation followed an internal guide that was uniquely her own.

She didn't.

Instead, for a long moment she simply stared past him, frowning a little. It unnerved him. He didn't have any idea what she was thinking, if she considered him the worst sort of cad, if she wasn't thinking of him at all. Maybe she was pondering her meal. And then she sighed, nodded to herself as though having realized something she should have already known, and pushed herself back from the table.

She dabbed at her lips, set the handkerchief down, and rose from her chair. He leapt to his feet to hold her chair back. Her hem must have become caught under the chair—she seemed to have trouble with hems—and she started to stumble; he caught her.

She looked up into his eyes. Her skin had turned a dusky, lovely apricot color. He could hear her breathe, see the rise and fall of the lace bodice, was too aware of it and the fact that now, finally, he knew that she smelled like vanilla and greenwood and sunlight, so much better than Fiji, so much—

"Excuse me," she said, laying a hand on his chest—to keep him away? Had she read so much in his gaze? He stepped back, nonplussed, chagrinned that she'd needed to recall him to his manners.

"If you'll excuse me," she said, her voice nervous, her gaze slipping away from his. "I shan't be a few minutes."

He watched her leave the room, trailing the interested gazes of a half dozen Frenchmen in her wake. He lowered himself heavily back down and raked his hand through his hair.

He should have said something about Cornelia the day he'd met Lucy, the moment he'd laid eyes on her. He should have gone up to her at the Savoy and said, "Excuse me, miss, I am about to become engaged. Can I have my pen?"

But he hadn't. And now . . . Now what?

He'd been raised to believe in a very strict code of honor and the importance of personal dignity. In the last few days he'd more or less jettisoned the latter, but he'd hoped to retain his adherence to the former. Now—

"Monsieur?" He looked up to find the waiter standing over him, holding a small silver salver with the bill. "The lady said you were ready for the reckoning." He set the little tray down and withdrew.

Had Lucy gone back to her room? She'd said she would be back but after reviewing his less than gentlemanly behavior perhaps she had decided she didn't need to spend more time in his company. He could hardly blame her.

He turned over the check. It was an exorbitant sum.

But then this trip had already proved far more costly than he'd ever imagined and in far more ways than one.

He reached inside his jacket for his wallet.

"At least you haven't said, 'I told you so.'"

"I'm biding my time." Lucy, who had in fact returned, once again sat across from him, her head bent forward over the table in a conspiratorial manner. She gave him a cat-in-the-cream sort of smile.

"I cannot believe that kid *robbed* me. I've a good mind to go back to his uncle's shop and—"

"I doubt the man was his uncle," Lucy hurriedly broke in. "He was probably just convenient."

Archie sighed. "You're probably right."

She regarded him sympathetically. "I also don't think there's a chance of your wallet being returned. You might as well chalk it up as a loss."

"I suppose. How much money did you say you had left?"

She winced. "Maybe five francs. I'm sorry."

"I must say you're being a real sport about this."

She demurred, her gaze falling modestly from his. "I don't see as it would help to sit around bemoaning our plight. And it's not really that awful a plight, after all."

"It's not?"

"No."

Even for Lucy, this seemed an unnaturally positive outlook. "Don't get me wrong, I find your attitude admirable, but we stand a very, *very* good chance of not being able to deliver your great-aunt to Saint-Girons within the proscribed time period."

It was her turn to look bemused. "Why? We still have days to gather them up and see them to the meeting place. France isn't *that* big."

For all her seeming worldliness, she really was engagingly naïve. "I wish things went as smoothly and quickly as they do in your imagination, Lucy, but I'm afraid they don't. I don't have any identification. It may take days for me to contact the proper bank authorities in England, have them determine my identity, and then wire funds here."

She frowned. "You're not thinking of waiting here in Saint-Malo, are you?"

"Ah . . . yes."

"But we can't. We need to deliver my great-aunts to Saint-Girons."

"Lucy, we have no money. Well, as good as none." He spoke very calmly, in measured tones, even as he felt his muscles tensing with foreboding. He picked up the chit. "We can't pay this bill. We won't be able to pay the bill for our rooms come morning. We have no money to buy train tickets. You've explained that you can't return an altered dress. Ergo, we have no choice."

"I see." She nodded in understanding.

He relaxed, but he was not happy. Lucy was right, the gravity of her great-aunt Lavinia losing out on her share of the rubies couldn't be overstated. "But what to do?" he murmured.

She smacked her hand, palm down, on the table. "We make a run for it."

He peered at her closely, certain he'd heard her wrong. She couldn't mean what he thought she meant. "Run for it?"

"Yes," she said decisively. "Clear out, vamoose, skedaddle. *Flee.*"

"We can't just run out on our bills. It's not only dishonest, it's criminal."

"We'll pay them when we return."

"Return? We're not going to return. We're going to stay here. With any luck, things will be squared away in a couple days and we can take a train to Châtellerault and then another to Saint-Girons. We'll ride at night, if need be."

She sank back in her chair, eyeing him disgustedly. "That won't wash. You just finished telling me about the inevitable loss my great-aunt is sure to sustain. You can't have it both ways."

Damn it. "There is a chance. Why, how many times have I heard you say, 'things will work out?' Don't you believe that anymore?"

"Of course I do. But having faith doesn't entitle one to take Fate for granted. You have to show a little appreciation by helping Fate along whenever possible. And that's what I'm doing." She said this last with a great deal of emphasis. "I'm not going to let my chance of happiness disappear because I didn't have the guts to act. I mean my great-aunts' chance for happiness."

"Lucy."

"No. I'm not going to cool my heels here in Saint-Malo doing nothing while a fortune slips from my great-aunt's fingers."

"You are the most wrong-headed girl I have ever met. You can't just steal away like a thief in the night."

"I can and will. I have to." She bit her lip. "And I was rather hoping it would be 'we' not just 'me.'"

"And how are *we* to get to Châtellerault without any money?" he asked, more desperate than hopeful that she would see reason.

"We'll beg a ride from someone on the road. Lots of people do it. Why Margery once traveled from Edinburgh to Chester without spending a penny."

Oh, yes. Margery. Lucy's "friend" who was accompanying her great-aunts. Why hadn't Navarre mentioned him, only this Mrs. Martin?

"Well?" she asked hopefully.

"No. I've already left one unpaid bill at the ferry office in Weymouth. I am not about to become a serial criminal."

"We'll pay all of them back as soon as we've seen Great-Aunt Lavinia to Saint-Girons."

"No." He shook his head. "Absolutely not."

CHAPTER
23

"Jump!"

Stuck halfway between the Hotel Ligure's first and second stories, clinging to some sturdy vines, Lucy peered over her shoulder to where Archie stood frantically beckoning her from below. She could barely make him out in the predawn darkness. In fact, were it not for some wrongheaded larks trilling unseen from the surrounding shrubs she would have sworn it was still dead of night.

She had been all for lighting out right after dinner. But Archie had convinced her that they weren't likely to find many people on the road so late at night, at least any that were willing to pick up wayfarers, or, more to the point, who were the sort one wanted to be picked up by. They'd likely end up sleeping under a hedgerow.

While she'd acknowledged his points were valid, she also thought she might like curling up with Archie, under a hedgerow or anywhere else. She supposed that made her a very fast girl, since Archie had revealed his intention to propose to another woman.

Except he wouldn't. He couldn't. He *mustn't*. And she had better be right because she was betting everything on that hope. No. Not hope, *belief*. Her heart was still thundering in her chest, either through fear of heights or in answer to her own audacity; it was impossible to tell which. She had convinced Archie to run out on a bill—amongst other things—a highly immoral act for a highly moral man. She had never done anything quite so . . . questionable. Would it matter that she'd done so in the best of causes?

The stakes were impossibly high. What if she lost? What if he *didn't* love her? No. No. NO. It was too late to reconsider, the die had been cast for better or worse, and she'd committed fully to her course. She took a deep breath.

"I can't see." She bent her knees and scooched down, groping for a foothold. She'd changed back into her disreputable clothes, pulling the skirt between her legs and up, tucking the hem under her belt to create impromptu bloomers. Despite Archie's protest that they ought to leave it behind, she'd wrapped Madame Tuttle's beautiful dress in a parcel and given it to Archie to stuff in his kit as best he could. It had been obscenely expensive, which was only to be expected. It was French, after all. But recalling Archie's expression when he'd first seen her in it had been worth the price she'd paid.

"Then jump," Archie reiterated. "I'll catch you. You're not five feet off the ground. At this rate you'll still be clinging to those vines when the iceman makes his rounds."

"All right." She took a deep breath and pushed free of the wall. The next instant she was in Archie's arms. She laughed breathlessly up at him. "You caught me!"

"Of course I did. Did you think I wouldn't?"

"No," she replied honestly. "I knew you would. I just wanted to hear you say, 'Of course.'"

"You are a very strange girl." He shook his head. But, she noted in delight, he hadn't released her.

"*I'm* strange? I'm not the one who climbs about the outside of buildings like it was second nature to me. What were you before you became a professor, Archie? A second-story man?"

"A sec—" She suspected if the lighting were better she would have seen his face go ruddy. "No. Let's just say that when I was at school I had an adventuring spirit."

"You climbed out of your dormitory?"

"Regularly. Oh, don't feign shock. How else was I to get where I wanted to go? They weren't going to hand me the keys. Besides, I always made sure to be back by morning."

She grinned, utterly charmed by the image of Archie as a tousle-haired, unrepentant miscreant sneaking out under the proctors' noses. It was an entirely new aspect of Archie, but not altogether unexpected. She'd just *known* he was a pirate! "Far be it from me to throw rocks. My house is made entirely of glass," she said.

"Hmm."

"Bless you."

"For what?"

"For not saying, 'You can say that again.'"

His mouth curved with humor. Lord, he was attractive! Especially when he smiled like that, black eyes snapping in the darkness. "I was thinking it."

She smiled back, thinking how odd it was that they could chat as easily as if they were on a church lawn after Sunday service, while all the time she became more aware of the tensile strength of his arms, his heart beating against her shoulder, the wool material that divided his warmth from hers. He was looking down into her face, his expression strained.

"Come on," he finally said, setting her on her feet. "We'd best get moving."

She fell into step at his side as he led them down the alley and out onto the thoroughfare. He didn't speak, but she believed she understood anyway: *his conscience is playing hell with him.*

She wanted very much to tell him not to worry.

He wasn't going to marry that other girl; he was going to marry her.

She hadn't realized it until last night, though she had probably *known* it since the day he'd shown up at Robin's Hall and dripped all over the carpet. He'd been so handsome and earnest, the fact that he had no idea he was gorgeous making him even more appealing. He'd been distracted by her, as though he saw in her something he recognized but couldn't quite place. Something he'd almost forgotten. She knew, because she'd had the same sensation, except she remembered what it was she saw in him: a feeling of being recognized, understood, and accepted. Which is why he always knew when she was acting: because he knew, on some deep ineffable level, who she was when she wasn't.

It was a feeling she hadn't had since she was a child.

She didn't know just what people had been telling him he was all his life, but they were wrong. He was so much more than duty-bound, overly conscientious, brilliant Professor Ptolemy Grant. He was Archie Grant, boon companion, should-be pirate, and suspected second-story man who could melt a girl with his smile but then would have no idea where the puddle at his feet had come from.

Archie Grant, with whom she'd fallen madly, deeply in love.

And she was *not* going to nobly step aside while he proposed to another woman.

She stared glumly at the road ahead, her conscience prickling annoyingly. Fine, she supposed she ought to spend some time, at least a few minutes, considering that other woman's feelings.

She tromped along and considered them.

They didn't change a thing. First, because whether or not this Miss Litchfield loved Archie, Archie categorically did not love her. She could not imagine any woman would want to marry a man who did not hold her in the same regard. In point of fact, she was doing the woman a favor.

And yes, she conceded that the argument had a specious element to it, but simply because something was self-serving did not make it untrue.

Second, and more importantly, if she had learned one lesson from Lavinia's oft-told tale of love lost, it was that silently hoping for your happily-ever-after only guaranteed you silence. If you so much as caught a glimpse of that ever-after sort of love, then you pursued it, you fought for it, you seized it with both hands and you never let go.

The only problem now was how to make Archie understand what she perceived so clearly? Likely he would take some persuading.

Luckily, she could be very persuasive.

⸻

"Whoa! Whoa!" The lead driver in a small caravan of gaily painted wagons pulled back the reins on his pair of shaggy ponies and leaned from his perch, craning his neck to admire the owner of the comely leg that had flashed winsomely from beneath a dusty, stained skirt.

Lucy flicked down her skirts and lifted a single brow at Archie in a "told-you-so" manner. He'd been trying without success for the last four hours to talk their way onto a wagon, a cart, or a lorry while they trudged along the road. Her feet were sore and she was getting hungry and it was only midday. No one was interested in giving a pair of Englishmen a free ride. Finally, she'd decided it was time to take matters into her own hands. Or legs, as it were.

As she'd known he would, Archie objected. As *he'd* known *she* would, she ignored his objection. And as she suspected they'd both known it would, her gambit had worked.

Now she waved madly at the driver, a wiry, middle-aged whippet of a man. "Can we ride with you?"

The man scowled.

"*Pouvez-vous nous emmener à la prochaine ville?*" Archie called out.

"What did you say?" Lucy asked.

"Don't you know?" he asked drily, then relented. "I asked if he could take us to the next town."

The man's head disappeared. A moment later an old woman's face appeared from around the other side of the wagon, iron-gray coils of hair escaping from beneath a battered felt hat. "*Pouvez-vous payer?*"

"How much money did you say you had left?" Archie asked.

"Five francs," Lucy said.

"What?"

"Good dresses are expensive." She lifted her chin. "It's a very good dress."

"*Oui ou non?*" the old lady demanded

"*Un peu,*" Archie called back and started walking again.

The woman disappeared.

Lucy might not know much French, but she'd picked up enough to understand that Archie had asked for a ride to town and in turn the middle-aged woman had asked if he could pay. '*Non*' Lucy had no trouble interpreting. She also had no trouble interpreting what the future held: blisters.

"*S'il vous plait!*" she shouted desperately.

The wagon started forward and Lucy's heart plummeted but then the wagon abruptly stopped. The man reappeared. "*Pouvez-vous gagner votre chemin?*"

Archie sighed. "*Non.*"

"What did he ask?" Lucy demanded.

He eyed her sardonically.

She blushed. "I'm a bit rusty. What did he ask?"

"If we could earn our way."

"*Oui!*" Lucy shouted and, lifting her skirts, ran to catch up.

CHAPTER
24

"Dark and burning eyes, dark as midnight skies
Full of passion flame, full of lovely game.
Oh how I love you, oh how afraid I am of you
The day that we met, is a day that I rue!
Oh, dark eyes, you are darker than the deep!
I see mourning for my soul in you,
I see a triumphant flame in you:
A poor heart immolated by you, untrue, so true!"

Lucy's lovely voice, clear in the upper ranges, smoky and elusive in the lower ones, pierced the night. If she'd been standing on a stage, hands clasped together as she warbled the evocative lyrics to the throbbing, melancholy tune, he would have been enjoying himself vastly.

But she wasn't. And he wasn't.

When she'd told the leader of what had proved to be a traveling troupe of performers that she would "sing for their supper," he hadn't thought she'd meant *this*.

The troupe's specialty was orchestrating shows performed out of doors—so as not to have to pay any theatre's rental fees—dinner and drink included in the price of admission. They were traveling south, as the evenings here in the north were growing too cold to perform out of doors. But today had been fine, the sun's warmth lingering into the evening so that when they'd approached the outskirts of the town where they'd intended to camp for the night, the leader had decided to take advantage of the unexpectedly mild evening for one last show.

In Lucy they'd found an opening act, one proving to be a great success with the townspeople.

She'd dressed as a Gypsy—despite their host-cum-employer denying that his troupe was Romani. Archie had been disappointed. Despite their appearance in almost every European country, the Romani remained an ethnic group as mysterious as ancient Egyptians. Due to generations of systematic oppression, the Romani's distrust of outsiders was legionary and impenetrable. He would have loved the chance to interview them. But it appeared Lucy was as close to the real thing as he'd come this trip. And that was plenty close enough.

The white blouse she wore beneath a heavily embroidered vest showed less skin than most ladies exposed in London's best restaurants, and the multilayered skirts that belled out as she twirled allowed only fleeting glimpses of slender calves above sturdy, high-topped boots. It didn't matter.

She didn't need to wear a revealing costume to be seductive, a point she was currently illustrating to a fine degree. She played the Gypsy temptress to the nines, dancing like a wicked ballerina. Lithe and graceful and sinuous and bold, she weaved in and out amongst the tables and benches set up beneath the forest's canopy, the trees' lower branches hung with paper lanterns that bobbed and swayed in the crisp evening air, scattering sequins of light on the diners below.

A brilliant blue silk scarf covered her hair, its fringe dangling over brows darkened with charcoal. She'd lined her eyes with a kohl stick, the black frame making her irises seem to glimmer like liquid gold, and painted her lips a berry hue that begged to be tasted. And from the loose-jawed wonder with which the male diners regarded her, he was not the only man who thought so.

And he hated it.

> "But I am not sad, I am not sorrowful,
> My fate is soothing to me:
> All that is best in life that was given me,
> In sacrifice I have riven from me,
> For you, my dark and fiery eyes!
> Always in my heart
> No further than my dream,
> I will wait for you.
> I will challenge Fate for you,
> My dark eyes!"

It was a ridiculous rendering of an old Russian song and in any other venue it might have been risible. But here, with autumn leaves rustling in the darkness, the yearning strains of the unseen fiddles playing ardent counterpoint to Lucy's tender voice, and the wind shredding the torchlight with passionate abandon, it felt heartbreakingly real.

She drifted between the benches, trailing her fingertips along the gentlemen's jackets and sharing sad, knowing looks with the ladies. But then, as capricious as the Gypsy lover the song alternately denounced and beseeched, the music abruptly shifted tone, going from melancholy yearning to fiery challenge. With it, Lucy's entire demeanor changed, too.

Her eyed flashed with scornful defiance. Her posture grew taut with tensile fury, her arms rising above her head and fingers snapping like castanets while her feet drummed the ground in an impassioned staccato. Her eye caught his and he raised his cup, silently commending her on her act. Instead of smiling back as he'd expected, her gleaming eyes narrowed and she tossed her head.

Then with the regal hauteur of a queen, she raised her hand and beckoned him toward her, clearly expecting him to join the performance. He gave a derisive snort and shook his head, returning his attention to the cup of hard cider in his hand. It was one thing for Lucy to dive headlong into a hackneyed, overwrought role; quite another for a college professor to do so.

Around him his fellow diners murmured. He kept his gaze firmly on his cup. Better than watching Lucy toy with some poor sot . . . A cool hand caressed his cheek. He froze at the touch, as soft and tantalizing as a dream. The crowd quieted, their hushed anticipation as loud as applause. Too bad. He wasn't about to be the cat's paw in Lucy's act.

Very calmly, without turning around, he reached up and pulled her hand away from his cheek.

The crowd broke into raucous laughter. The man beside him clapped him on the back while around him people cheered or snickered, depending on their gender. One woman loudly proclaimed that he was certainly a heartbreaker and her husband countered that he "*une centaine de sortes de imbécile!*" He'd have to give his nod to the husband because he didn't feel like anything but a fool, caught on tenterhooks of anticipation, while Lucy seemed determined to undermine any shred of dignity he had left.

And she hadn't finished. She grabbed his shoulder and jerked him around. The diners' commotion ended as sharply as if a needle had been lifted from a gramophone record.

Gaze locked with his, Lucy slowly sank down onto his lap. He froze, certain that any movement might lead to disaster. She reached up and bracketed his face between her hands, eyes shining with mystery and challenge. Even knowing it was an act, his heart beat faster in response.

"I will wait for you.
I will challenge Fate for you,
My dark eyes!"

Her eyelids slipped halfway shut. Her cool fingers shivered against his cheek. His heart thundered in his chest as he dragged in a ragged breath. She tilted her head and melted toward him, her lips parting, gold eyes lambent with promise as she pulled his face closer—

A woman suddenly tittered nervously.

More roughly than he'd intended, he grabbed her wrists and wrenched her hands away. The crowd erupted in mixed hoots of approval that he'd resisted the *femme fatale* and disdain that he could be so dim-witted.

"Brilliant, Archie!" Lucy whispered sotto voce. "They're eating it up! Keep playing along."

She thought . . . She didn't realize . . . Archie stared at her, amazed she could be so . . . *dense*.

With a covert wink, she snatched free of his grasp and leapt to her feet, glaring down at him. Then she snapped her skirts back and spun around, turning her back on him.

Oh, he'd play along all right.

She made it two steps before he caught her arm. He jerked her back, toppling her onto his lap, catching a glimpse of eyes wide with surprise just before his mouth descended on hers.

The crowd went wild.

"How much to stay and do the same again? I pay you fifty francs a week." The troupe's impresario, Luca, had suddenly recalled he did know a bit of English and he used it now to try to convince Lucy to join their "family," it apparently being a foregone conclusion that where *le femme* went so went *le homme*.

"We are *not* going to do the same again," Lucy replied severely, amazed that *she* was saying such a thing. It seemed more like something Archie would declare.

To say his kiss had flustered her would be a gross understatement. Shaken her to her very core was more like it. No one had ever kissed her like that, open-mouthed, searing, passionate, his tongue stroking hers . . . every bone in her body had seemed to melt with yearning. Had he become drunk on the sensation, too, an instantaneous inebriation, craving more before the first taste had even ended?

She released a shaky breath and peeked over at where he stood, leaning nonchalantly against the wagon's side, chewing on a splinter of wood, his hands in his pockets. He looked particularly piratical this morning, a dark lock of hair falling across his forehead, his hard jaw unshaven, the sleeves of his shirt rolled up over muscular forearms lightly covered with dark hair. And his hands . . . Lord! He had beautiful hands!

She raised her brows, inviting him to join the conversation because, yes, he should *definitely* be the one telling this fellow that they were not going to kiss for public entertainment—*God*! When had she become such a prude?!

He didn't seem to notice. In fact, he didn't seem to be paying any attention at all.

"Tell him," she said.

"Hm? I'm sorry, I was thinking of something else."

"Tell this chap we aren't going to—" She broke off in frustration, utterly discombobulated by her inability to say "we aren't going to kiss in front of people for money." It was beyond ridiculous. She'd been kissed on stage before. Eighty-two times! Which was the full run of *Lady Treetop's Secret*. What was *wrong* with her?

"Aren't going to what?" Archie asked.

"Aren't going to join his merry band and spend the rest of our days wandering about Europe reenacting last night's performance."

"Good heavens, of course not."

Well, she'd wanted his agreement, but he needn't sound so horrified by the idea. It wasn't as if it had been a disagreeable experience.

Abruptly, her irritation turned into dismay.

Oh, she knew well enough Archie didn't think their *kiss* a disagreeable experience. She was not so green that she didn't realize he'd enjoyed it—no one was *that* green—but perhaps he thought her vulgar for instigating it? She didn't know.

He'd kissed her thoroughly, deeply, just long enough to teach her that everything she thought she knew about kisses amounted to nothing. And then he had jerked back his head as if stung and dumped her from his lap. Her bum still hurt. The dinner audience had burst into applause and showered them with coins—most of which had ended up in the troupe leader's purse.

It had been bloody good theatre—except for her, it hadn't been theatre.

"But, monsieur," Luca was saying to Archie, "this is festival season in the south of France. Everywhere, everyone has some sort of fair. We could make a fortune!" the impresario pleaded. "I pay you a *hundred* francs a week."

"Terribly sorry," Archie said. "We have an appointment we cannot miss. Don't we, Lucy?"

"Yes, we are expected," she agreed. "So, if you'll just give us our share of last night's take and point us in the right direction, we'll pop off to the nearest train station and be on our way."

The little troupe leader held up one finger. "First, the nearest train station is in Lamergeaux, which is thirty miles from here.

"Second, there is no 'your share.' That was not the deal we struck. The deal, as mademoiselle and monsieur will recall, was that we would give you a ride and *la petit fille* Gypsy would sing in our evening performance. He lifted his hands. "Well, you rode; she sang. The contract is fulfilled."

"But that's not fair!" Lucy exclaimed. "You must have made two hundred francs last night, just from what people threw at us!"

"Two hundred forty-three," he said. "And life, *mon cher*, is not fair. Now, if you would like to negotiate, perhaps we can come to some accord, *n'cest pas?*"

"I told you, I am not singing again. What is it with you people?" she burst out. "First those greedy people on Sark, then Mr. Navarre, and now *you*! Threatening to abandon us on the road unless I agree to do something I do not want to do!"

"Lucy, I don't think it's quite that—"

"Please, Archie. Let me have my say." She held up a hand and closed her eyes and marshaled her acting ability. When she opened her eyes again she treated the impresario to a prime representation of Affronted Virtue. At least, that was what she was going for. "I have dreamt of visiting France my whole life—and don't even bother, Archie! I know you know I've never been here before. Bully for you!—and now, finally, when I am here, what do I find? It's filled with the grasping, pinch-penny opportunists!"

At this assault on his national pride the impresario's hand flew to his chest as though he'd been mortally struck. He drew himself up, striving for as much dignity as his meager height allowed. "Mademoiselle, I beg to differ. We . . . French are nothing like *les Anglais*."

She sniffed. "It doesn't look that way from where I'm sitting."

The impresario looked to Archie for a translation. "What does she mean 'from where she is sitting'? She is not sitting anywhere . . . Oh. I see. She is making an irony. She has no place to sit."

Archie opened his mouth to correct him then closed it again, shook his head, and sighed, clearly having decided it was not worth the effort of an explanation.

"Mademoiselle." The Frenchman returned his attention to her. "I said we negotiate, not for *what* we negotiate. Even though a deal is a deal and you said you would sing but now refuse, yet still," he stabbed a finger at her, "*still*, I will not leave you marooned on the side of road. Because I am a gentleman. A *superior* gentleman. I only meant we could negotiate the possibility of your next performance while we rode."

The liar. He'd been all set to abandon them until his pride had been pricked. He lifted his nose, playing the injured party to the fullest.

"That's awfully decent of you," Archie said, quickly grabbing Lucy's elbow and spinning her around to face him, his gaze drilling into her. "I say, isn't that awfully decent, Lucy?"

"Yeah. Just swell."

CHAPTER

25

Archie was fairly certain Luca was purposely driving over every rut in the road as punishment for their having snatched an anticipated windfall out from under his nose. He and Lucy sat side by side on the lowered back gate, facing backward, their legs dangling, while Lucy alternately gnawed on the chicken leg she'd kept from lunch and kept up a bright, inconsequential prattle. While not precisely odd, Lucy being the unchallenged queen of tale-telling, this was unusual in scope. She didn't stop talking once. It was almost as though *he* disconcerted *her*.

And perhaps he did. God knew he'd probably scared the girl silly with that kiss. He'd practically forced himself on her. No, he *had* forced himself on her. And she hadn't done a thing to stop him, which meant either she'd been too shocked to do so or she hadn't wanted him to stop.

He couldn't decide which was worse.

Every minute he spent with her turned him into the sort of man he had been trained to despise: inconstant and false, without dignity or honor. A man reacting to life on the most visceral level, passionately, impulsively. *Cornelia expected him to ask for her hand!* Why couldn't he hold that thought at least until . . . until . . . He nearly groaned, but years of schooling came to his aid, helping him keep his expression impassive. He could not excuse his actions.

He'd told himself he'd only done what she'd prodded him to do, but now he added liar to the list of grievances he was compiling against himself. He'd kissed her because he wanted to feel her in his arms, to feel the moment her mouth woke beneath his, physical hunger ignited by the wildfire of his own desire. And he had! He had . . .

He should never have touched her.

When he'd finally come to his senses, recalled to their surroundings by the diners whooping like spectators at a burlesque show, he'd been so stunned by his own actions he'd actually dropped her. She'd handled the whole thing with far more aplomb than he had, hopping to her feet, dusting herself off, and curtseying to the madly applauding spectators before disappearing for the rest of the night.

Or fleeing.

"And then I said to him—"

"What is going on?"

The bright flow of chatter stopped. She eyed him candidly, a clear sign she was about to tell a hummer. "Nothing. Why do you ask?"

"There's something odd about how you're acting today. Look, if it's about that kiss—"

"No! No." Her face grew bright. "Please. I understand. It was just a kiss for show is all." She gave a little laugh then peeked at him sidelong. "Right?"

For once, he couldn't read her tone. Expectant? Anxious? Hopeful? Guilty? Nervous? He could read each one in that single word.

"Aren't you having fun?" she asked in small voice when he didn't answer.

"No," he bit out. It was torture.

"Oh." Her shoulders slumped but then she darted a quick glance at him and smiled. "We'll just have to try harder is all."

"Please, don't." He didn't know if he could survive Lucy's concentrated efforts at fun.

He must not have sounded sincere because she grinned and he decided to give up trying to figure out what was going on with her. Instead, he went back to listening as she took up the interrupted narrative with some bit of doggerel that wrung a smile from him with one of her overblown impersonations.

They'd been traveling since morning with only one stop for a midday meal. Rather than stay with him, Lucy had sought the fiddler, the only other member of the troupe who spoke any English, and spent the meal with him. Archie had watched, fascinated by how naturally she drew the portly musician out, in the same way she had the old man on Sark.

"What was the fiddler telling you at lunch?" he asked when she finally fell quiet for a rare few minutes.

"The fiddler?"

"Yes. You looked positively riveted."

"Oh." She finished tearing off the last bit of meat from the chicken leg and tossed the bone to the side of the road. "He was telling me that because of the recent persecutions against Romani, Luca has convinced his family to reinvent themselves as a traveling troupe of entertainers."

"Wait. They're *Gypsies*?"

She nodded, then scowled. "It's disgusting what they must endure. Why, they aren't even allowed to—What? What's wrong?" She glanced down to see if she'd dribbled on her blouse.

"Why would he reveal this to you?" he asked, amazed.

"Why wouldn't he?"

"Because the Romani are notoriously close-mouthed with outsiders."

"Oh, that," she said nonchalantly, digging in the wagon well behind her before producing a wizened little apple with an air of triumph. "Want some?"

"No and yes, *that*."

"He thinks I'm Romani."

"You told him you were a Gypsy and he *believed* it?" he asked incredulously.

She gave him a flatly disgusted look. "No. I never underestimate my audience, Archie. You'd do well to remember that. He thinks I have Romani ancestors. He said only someone with Romani blood could sing that song like I did. I simply didn't deny it." She preened a bit, a small sign of vanity he found inexplicably enchanting.

"And so he just told you everything. Just like that?" He was afraid his doubt was apparent in his voice. "*How?*"

"I don't know. I asked him a few questions, such as whether he played any other instrument, who'd taught him, what his favorite song was. You know. And one thing just led to another." She took a bite, eyeing him curiously. "Why does this surprise you so much?" she asked around a mouthful of apple.

"I'm a trained anthropologist. I've spent most of my adult life observing people, investigating societies, and attempting to understand them. I gain my subjects' trust by not intruding upon them, then unobtrusively recording their lives from the fringes. And here you come, chattering away, pretending to be one of them and—"

"Hold on there," she stopped him. "I did not pretend anything. Yuri drew conclusions and I did not correct them. For all I know I do have Romani blood.

"You make it sound as if I did something suspect, or at least unethical. All I did was become part of his world, I . . ." She searched

for the word and snapped her fingers when she found it. "I assimi-
lated. People are not subjects. They're people. How can you possibly
understand something if you don't experience it, Archie? Recording
something isn't *knowing* it."

"You misunderstand. I wasn't criticizing you. I was trying to
understand your process."

"Process?" She laughed. "I don't have a process. I'm simply
interested in people."

He frowned. She'd said something similar before. Something
about how they did nearly the same thing, how she delved into other
people's lives to be able re-create a facsimile on stage, while he did
the same for science. Both of them strove to understand how people
connected, how a society is formed of individuals . . . Good Lord.

"A penny for your thoughts."

He looked up. "Lucy, you brilliant girl, you said a person cre-
ates society."

She stared at him as if he'd gone daft. "What are you talking
about?"

"On Sark, you said that a person not only comes from a place
that molds him but that he, in turn, has molded."

"I did?"

"Yes. You were explaining to me how you went about develop-
ing your characters for the musical stage."

"You listened to me that closely?"

"Of course," he said, distracted by the idea burgeoning in his
mind, something monumental, something extraordinary.

She shrugged. "What of it?"

"It's brilliant."

"It is?"

"Yes," he said excitedly. "It's revolutionary, is what it is."

"Oh?" She straightened her spine, preening a bit. "How's that?"

"It's generally accepted by the anthropological community that culture's purpose, the reason it exists, is to meet the needs of the group. *Group* is the main player, has the starring role, if you will. The individual in that group is secondary.

"But what you have hypothesized is that the individual shapes as much as is shaped by the society." The idea had caught fire in his imagination. "If society exists to meet the needs of the individual it fundamentally changes how we see . . . *everything*. Am I making a bit of sense?"

She nodded.

He raked his hair back with both hands and laughed, convinced he'd discovered something important. "It'll take years of research to prove, of course."

"The prospect doesn't seem to discourage you."

"Discourage me? Why would it? It's exciting!" His thoughts were racing ahead, already formulating new methodologies.

"You really love it, don't you?" she asked in an odd voice.

He turned toward her. "Yes. Yes, I really do. I know most people don't consider anthropology terribly useful. I don't make anything, or deliver a service to anyone, and any benefits I provide are only in the most indirect ways, as insights. But I can't imagine doing anything else." He gave her an apologetic smile. "I suppose that makes me fatuous."

"No," she said softly. "It makes you lucky. You're able to do what you love and you're good at it." She paused. "At least I assume you're good at it. I mean, a college wouldn't just hire any young man who enjoys tromping about the world and chatting up anyone who'll let him in the door. Really, I'm quite jealous."

He looked at her in surprise. "You're kidding."

She shook her head. "No, I'm not. Cross my heart."

"But why should you be? I could say the same about you. You love what you do and you are better than good at it."

Her extraordinary eyes lit with pleasure. "That's awfully swell of you to say and I do like to sing. But as for the loving it?" She shrugged. "Sure, I enjoy pretending to be someone else for a few hours. It's sort of fun to try on another life." She shrugged.

"*Like* to sing? *Fun?* That's rather damning what you do with faint praise."

"Well, then, how about if I say I find it interesting?"

"No," he said decisively. "No one could be as good as you are if there weren't more to it than that. There must be more driving you. What is it?"

She squirmed a little, clearly unused to being questioned so closely. Or, he thought with sudden intuition, to having anyone insist on delving deeper into her answers, unwilling to accept that whatever she was *willing* to share was all she *had* to share.

"Maybe I'm just not as deep, passionate, and intense as you are," she suggested blithely. Flags of color had risen to her sharp cheekbones.

Three days ago he would have left it alone, believing that, as a gentleman, whatever line she drew in the metaphorical sand was one he'd be forced to respect. But three days ago he'd only been intrigued. As a young scholar confronted with something inexplicable, he'd been filled with a passionate need to comprehend. Now he was something far more.

Now, he wanted to understand Lucy. He *needed* to understand her.

She fascinated him, charmed and alarmed him. Even when she made him feel befuddled—which was most of the time—he still had this insane conviction that she made sense. It was only when they were apart that he recognized otherwise.

It was the very opposite of how he felt about Cornelia. When they were together he felt out of sync; when they were apart they made sense.

He hadn't given much thought to his would-be intended in days. Not really *thought* about her. But then it wasn't all that unusual. In fact, he rarely did so when they were apart. He'd never once questioned why. But now he did. Because when he was not with Lucy, however briefly, he thought about her all the bloody time.

It could only end badly. He'd spent his life learning to keep his passions tamped down, under control, out of sight, buried. Passion was the antithesis of reason and reason was civilization's bulwark against anarchy. He should just stay mute, distance himself from her and everything about her, start the process of tearing out the hooks she'd buried deep in his—no! he would not say *heart*. Psyche—deep in his psyche.

So, of course, because this was Lucy and he seemed categorically incapable of doing what made sense where Lucy was concerned, instead he took a deep breath and said, "That's a lot of rubbish. If you don't want to tell me about yourself, fine, but don't put me off with that . . . bunk."

She blinked, feigning shock. "Why, Professor, fancy you using slang."

"I do have students, you know," he said. "Occasionally I'm forced to communicate with them. I find both parties are best served if I use the students' preferred argot. Besides, I'm discovering that linguistics could present a rather intriguing area of study. I'm surprised no one has thought to treat it as a completely separate subspecialty."

"You've never showed off this talent before."

"The slang you employ doesn't have that many terms in common with the one my students use. I suspect yours is a more dated form."

She gave him a slow grin. "I believe you just called me old."

Good God, had he? "I . . . *No* . . . I mean . . . Of course, you're not old. You're hardly older than my students. I only meant that the slang you use is perhaps specialized to the traditions of the theatre. And, lest you think differently, your rather heavy-handed attempt to distract me won't work."

"Piffle," she said.

"Now, if you please."

"Please what?"

He fixed her with a firm stare. "If it's not acting and not singing, what is it about the musical theatre that draws you?"

She made a very unladylike noise. "I suppose if I invented a reason you wouldn't believe me. It seems to be rather a peculiarity with you."

He wasn't sure why his ability to see through her thin charades should surprise her—it really wasn't all that hard—but he was always happy to impress her. "Yes."

"All right, then. Fine. But it's a tad embarrassing. I'm afraid you'll think me terribly shallow." She strove to sound nonchalant, but the color was back into her cheeks and her gaze kept skittering away from his, telegraphing clear as day she was about to admit the unvarnished truth.

He waited, uncertain what she thought might lessen her in his eyes. That she liked dressing up in pretty clothes? That she liked the bouquets given by admirers? He didn't care.

"I like the applause," she blurted out.

"The applause."

"Yes," she said with a touch of defiance. "The cheers, the whistles, the *applause*. I like standing in front of the curtain after the last act, when we no longer are in character, and they applaud and I know it is for me. *Me*. Not the part I played or the songs the composer wrote, but what I did with them." She broke off suddenly and swallowed, a tremulous smile flickering. "I love that."

Her gaze met his and danced away. She caught her lower lip between her teeth and once again strove for a light tone. "I like feeling that I matter, I guess. That I've done something people fall in love with, even if it's just on stage. Because after the curtain, when you're just standing there and they can finally see you . . . it feels real."

Of course, he thought. How many roles had she played, in how many places, long before she'd ever stepped on a stage? She'd told him about a few: the songbird, the tomboy, the obedient niece. But beneath it all she'd wanted to be recognized, to be seen. "It is real," he said. "And there is nothing shallow about wanting to be seen for who you are, what you are."

He saw her.

Even if he didn't want to see her. Nothing good could come of his seeing her.

She smiled at him, a little shy, immensely gratified. "You're a nice man, Archie."

No one had ever called him a nice man. Sometimes Lionel cautioned him that he became too emotionally attached to the subjects he was studying, but he called it "unprofessional," not "nice." His pulse quickened and a mad sort of apprehension seized him.

No. No, no, no.

He hopped off the back of the wagon.

"What are you doing?" she called back, startled.

"God only knows."

CHAPTER
26

"You've already been far too kind to us," Lavinia said, determined to resist Marjorie's all-too-tempting offer. She perched on the end of the settee in her friend's hotel room as Marjorie carefully packed her extravagant costumes between scented sheets of tissue paper.

She wished she could have seen Marjorie's performance at the theatre last night—the manager at the hotel had kissed his fingertips in tribute to their new friend this morning when they'd come down for breakfast—but there had been no last-minute seats available.

"Kindness, piffle," Marjorie said, waving the air as though to clear it of something distasteful. "I am being utterly selfish, my dear."

"Yes. Just as selfishness prompted you to lend me your beautiful dress after seeing how clumsily I stained my own in Saint-Malo."

"First of all, the stain was not your fault and second of all, it is not a loan. It is a gift." She looked a little taken aback as she spoke, as though she hadn't intended to say any such thing.

Still, Lavinia flushed. "I could not accept such generosity."

"Once again, you mistake me for a far better . . . person than

I am. The dress suits you more than it ever did me. How could I wear it again, knowing it looks better on another woman? My vanity would not stand for it."

Lavinia suspected Marjorie was only attempting to persuade her, but secretly, she agreed. The little threads of shimmering graphite shooting through the soft orchid-colored material kept it from being too *jeune fille*. Instead, the color made her gray hair look silvery and lent her skin a radiant glow. The easy drape of the material concealed the less salubrious effects of time on her figure yet accentuated the posture her parents had so rigorously imposed on their daughters.

And the hat—oh! that ridiculous, extravagant, silly hat, with the shadow of its wide brim softening the lines time had etched in her face, and the crowning heap of ribbon, net, and feathers that lent her height! While she knew that words like "pretty" or "beautiful" would never truly apply to her looks, in Mrs. Martin's clothing she thought she might be called handsome.

And she liked it.

She liked it very much.

She was not so humble that she hadn't noticed the covert expressions of admiration on some men's faces when she walked by, or the glint of critical appreciation in the eye of certain well-disposed madames . . . She gave up all thoughts of returning the gown or hat.

"I can't think what to say other than thank you."

Marjorie smiled happily. "You're welcome. Now all we need is for you to agree to come to Bergerac for me to be happy. Don't you want to see the town that gave its name to one of theatre's most memorable lovers?"

"Cyrano?"

"The very same."

"You must know how much we would like to, but I don't see how we can. We have to wait here for Lucy."

"I understand, my dear. But the fact is, we don't know where Lucy is." She sank down next to Lavinia and secured her hands in her large, gloved ones. "The telegrams I have received in reference to my inquiries have been very confusing. We only know that she disembarked from the ferry at Saint-Malo. After that . . ." She shook her head.

"But she checked into the hotel."

"*Someone* checked into the hotel. It is all most suspicious. However, I strongly suspect that that miserable little innkeeper Navarre is attempting to hold us up for someone else's unpaid bill."

Lavinia started in shock.

Marjorie nodded grimly. "From what I can piece together from Navarre's histrionic telegrams, a girl he mistook for Lucy Eastlake came in accompanied by a man. The pair of them proceeded to tally up a sizeable bill, not only at the hotel's restaurant but elsewhere, then decamped in the middle of the night."

"How awful!"

Marjorie blew out a long, low sigh. Whether she was sighing over Mr. Navarre's gullibility or the iniquitousness of the young woman posing as Lucy, was impossible to say.

"But why should this girl pretend to be Lucy? And how would she know to pretend in the first place?" Lavinia asked.

"I have it all worked out," Marjorie said going from aggrieved to chipper in the blink of an eye. "*I* think this girl was an English adventuress. Who knows what duplicitous scheme she originally intended. But when she walked into the hotel Mr. Navarre, recognizing her nationality, jumped to his own conclusion. Very likely, he asked her if she was 'Miss Eastlake' for whom he was holding a room."

Lavinia's eyes grew round.

"The adventuress, seeing an opportunity to dine well at someone else's expense, went along with his assumption." Marjorie's eyes narrowed knowingly. "As did her male companion. Whoever *he* was. Which is another reason I do not think this young woman could possibly be Lucy. Can you imagine Lucy being squired about France by some strange man?"

"Good heavens, no!" breathed Lavinia, shocked to her core. "But I can scarce believe an Englishwoman could act so wickedly."

"It's sad but true," Marjorie said, discreetly adjusting the fit of her bodice, "Girls are simply not what they used to be."

"But if what you surmise is true, *where is Lucy?*"

"It's hard to say, but I could well imagine Lucy coming into the hotel at some later point and making inquiries of some person other than Mr. Navarre. Perhaps a night clerk. Upon discovering we were gone and there being no rooms available, she went elsewhere. We simply don't know."

"But then we should go back to Saint-Malo and find her!"

"My darling, once she realized you were gone, she would have no reason to stay. She would assume that you had gone on to Saint-Girons and be traveling there to meet you, which is just what I suggest we do."

"*We?*" Lavinia asked, hardly daring to believe her ears.

"Yes. As soon as I have completed my little performance in Bergerac."

"Oh, Marjorie!" Lavinia squeezed the broad hand covering hers, touched by this show of kindness.

"If you say I am too kind once more I shall be forced to propose myself for sainthood, which will interfere greatly with my career, sainthood and the stage being mutually exclusive. And *you* shall be responsible for having disappointed the vast unwashed rural population of France. Not to mention Paris."

Lavinia smiled at her nonsense. "Dear Marjorie, we couldn't impose."

"Why not?" At the sound of Bernice's voice, the two ladies looked around to find Bernice standing in the doorway adjoining their two suites. At night Marjorie had courteously kept it closed tight so that when she returned from her performance at the theatre she hadn't disturbed them.

"Where have you been?" Lavinia asked.

Bernice beamed happily. "I was touring the ruins of a thirteenth century abbey just outside of town. Fascinating stuff. Then I popped in to the cathedral. Papist, I know, but still . . . The choir was singing compline. It was transcendent!"

Somewhere in the last few days, Bernice had emerged as an inveterate sightseer, always ferreting out some obscure museum or local attraction or other, rambling about here and there, returning tired but invigorated by her solitary explorations. Lavinia had never suspected her sister's interest in travel. As far as she could remember, Bernice had never once suggested she wanted to step foot out of their little town, let alone England.

Now, stomping the leaves from her feet, she peered around brightly from beneath the unexpectedly jaunty little red toque perched atop her head and said, "I don't see what good staying here will do us, Lavinia. Marjorie is undoubtedly correct in assuming Lucy will be heading for Saint-Girons. So that is where we must go."

"You're both probably right."

"In which case, I suppose we had best take Lucy's things with us once more."

Lavinia nodded. "I don't see there's any choice."

"I'll tell you what," Marjorie said. "Though I am sure everything is fine—Lucy is one of the most resourceful young ladies of my acquaintance—just in case she does find her way to Châtellerault, we shall leave a letter for her here at the hotel."

Lavinia blew out a soft sigh of relief, satisfied. Marjorie was right; Lucy was an exceptionally capable young woman.

"Good," said Bernice. "The only question now is whether to accept Marjorie's generous offer to accompany us. While of course we would delight in her company, we mustn't be selfish and inter-fere with her scheduled performances."

"Of course not!" Lavinia exclaimed, turning to Marjorie. "We would never allow you to disappoint your public for our sake."

"Never!" Bernice added.

"My dears," Marjorie said, smiling munificently. "If I may? After tomorrow I *have* no performances until next week. You are to meet in Saint-Girons on Monday, which leaves plenty of time for me to travel from there to Toulouse where I am next scheduled to appear.

"And really, I am being utterly sincere when I say I would be delighted to go with you. The thespian in me is enthralled!" She surged to her feet. "It's a story tailor-made for the stage, darlings! A valiant and doomed boy hero arrives with a saddlebag full of mysterious rubies—"

"It was only a pouch, not a saddlebag."

Marjorie's mouth puckered with disappointment but then she rallied. "Pouch, you say? All right." She clasped one hand to her bosom, lifting her other arm as though sighting along it and peer-ing dreamily into the past. "He arrives with a pouch of mysterious rubies which he then cavalierly leaves behind with the entrenched and desperate survivors of a siege.

"Thus ensues the tale of a fifty-year-old pact, ill-starred lovers"—at this Bernice shot a startled glace at Lavinia, who pinked up—Mar-jorie was such a sympathetic listener—"their unexpected and dramatic rescue, and the would-be lovers' final parting. Then, years later, the unexpected bequest from the Englishman to the valiant lady he once obviously admired. Monday will provide the final act." She sighed rapturously before her gaze snapped to Lavinia and Bernice. "Please. You really *must* allow me to come with you!"

CHAPTER

27

"This is, how they say, the end of the line," Luca told Lucy flatly while around them the rest of the caravan watched with oblique interest. "Even though you have not paid me a *sou*, out of the generosity of my heart I have fed you lunch, I have driven you and your whatever he is—clearly not your lover, a lover would not walk five miles when he could be with you—all the way to Lamergeaux. Again, out of the generosity of my heart and with no hope of recompense. Why? Because I am a French gentleman." He turned to his troupe, inviting their appreciation.

"You're Romani."

Luca did not deny it. Instead, his chin notched even higher. "Ah. But *French* Romani. You cannot say you were ill-served at my hands." He stared at her.

"No. I could not and would not."

"Good, then we are finished."

She glanced over her shoulder, hoping to spy Archie. Revelers and merrymakers, peddlers, food vendors, and entertainers crowded the little market town's central square, all come to partake of the annual harvest festival. Archie was nowhere to be seen.

She'd spotted him earlier when they'd first stopped but since then he'd disappeared. She didn't worry that he'd abandoned her; his having sprouted wings and flown away was more likely. He simply wasn't the sort of man who could leave a woman stranded on her own, no matter how much he might want to.

Something painful twisted in the vicinity of her heart. She might well deserve it if he did. She blew out a quick, steadying breath. No use crying over spilt milk. What was done, was done.

"Au revoir."

"No!" She came back to the present with a start. "Please. We're still miles from Châtellerault."

Luca could not have looked more bored. "And this is my problem how?"

"It's not but—"

"*Exactement*! Not. My. Problem. If you want to go Châtellerault I suggest you buy a train ticket. One comes through town daily. In fact, the train from Châtellerault is due soon. Not that that will help you. You have missed today's outgoing train."

"We don't have any money."

His smile became suave. "I offered you a remedy for that problem, too, but you refused. However, I might be persuaded to reconsider. There's a good crowd here. It will be a fine evening. We could all benefit from another performance."

Archie would never go for it. She shook her head

"Then I wish you *bon voyage*, mademoiselle." He swung around and stomped off with imperial disdain.

"Here, little Gypsy." The fiddler slipped a sandwich wrapped in waxed paper into her hand, winked, and was gone.

She looked at the oily package, shrugged, opened it, and took a bite as she started to wend her way through the fairgoers. The fair was taking place in a huge field that divided the town proper from the railroad tracks. Booths selling cakes and pastries, meat pies and cheese wheels, ribbons, hats, leather goods, and toys lined the perimeter. Mothers held tight to the hands of children straining to drag them to the puppet show, while men ruminated over displays of tobacco pouches and pipes.

The far end of the field served as a venue for various contests being held, one for the largest aubergine, and another for the ripest cheese. There were prizes for the fattest duck, the biggest bull, the wooliest sheep. A number of competitions designed to test the local male population's strength and athleticism were starting, men queuing up to try their hands at hammer throws and skeet shooting.

Under other circumstances Lucy would have enjoyed the spectacle tremendously, intrigued by the similarities and differences she noted between such an event in England and France. But she wished Archie was with her to share her pleasure. The scent of caramel, cinnamon, and wine perfumed the air, while hawkers vied to be heard over the shouts and screeches of riotous children, and all around the press and motion of people at play infused the blood with the spirit of carnival.

She'd wound her way to the competition field, still munching on her sandwich when she saw a man standing atop a raised podium. He was waving a heavy-looking pouch over his head and extolling a quickly swelling crowd to do who knew what.

Curious, Lucy moved closer. "What's happening?" she asked, not really expecting an answer.

To her surprise the stout, matronly looking lady beside her answered in heavily accented English. "It's the annual prizefight. The festival board issues a challenge to any and all comers to fight our local champion for three rounds, the winner to take the purse."

Lucy had absolutely no interest in blood sports, but since the lady had been generous enough to answer her, she felt it only courteous to evince a little polite curiosity. "Is he any good?"

"Our champion? *Mais oui.* He is most robust. Most virile." The woman fluttered her hand at her face, leaving little doubt as to her feelings on the subject. "No challenger stands a chance. For three years now he is undefeated."

"Oh." Having felt she'd observed the rules of etiquette, Lucy nodded at the woman and started back the way she'd come when her eye was caught by a man in a white shirt, climbing unceremoniously to join the emcee on the podium.

She peered closer. And froze.

It was Archie.

He said something. The woman beside her crowed delightedly. "Aha! Here is a challenger!"

At once, Lucy started shoving her way to the front of the crowd. She had to stop Archie before he got killed!

———

Now that a sacrificial lamb had appeared, the local population was showing up in droves to see what self-deluded idiot had volunteered for the slaughter. Undeterred, Lucy ruthlessly elbowed her way through the thick of the crowd, finally making it to the front where a rope cordoned off the makeshift ring set up beneath the podium. She lifted the rope and was about to dash across the arena when two pairs of strong arms grabbed her and hauled her back. She jerked around to find herself facing a pair of stalwart-looking members of the local constabulary, the older of whom promptly launched into what Lucy recognized as a lecture. Odd how the spirit of a thing came through even when one couldn't understand more than a few words.

"*Mille pardon. Non parle Frances.*" She batted her eyes winsomely.

The younger constable's severe expression melted; the older one's mouth flattened as he shot a disgusted glance at his colleague.

Immediately, the boy cleared his throat as he recovered his missing authoritative glower.

The older man pointed at her, pointed at the rope, and then stuck his finger under her nose and shook it. Well, that was clear enough. In the meantime, up on the podium, Archie was listening to a series of instructions being given by a pair of official-looking men. She had to put a stop to this before he got hurt.

She glanced left and right, but the place was packed now, jammed full of people, making it almost impossible to move, certainly not quickly enough to make it to another area where she might slip under the rope without being stopped. And, drat it all, the older constable wasn't going anywhere either.

She gnawed her lip. Archie was fit. He was also strong. He'd carried her easily enough. Perhaps it wouldn't be so bad, after all. Perhaps he might even—

A man suddenly appeared beneath the podium. Lucy's jaw dropped. He was enormous, a monster of a man at least six and a half feet tall. Making a great show of it, he stripped down to his undershirt, revealing shoulders as broad across as most ponies', capped with muscles that looked like ham epaulets. *Hairy* ham epaulets, since his whole upper torso, including his back, arms, and neck seemed to be covered in a black pelt. His chest was round as a rain barrel. His blunt, square face sat atop a neck as thick as a beer keg, while the thighs straining the fabric of his pants were round as hogsheads.

"Archie!"

Archie, still in the process of agreeing to his own murder, looked around at the sound of her screech. He spied her and frowned, lifting his hands in the universal gesture that asked, "What?"

Frantically, she pointed at the monster lumbering up the podium steps, each riser sagging under his weight. He gave the man a quick assessing glance, looked back to her, and shrugged.

"You'll be killed!" she wailed. She bolted and the horrible old constable, as though waiting for just such a move, snatched her back. "*Ar-chie!*"

Looking unreservedly disgruntled, Archie said something to one of the officials, then turned and stomped down the steps, sparing no more than a nod to the monster still lumbering up the stairs. His opponent, clearly unused to such an obvious lack of appreciation—or maybe terror—vacillated a few seconds before following Archie back down. The two officials on the podium traded confused looks, then shrugged and fell into line.

"Lucy, please stop shouting at me. It's unnerving," Archie said as he strode across the ring toward her. The constables, seeing that there was no longer any threat of her running into the arena, withdrew.

"*You're* unnerved! You're not the one being asked to witness the terrible end of someone you—of someone."

"Oh, for Pete's sake. No one is going to meet a terrible end. Don't worry."

"Have you lost your mind? Look at him!" She raised her hand and pointed at the local champion, unsuccessfully pretending not to be eavesdropping a few yards away.

Archie looked. He didn't appear in the least bit impressed. Maybe something was wrong with him. She'd heard that intellectual types' brains sometimes overheated, resulting in brainstorms where they lost touch with reality. It seemed a viable explanation.

"Yes?" Archie said, turning back. "He's very large."

"Large? He's *enormous*. He's a veritable minotaur!"

"Exactly. Which is why I—"

She grabbed his hand across the rope. "Please, Archie. If anything happened to you I couldn't forgive myself and it's not *necessary*, Archie—"

"*Qu'est-ce que signifie* 'minotaur'?" the giant asked. No one answered.

"Look," Archie said, giving her hand an awkward pat, "Two train tickets will stand us eighty francs and then we'll need to pay the hotel because, despite what you think, we can't keep skipping out on our bills and—"

"But that's just it, Archie. I have—"

"*Quelle es* minotaur?" the Minotaur interrupted loudly, now beginning to look seriously aggrieved.

Archie spun around. "Do you mind? I am trying to have a conversation with the lady."

"*Il est une créature mythologique, mi-homme, mi-taureau.*" Apparently the giant's number one fan, the same lady who'd apprised Lucy of just who, or rather what, Archie was going up against, had followed in Lucy's wake and was now explaining something to the man.

The boxing champion fairly blew smoke out of his flaring nostrils and spat something to the lady, then jerked his head in Lucy's direction.

"Oh, dear," the lady said.

"What?" demanded Lucy.

"He says he will give the young man here a drubbing worthy of mythology."

"Oh, dear," Lucy echoed, looking pleadingly at Archie. "Now look what I've done. Please Archie, if you'd just let me explain—"

"Oh, no!" he said, backing away and shaking his head. "Oh no, you don't. Every time you explain something I end up thinking it sounds reasonable right until the time I regret it. *No.*"

The crowd, clearly having had enough of these blatant delaying tactics, began making catcalls. The officials, attuned to their audience's impatience, took hold of Archie, one on either side, and dragged him a little distance to finish their instruction.

"Do you have children?" the middle-aged lady asked in deceptively mild tones.

"No," said Lucy, her eyes still on Archie. If she could just have two uninterrupted minutes, she could put an end to this nonsense.

"Whew!" The woman expelled a relieved sigh and crossed herself. "Well, that is a mercy. Your children will not have to see their father—"

"What? Oh, we're not married."

"*Non?*" The woman surveyed Lucy sympathetically. "Perhaps it is for the best. You are young. There will be others."

"No, there won't. He's the only one," Lucy said, her gaze still on Archie.

He nodded as he listened intently, then casually shed his white shirt. Even through her worry, Lucy could not help inhaling with appreciation. If the champion was a minotaur, Archie was Theseus, superbly muscled and perfectly proportioned. When he moved, his broad back rippled beneath his close-fitting undershirt, the short sleeves riding above the bulge of biceps. He lifted his arms over his head, bent from side to side, stretching and revealing the play of hard muscle slipping beneath smooth, clear skin.

He looked so capable, so virile. Perhaps he could . . . But then she recalled how Charlie Cheddar had laid him out with one blow. And not only had Charlie been drunk, he was at least three inches shorter than Archie.

Archie was doomed.

If Charlie could knock him out with just one—her eyes widened on sudden hope and inspiration. It seemed likely to her that Archie would fold up like an accordion with the first blow. And if it wasn't too hard a blow, just enough to—

She waved madly at the local champion who was strutting around the perimeter of the ring, extolling his fans and beating at his chest.

"*S'il vous plaît!* Monsieur! *S'il vous plaît!*"

The monster stopped strutting and turned to eye her. His gaze grew appreciative as he sauntered over. "*Oui?*"

"Don't hit him too hard. *Please*. Just knock him out and call it a day."

The huge man looked over her to her middle-aged companion and said something. "He wants to know what you want," she said.

Lucy told her.

The woman quickly translated. When she'd finished, the champion threw back his head and roared with laughter. Then, spreading his arms wide, he made a slow circle, hollering to the crowd, clearly encouraging them to join in his hilarity. Archie, too, had turned. He stared at her in stunned incredulity.

Oh, dear. "He's telling everyone what I said, isn't he?" she asked the lady at her side in a small voice.

"*Oui*," the matron answered sympathetically.

Having finished amusing the crowd, the champion completed his previctory lap back to where Lucy stood. He winked at her and said something in tones so universally smarmy she didn't need a translation. Then he reached across the rope and chucked her under her chin.

The matron tittered. "He says he will not hurt your boyfriend too badly if you promise to kiss him when he wins."

Lucy tried not to grimace. The brute's hair was oily—all his hair, including the shoulder tufts—and stains darkened his undershirt beneath his arms. But to save Archie? She smiled weakly. "*Oui*."

"What?"

Her head snapped around to see Archie stalking towards her. The sun kissed his blue-black hair and his jaw had a hard and angry set to it. Behind him hurried the two harassed-looking officials and behind *them* a train came into view, hiccuping smoke and whistling a mournful warning.

She racked her brain for something to assuage his vanity. Men were such touchy creatures. She'd wounded his masculine pride and now he was going to sulk. A man who stood in peril of being beaten to death couldn't afford the luxury of sulking.

"Well, thank you very much," he said. "Nothing like a vote of confidence to buoy a fellow's spirits."

"Now, Archie. It isn't like that."

One of the officials tapped Archie on the arm.

Impatiently, Archie swung on him. "You again. Look, can't you see I'm having a private conversation with this young lady?"

The poor little official shrank at his whiplash tone. "But . . . how can it be private? We are surrounded by more than two hundred people, monsieur," he gingerly pointed out.

"That's beside the point. I'll be with you in a moment."

The other official, clearly made of sterner stuff, stepped forward. "In one minute, whether or not you have finished your oh-so-private conversation, this match begins!"

"Fine," Archie said tightly. "Now, if you don't mind?"

The man snapped forward in an angry little bow and withdrew, leaving Archie to turn his black gaze on Lucy. She cringed.

"I'm sure you'll make a wonderful showing," she said, praying she sounded sincere.

"Do *not* patronize me."

"I'm not. Really. It's just a contingency plan. You know. In case something goes wrong. Like if you trip."

"You mean while I'm running away?" Archie asked sarcastically.

"No, not at all," she said in her most pacifying voice, which did not have any visible pacifying effect on Archie at all. In fact, if anything, it only made his swarthy skin go darker. Behind them a bell clanged.

"You know, Lucy, I am—"

She was never to know what Archie was or was not because at that instant a huge arm swung out, aiming straight for Archie's head.

CHAPTER
28

Lucy's eyes went round as saucers and Archie ducked.

An enormous arm swept over his head, the breeze ruffling his hair. He started back up just as his opponent's other arm swung from the opposite direction so he waited an instant before straightening.

This was going to be ridiculously easy.

The behemoth just kept swinging and Archie just kept ducking, letting the Frenchman wear himself out. He was a country brawler; Archie had been trained by some of the best pugilists in England.

True, he caught an occasional glancing blow to his ribs. He would have been spared even these if Lucy hadn't kept distracting him by shrieking, "Watch out!" "Oh my God!" or some variation thereof. He kept track of her out of the corner of his eye, a manic figure in a bedraggled blouse and shrunken skirt, darting along the rope line, hopping up and down as a pair of dark-uniformed police thwarted her attempts to hurl herself into the ring.

In fact, he was much more worried about her actually breaking free and throwing herself between him and the Frenchman than he was about himself.

Lucy could get hurt.

With this a distinct possibility—because the police were seriously outclassed in the matter of evasion—he set about ending the match. Initially he'd decided to let the man hang in there for all three rounds. There was no sense in needlessly humiliating the local hero. But Lucy's continued and fervent efforts to save him put an end to that plan. Like many a plan she'd put an end to, he thought as he ducked yet another mighty punch and came up beneath the Frenchman's unguarded chin with an uppercut designed to take him off his feet.

It didn't have the desired effect.

The Frenchman's arms dropped, true, but he only swayed, looking more baffled than injured. There was no help for it; Archie hit him again. The fighter's eyes rolled back and he toppled over, dropping flat on his back in a little puff of dust.

Stunned silence met his fall and then a rapturously amazed voice called, "Archie! You *won*!"

He turned to see Lucy duck under the rope, hike up her splotchy skirts, and sprint toward him. She skidded to a stop right in front of him, her shining face turned up to his, smiling broadly, her eyes wide with wonder.

"You won!" she reiterated.

"You might at least make *some* attempt not to sound so astounded."

"But you won!" She pointed at the behemoth climbing painfully to his hands and knees. "Against *him*!"

"I know." He'd thought he had himself well in hand. But the excitement of the fight must have affected him more than he'd realized because his heart was still pounding, his muscles still coiled with readiness.

"But *how?*" She patted his chest as if to reassure herself he hadn't somehow died in the last few minutes and she was seeing a ghost. "Wait. Don't tell me. The deans at your boy's school thought fisticuffs would be a bully way to dispel your excess energy."

"Hm? Oh, I boxed at the '04 Olympics," he said, distracted. He was too busy tallying up the freckles on her cheeks, the vibrant flush on her skin, the curl of her gold-tipped lashes. And his pulse, rather than slowing, had quickened as a sort of ebullience, an irrepressible recklessness, filled him.

He remembered this feeling from long ago; it had never boded well. He'd felt like this before accepting Hinny Mickfert's dare to scale the bell tower, before touching the flame to the methane gas tube in the college laboratory, before diving off that cliff in Abereiddy.

In short, he felt on the cusp of doing something very rash.

"Archie?"

"I won." He should look away. Walk away. *Be* away, before it was too late. "I won the prize."

"Yes," she agreed, nodding happily. "A substantial purse, so I'm told. Well, done, Archie. Well done!"

Too late. "That's not what I meant."

"No?" Her extraordinary eyes widened in surprise. "What did you mean?"

"This."

CHAPTER
29

"I was thinking that perhaps, some time in the future, it would be interesting to tour Italy," Bernice said, softly so as not to wake Marjorie.

Their friend had secured them the compartment they occupied, but, lulled by the soft sway of the carriage and the unremitting green of the countryside, she had fallen asleep soon after the train had left the Châtellerault station. Bernice and Lavinia shared the seat opposite her, Lavinia taking the place closest to the window to enjoy the view as reading en route made her queasy.

"Baedeker's says there are very reasonably priced inns catering specifically to English ladies traveling unaccompanied."

"Italy?" Lavinia echoed, still surprised by her sister's nascent wanderlust. "I . . . I don't know. I suppose so. We will certainly be able to afford it."

"Oh." Bernice's round face flamed with embarrassment. "I keep forgetting that you are going to be rich, Livie."

"*We* are going to be rich, my dear. You know it has always been my intention to settle half of whatever those rubies fetch on you."

Bernice regarded her sister fretfully. "I know, but I couldn't feel right accepting—"

"Good heavens, Bernice, don't be a juggins."

"A what?" Bernice asked. If Lavinia was surprised by Bernice's taking to travel, Bernice was equally dumbfounded by her sister's transformation from frail maiden lady to self-possessed cosmopolitan.

"A juggins. Someone who is unnecessarily circumspect."

Bernice was a tad offended. She had only meant to make clear that she didn't expect anything. "Forgive me for not presuming."

Lavinia smiled. "And now you are being a double juggins. Or perhaps a widgeon."

Widgeon, Bernice understood. In many cases, it could be considered a fond term.

"You know very well were the situation reversed you would do the same and insist upon the same. So, let's speak no more of it, shall we?"

How could she be offended? Lavinia would never purposely hurt her feelings. It was just that she had recently discovered the pleasure of speaking her mind.

She was changing. They were both changing.

How odd that, so late in life, one could begin to . . . well, bloom. But then, even at Robin's Hall, November roses were not all that rare.

"Now tell me about Italy. Where would we start?"

Bernice flipped to the map at the back of the book, her finger traveling slowly along the coastal towns.

"Good heavens. Do you see that, Bernice?"

"See what, Livie?" Following her sister's wide-eyed gaze, she leaned forward and peered out of the train window. She jerked back with a thump.

"Oh. Oh, *my*!" Bright pink circles arose on her soft, round cheeks as she fussed with her blouse cuffs. She cleared her throat.

"Now, Lavinia, it is only to be expected that the inhabitants of these small French burgs would have a different notion of decorum than that which we are used to at Robin's Hall. We mustn't judge them by our standards, and instead allow for the Frenchmen's looser moral understanding."

Now that she'd composed herself and could consider the goings-on objectively, Bernice permitted herself a somewhat longer look back at the couple, still locked in their passionate embrace. Lavinia, who hadn't so much as blinked, lifted slightly from her seat, allowing herself a clearer view.

A small crowd gathered in a cordoned-off area had surrounded a young man and woman thoroughly wrapped in one another's arms. A few of the male spectators actually clapped the young man on the back. He didn't appear to notice, being entirely engaged in . . . well, entirely engaged.

"He looks like a young farm hand, don't you think?" Bernice asked. He was certainly built like one, or at least as Bernice imagined—not that she'd ever imagined—one would be. Lean and muscular, the young man wore only the top half of his gentleman's combinations and a pair of dusty looking trousers. As his broad back was turned toward them, all they could see of his head were thick black curls.

Even though the object of his affection faced them, it was impossible to see what the girl looked like due to the young man's head completely eclipsing her face. But, judging by the slender arms clinging round his neck and the narrow form he held lashed so tightly to himself, she was slight and small. Her poorly made, ill-fitting clothing suggested that she, too, came from a simple background.

"Country sweethearts," Bernice opined.

The young man suddenly dipped down and plucked the girl right up off the ground and lifted her high against his chest, his mouth never leaving hers. A pile of tawny brown hair spilled over his forearm as he turned and strode off through the crowd just as their train headed around a curve.

"If this is how they act in France . . ." Lavinia murmured.

"Just think what it must be like in Italy!" Bernice breathed.

CHAPTER

30

He really had to stop grabbing Lucy and kissing her. It was becoming a very bad habit.

The thought flickered, the dim light of reason trying to illuminate his thoughts. But then the feel of her mouth, soft and voluptuous beneath his, and the press of her supple form yielding against him extinguished that sputtering light and ignited a blazing fire instead.

He wrapped his arms more tightly around her, bending her backward over his forearm, his mouth slanting urgently over hers. He cradled the back of her head, his fingers spearing through the thick, glossy hair. God, she tasted good. She smelled, she felt, she was . . . Impossible to find words while a tidal surge of sensation and desire swept through him.

Long, long minutes later he became dimly aware of some ill-mannered idiot poking his back . . . Damn! Here he was, once more putting on a show for the locals. He broke off the kiss and snapped upright, carrying her with him. What must she think?

She didn't seem to think anything.

She wobbled on her feet, dazed, her eyes soft and unfocused. He steadied her with a hand on her elbow. She stared down at his hand with an unreadable expression. Any second now she would slap his face in the time-honored tradition of a lady insulted. He richly deserved it.

But instead she looked up at him and gave him a barmy sort of half smile.

Silly, silly, unwise girl. The rabbit hole he'd entered five days ago turned into a bottomless abyss, one from which there was no return.

"Here now, lad," a hearty English voice said from his side. "It's still daylight, for the love of Mike!"

A pot-bellied, redheaded bantam of a man with bright blue eyes grabbed his hand and shook it violently. "Bless you, lad. You just won me a tidy sum, a tidy sum indeed! I knew you were a contender, the minute I saw you lift your fists. 'There's a stylist, Ned,' I said to meself. I recognized it, you see, counta I went a few rounds on the canvas meself when I was a youngster.

"So I hightails it over to where the boys are takin' odds and hands over me whole month's earnings. Eighteen to one. *Eighteen to one!*" He broke off in delighted laughter. "Come along! You and your sweetheart."

"Come along where?" Archie asked, feeling stupid.

"To me pub, lad! The Wayfarer."

"You have a pub?"

"More of an inn. Lost me senses over a French girl and followed her here. She inveigled me into marrying her and working on her dad's farm. Turns out I'm not so good at farming. Luckily, I am good at running an inn. But I missed the taste of good ale so much I turned the bar into a proper pub where a man can enjoy a pint. And you'll be my guests there for the night."

He caught Archie around the shoulders with one arm and Lucy with the other. Then, shouting, "*Suivez-moi, mes amis!*" to the spectators who still milled about in disappointment, thus instantly heartening their mood, he shepherded Archie and Lucy off the field, trailed by a large and growing crowd.

———

Merrymakers and fairgoers, regulars and first-timers, witnesses to the fight and those who had just heard rumors that Ned Cleary was standing drinks to anyone who could make their way through the tight press of bodies in his bar to collect, filled the Wayfarer Inn, spilling out the wide-flung doors and into the street. Ned, flush in more ways than one, sent his barmaids to buy "whatever's left that looks good to eat" from the booths around the field before they closed down. When they returned he set it all out as a free feast.

The festival air in the Wayfarer grew and expanded as people drank and ate, laughed, and enjoyed themselves. Someone called for a fiddler and soon couples old and young, and a few who were one of each, were stomping the floorboards. The women raised their skirts; the men, a cloud of dust. Tall tales, squeals of laughter, and congratulations passed freely. Within seconds of Archie's glass being emptied, someone refilled it with a clap on the back or a nod of his head. More often than not it was his erstwhile opponent, Denis, who turned out to be a very pleasant baker with a philosophical bent.

"I only won for so many years because I am strong," he confided reflectively from across the table they shared. "The strongest. I have no idea how to fight. What sort of person goes about trying to learn how to pummel another man more efficiently? Not that I begrudge you the knowledge, monsieur," he hurriedly added. "We have all heard of stories about your English boarding schools. Had I gone there, I, too, would have learned the art of pugilism. But here? In France? Phff."

"Ish true," Ned agreed stoically, if a little blearily. "Only Englishmen and Americans have schools to teach fisticuffs."

Archie, his thoughts having grown a little muzzy and filled with bonhomie, smiled sympathetically.

"*But*"—the giant wagged his finger playfully under Archie's nose—"had we been involved in a weight-lifting competition, my friend, *then* I would have won the beautiful girl's reward." His eyes danced to where Lucy perched on the end of the bar, her legs swinging merrily. And lovely legs they were.

All three men fell into a silent, cow-eyed appreciation that lasted until Lucy felt their scrutiny and turned her attention their way. She'd been laughing at something someone said and her lips were parted in a broad grin, her eyes sparkling, her skin pink with warmth and ale.

"No, you wouldna," Archie said, his eyes never leaving Lucy's face. She tipped her head inquiringly, a mocking lift to her brow. She knew they'd been imbibing. And when he couldn't think how to respond, his thought processes having been temporarily disabled by her beauty, his drunkenness, and a multitude of other factors for which he couldn't account, she gave him a saucy wink and went back to listening to the old geezer filling her ear from the bar stool at her side.

"Ah. So it's like that, is it?" Denis said knowingly.

"Yes. Like that." He didn't even try to deny it. But neither did he explore too closely what "like that" meant.

He'd never met anyone like Lucy. He wouldn't ever meet anyone like her again. She filled his mind, crowding out his every resolve to act sensibly. It was like being drawn to the edge of a waterfall. No matter how dangerous you knew it was, you couldn't keep from looking over the edge.

As a lad, he'd always had a hard time "not looking over." He'd imagined he'd gotten over that tendency.

It appeared he hadn't.

"Then, because I am Frenchman and you are only a poor Englishman but a damned fine boxer, then perhaps I will not try to
steal her from you," Denis stated magnanimously. He quaffed
down the rest of his beer. "She made eyes at me, you know."

Archie burst into laughter. "Yeah, in order *to save my life.*"

As flirtatious as Lucy was, and she was flirtatious, he didn't for
a minute believe she was interested in Denis. Or any other man . . .
The thought gave rise to another notion—one not yet fully realized—
that clamored on the edges of his consciousness, shouting to be
heard. Something important, very important, that he should stop
to consider.

But then Denis, after trying unsuccessfully to look offended,
joined in his laughter, clapping him on the back.

Archie peered around at the revelers, the dancers, the fiddler, the
piper, and the barmaids swatting at hands. Farmers swayed in unison
to some old drinking song, children skittered in and out amongst the
tables, dogs barked, and Lucy, always Lucy, now sang some naughty
music hall ditty, and he realized he was having the time of his life.

"This is fun," he said, apropos of nothing.

Denis nodded.

"Ya know, I'm a profeshor."

"I should say so," Ned agreed. "Professor of the Right Uppercut."

"Well, that, too," Archie admitted modestly, "but I'm also an
anthra . . ." No, that wasn't the word. His mouth was having a hard
time forming what his brain wanted it to. "I'm an anthree . . . I
study culture. I'm a trained observer.

"'N one of the first things an anther . . . an antro . . . a guy
who studies cultures learns is never to become involved with your
subjects. Leads to all sorts of meshy, unscientific stuff. Right?"

His audience regarded him with gratifying—or was that stu-
pefied?—attention.

"Mustn't interact, ya know? So, I haven't. Always been careful to stay detached. Objective. Like a well-mannered audience member. Observin', not participatin'," he finished sadly.

"Sounds deadly dull," Ned opined.

"It is!" Archie cried in agreement then immediately reversed himself. "I mean, no. No. It's fascinating. But"—he leaned across the table and motioned his two companions closer—"observin' isn't *fun*."

He sat back as though he'd just delivered the answer to one of life's crowning mysteries. "*This*"—he slapped his palm on the table— "is fun."

"Hear, hear!" Ned raised his tankard in the air.

"Tonight . . ." Archie started to say and then thought a second and made an amendment, "today," he thought again, "well, ever since I jumped from the wharf onto that ferry—"

"You jumped onto a ferry boat?"

"Yup."

"Why?"

"To get to her." He nodded toward Lucy.

"Oh." Both men nodded as though this made perfect sense.

"Anyway, ever since I jumped on that ferry and straight into the maw of madness," he paused, rather liking the poetical sound of the phrase, enough so that he repeated it, "straight into the maw of madness, I've been smack-dab in the center of things.

"You know, Lucy's right." He looked from Ned to Denis. "She is. You can't understand something unless you live it. Or a person."

"You can live a person?" Denis asked doubtfully.

Archie nodded owlishly. "Inhibit, I mean, *inhabit* their skin. Walk a mile in their shoes. That sorta thing."

"But of course," Denis said.

"Your shoes," Archie said, "are fun."

"The night is still young, my friend. There is much more fun to be had."

"Oh, I think he's had plenty of fun for one evening."

At the sound of Lucy's smoothly amused voice, Archie looked up, blinking as the room seemed to swim around him.

"Lucy!" he cried rapturously.

"That's my name," she said, taking his hands and hauling back on them so that he was forced to stand. "Come on, Champ."

"Are we going somewhere?"

"Uhm-hm," she said.

"Where?"

"To bed."

CHAPTER
31

Lucy hadn't intended to do anything more than guide Archie to his room, topple him onto his bed, pull off his boots, and leave him in a beer-induced slumber. Though because they'd spoken in French, and fairly slurred French at that, she hadn't been able decipher what the ex-champion, the Irishman, and Archie were talking about. But from the overly friendly exclamations, the pledges of lifelong friendship, manly slaps on the back, and slow-blinking affability, she had a pretty good handle on one thing: Archie was blotto.

But apparently not as blotto as she'd thought.

Once she maneuvered him through the door, he wheeled around to face her, grinning with a sort of boyish disingenuousness that she couldn't help but find appealing.

"That was fun."

"It was," she agreed, manhandling him around again so she could start peeling off his jacket. He looked over his shoulder at her. He smelled of ale and sweat and, well, Archie, and it shouldn't have appealed to her nearly as much as it did.

"*You're* fun," he said as though he'd just awarded her the highest of compliments.

"Why, thank you. I think."

He frowned. "Whaddaya mean 'You think?'"

"Well, in certain circles, a 'fun girl' is the same as a 'fast girl.' I hope you don't think I'm fast?" She gave him her best big, reproachful doe-eyes. She didn't really think he'd buy it—Archie had unerring sense of when she was putting him on—even though those doe-eyes had sold a lot of tickets to a lot of shows.

But she had reckoned without taking into consideration how much he'd drunk. An expression of such shocked contrition filled his handsome face that she couldn't bear to play the scene out. "Maybe just a trifle racy," she amended.

"I don't think you're racy," he said earnestly.

She'd finally wrestled his jacket off and propelled him toward the bed. Once there, she carefully positioned him facing her with the backs of his knees against the mattress. Then, with an impish grin, she set her hands against his chest. "Oh," she breathed, "but I am," and pushed.

Nothing happened.

He stared down at the hands splayed over his very hard, very masculine chest. She put a bit more weight into the endeavor. Nothing. Except now a loopy grin had appeared on his face, a grin that, were it just a tad less loopy, would have been brutally sexy. He covered her hands with his own, flattening her palms hard against his chest. His smile crooked up just a little more at the corners, making her breathlessly reassesses her former opinion. Goofy smile or no goofy smile, he was incredibly sexy.

The heat of him soaked through the thin shirt, toasting her palms. His chest rose and fell in deep, even breaths, and uncontrollably, her fingers curved and pressed, testing the dense texture of his pectoral muscles. Her eyes tripped up to meet his. Black as tar, wicked as midnight sin, they gleamed with an unsettling light, regarding her with an expression that heated her from fingertips to belly, lips to thighs. He bent his head, bringing his lips within inches of her ear.

"Try harder," he whispered, the warm wash of his breath making her tingle.

She did as instructed. He pitched backward like a falling tree, at the last second grabbing her around the waist and pulling her down on top of him. She landed with a surprised "oof!" and pushed up onto her forearms, her hair spilling over her eyes.

A gentle hand swept her hair back and lingered to cup the side of her face. Lucy found herself staring into Archie's eyes, drowning in them, helplessly transfixed. Slowly she became aware of her breasts against him; of their hearts beating in duet, hers a rapid staccato, his slower and heavier.

His hand trailed back from her temples, his fingertips spearing through the tousled locks to cup the back of her head. Gently, he urged her head down toward his. He angled his face and with exquisite tenderness touched his lips to hers.

She trembled.

"That's for the clumsiness of the last two kisses," he murmured. He touched his mouth to hers again, a soft buffing of her lips. "That's for the clumsiness that is sure to come."

His mouth ambushed hers in a rough, voluptuous kiss. Her thoughts went muzzy, reason fleeing before the onslaught of a melting pleasure, filling her like candle wax, turning her warm and pliant. Her arms slipped around him, provoking a breathless, gratified laugh.

She answered with her own ardent kiss. Her lips parted to his tongue, warm and insistent, brushing the roof of her mouth and the inside of her cheek, then tangling in voluptuous combat with her own. Her head spun, drunk on sensation. Vaguely, she became aware that he was rolling her beneath him; she went willingly. His thumbs brushed the corner of her mouth as his large hands bracketed her face before tipping her chin higher, stroking back her hair. He kissed her, then kissed her again. He lifted his head, breaking away from her mouth to taste the hollow at the base of her neck, his tongue swirling in luxurious exploration and then moving lower, to the swell of her breast exposed by the modest neckline.

She arched into the glorious sensation, her fingers digging into his back, the shirt keeping her from that marvelous, corrugated muscle. She popped the top buttons free of their holes and slipped her hands beneath the opening only to find herself further thwarted by his undershirt.

With a sob of frustration she jerked his shirt off his shoulders.

He lifted his head. His breath came heavy, his hair falling in dark, disheveled curls over his forehead, his dark beard shadowing his jawline and smudging the cleft in his chin.

"Lucy," he said, looking down at her. "Lucy, we—" He groaned and dropped a kiss on her mouth that she returned even as she continued working to free him of his shirt.

"We shouldn't," she finished for him as soon as he raised his head again. She undid the last button and tugged the shirt off of him.

"No. I mean, you're right," he said. "We mustn't."

"Mustn't." Now she tugged at the undershirt, but then his head dipped to the lee of her neck. She buried her fingers in the cool, silky curls, holding his head tighter, panting softly.

His hands slipped up her back to peel her blouse from her shoulders, the cool air sifting across her bared flesh. Bared flesh . . .

She grabbed the material at his waist, yanking it up.

"Our society frowns—" he rasped, then there were more kisses; wilder, wetter, longer kisses. He tore his mouth free. "Not all societies."

"Really?" She could barely hear her own voice. He raised his arms and she pulled the soft undershirt off and now, finally, her hands were free to explore his gorgeous physique: to plumb the density of his pectoral muscle; stroke the velvet ladder of his rib cage; rake the soft, light smattering of fur that crossed his chest and speared in a thickening line down into his trousers.

"This is madness." He was working on her blouse now, trying with clumsy fingers to push her blouse buttons free and failing miserably.

"Madness." She proceeded to demonstrate more madness by launching a battery of kisses on his mouth and throat, chest and shoulders. Then she abruptly pushed him away and searched his face worriedly, earnestly. "I want you to know, I have . . . I'm not . . ."

He shut her up with a long, hard kiss, broke it off, his forehead pressed to hers, eyes half shut with pleasure. "I don't care." A tender smile flickered across his face. "Me, either."

She gave him such a rapturous smile he groaned again and slewed his mouth over hers, his hand fumbling with her blouse. She only wanted to be free of the thing, to feel every inch of her flesh against his. And then . . .

"I can't get the stupid thing off," he growled.

She must have made a sound—dismay or frustration or simply encouragement—for all of a sudden he took the bottom of her blouse and stripped it off over the top of her head in one motion. He tossed it aside, his gaze locked with hers.

For one brief second he went absolutely still, his eyes afire, his face almost reverential.

He took a shuddery breath. "God, you're beautiful."

And after that, the only conversation they had did not need words.

CHAPTER

32

Thump! Thump!

"Get up or you're going to miss the train!" Ned shouted through the door.

Archie came awake with a start, snapping upright on the bed—*Lucy*. He swiveled round and there she was beside him, lying on her side beneath a blanket, snoring lightly. A corona of rich brown curls surrounded her face and she'd tucked one hand beneath her cheek.

Jesus. He raked his hair back with his hand, staring down at her. She looked ungodly beautiful, wholly appealing. *Jesus!*

"Are you awake? Answer me!" Ned renewed his pounding. "You have twenty minutes to get to the station!"

"All right! All right!"

Beside him, Lucy stirred. He looked down again to find a pair of gorgeous green-and-gold-shot hazel eyes calmly regarding him. Without thinking, he bent to kiss her, pulled along on a rip tide of attraction. Somehow he found the wherewithal to stop himself.

"What did he say?" she asked.

"What?" He couldn't help it, he looked at her, tousled and sleep-muzzed and sex-flushed in his bed—or was it her bed?—and all he could think about was that he knew there was a mole on the inside jut of her left hip bone, that the backs of her knees were ticklish, that she laughed even as tears spilled from her eyes as she reached her climax, that her nipples were silky and that her skin tasted toasty.

"What is he shouting about?"

He came back to his senses with a start. "He says the train is leaving for Châtellerault in twenty minutes."

Her eyes flew wide with alarm. She bolted from the bed, dragging the blanket with her, covering herself.

"Don't just stand there," she said, grabbing up her discarded clothing. "We have to go. *Now.*"

She was right, of course. There wasn't a second to waste. But this was not how he envisioned or wanted this morning to play out.

He snatched his trousers off the floor, and, still sitting, stabbed his feet through the legs. Behind him he heard the sound of clothes hastily being donned. "Lucy, about last night—"

"Archie, we don't have time for this. Not now."

Damn, but she was being cavalier about this. Which was fine for her, but he didn't have quite her, well, considering the situation he couldn't call it worldliness, could he? Her *laissez faire*?

"Look, I'm . . . I appreciate—" No, he didn't. "I, ah, defer to your pragmatism but this—" He stopped, feeling stupid and frustrated and worried, worried sick.

He didn't have a clue what to say. He had no idea what she was thinking, what she expected or even if she expected anything, let alone know what she wanted. Or what she felt.

In other words, he had no idea where to start but he had to start somewhere. So he started with the one certain, unassailable fact. "Why did you say you weren't a virgin?"

The rustling abruptly stopped. "What?"

"Why did you say you weren't a virgin?" All the shock and dismay and sense of betrayal he'd felt upon making this discovery last night—which, granted, had lasted all of five seconds before other thoughts, or rather feelings, banished them to the background—filled his voice.

"*What?*" She sounded as amazed as he'd felt.

"Didn't you think I'd notice?"

"I didn't think."

Which made two of them. He snapped his shirt off the bed's corner post and shoved his arms through the sleeves before turning to face her again. She was stuffing the ends of her blouse into her skirt's waistband. Twin brackets scored the area between her eyebrows.

"Just before . . . before things became . . ." God, if only he had Lucy's gift of frank speech. "Became intense, you said you wanted me to know that you weren't a virgin."

Her scowl became more pronounced.

Ned shouted through the door again. "*Ten* minutes!"

"I most certainly did not." She sounded flabbergasted.

"You said you wanted me to know you weren't a virgin."

"I can't think how you—" The frown disappeared, replaced by dawning comprehension. "You have it wrong. I had been about to say I wanted you to know I didn't have any regrets over . . . you know." Amazingly she blushed, enchanting him anew. "And that I'm not going to."

"*What?*"

She scooped up a half boot and stuck it on, hopping one-footed as she tried to push her heel into place. "Of course, I was a virgin. I—" She broke off suddenly and stopped hopping and stared at him. "You thought I was *apologizing*?" She gasped. "You did! For not being a virgin! Save me from the hubris of men. That is the most conceited—"

"No, no! I swear—I mean, yes, I did, but I swear I didn't think you *needed* to apologize, that's why I said—"

Her eyes grew round as she finished his sentence, "'Me, too.' Archie. You mean you *weren't* a virgin?"

He closed his eyes. In his worst imaginings, he could never have envisioned this conversation proceeding as it was. "Does it matter?"

"I suppose not." She finished lacing up one boot and made quick work of the other before hastening about the room, snapping up sundry articles of clothing and stuffing them in the kit he'd purchased.

"Honestly, Archie," she muttered as she worked. "What sort of woman goes about declaring she's *not* a virgin?"

"Lucy, please. I just need you to know that I am so—"

The look on her face cut his words off midsentence. "If you say you are sorry, I shall never, ever forgive you. I will consider it the most . . . the most caddish thing ever."

"Lucy, I—"

"Come on, Archie!" Ned yelled through the door. "I've sent a lad to see if he can delay them but they won't wait long."

"Yes! I heard you the first time!"

Lucy glared balefully at him.

Things had gone from bad to worse and he hadn't even said anything yet. At least, nothing important. And he needed to, he could see that. He needed to say something and he needed it to be far more eloquent than anything he'd managed thus far. Probably in his entire life. But with Ned banging on the door and Lucy shooting daggers at him, eloquence just wasn't going to happen.

So, he opted for the only sensible course open to him: he kept his mouth shut.

He seized the kit in one hand, strode to the door, and yanked it open. Then he went back into the room, grabbed Lucy's hand, and pulled her after him.

The daily train stopping in Châtellerault had no private compartments but they did have semiprivate ones. Even so, Lucy thought the tickets expensive. After paying for the tickets from Archie's winnings—and wouldn't you think the purse offered for the winner of a regional boxing championship would be more than a hundred francs?—they had little money left, a fact Archie swore he'd sort out with a local bank as soon as they'd reunited with her great-aunts.

Lucy crammed herself onto the bench seat alongside a pair of men in checkered suits and bright yellow vests engaged in an animated discussion. Judging by the leather sample cases piled on the racks above them, Lucy supposed them to be traveling salesmen. Across from her an apple-cheeked English nanny clasped a wiggly toddler on her lap while a boy sandwiched between the girl and Archie regarded Lucy with round, somber eyes.

Archie was frowning. Oh, not at her, but at the unfortunate floor, as though it could offer up some answer to a vexing problem but refused to do so. Lucy suspected *she* was the vexing problem.

She shouldn't have been so flippant about last night. But she'd awoken to find him staring down at her with what only an idiot would recognize as something, anything, other than desire. Every fiber had responded to that in kind.

Until she'd also recognized his dismay. It wounded her in a place she hadn't known existed, and then the innkeeper had started shouting again and so she'd done what had become second nature to her: she'd donned a persona, that of a thoroughly modern, thoroughly unsentimental girl with a train to catch. Because the last thing she wanted to do was listen to Archie's litany of self-recriminations.

What if she had made a horrible mistake? What if he thought she meant to trap him into a marriage proposal? While she had every intention of marrying Archie, she didn't want it to be because he'd *deflowered* her—and there really ought to be some better term. She felt like a well-pruned rose bush. Apparently, he'd been concerned about taking her virginity—again, why must it sound so awful? As though Archie was a thief? She'd freely given her virginity up—but she'd cut him off with a precipitous answer. Which is why he'd thought she wasn't a virgin. By the time he'd realized she was, things had been far beyond the point of no return, at least as far as she was concerned, and even though he'd hesitated at that exact instant, he hadn't needed much convincing to continue . . . pruning.

And she had encouraged him. There were no ifs, ands, or buts about it. She had been eager, no, *beyond* eager. She had been frantic to discover what lay at the end of the tsunami of pleasure she'd been riding.

So, yes. Yes. And yes. Last night *had* been imprudent, reckless, and heedless. She hadn't been thinking. But the moment they'd kissed, thought had simply ceased to be a factor in anything that followed and what followed had been, in a word, wondrous.

Desire had ignited the intense, sensation-charged journey from kiss to culmination, from wanting to knowing, and had taken her to a culmination so rich, so exquisite, so potent she'd started laughing like a loon and then burst into tears of pure gratification. And then? And then it had begun again, a new journey. And when Archie reached that same destination and his body strained, taut and glistening above her, his face suffused with dark color, his eyes glittering—

"Why's that lady look so funny, Miss Pritt?" the little boy across from her asked in charmingly accented English.

Lucy's vision telescoped back into focus. The little boy was staring at her with unabashed curiosity while his nanny shushed him. Heat exploded up her neck and into her face.

Archie glanced up from his determined study of the floorboards. She smiled hopefully at him.

A brief, involuntary smile flickered across his firm, well-molded, warm, pliant—she gave her wrist a vicious pinch—across his lips.

It died as quickly as it had been born, leaving his face once more a study in preoccupation and guilt.

But guilty about what? Or about whom?

The woman he'd imagined he was going to ask to marry him? Did he feel that he had been disloyal?

A dark mood fell over her. Last night, Miss Litchfield might as well have not existed for all the thought Lucy had given her. Perhaps she should have. Archie would not take vows, even ones he'd not yet spoken or even promised to speak, even ones he simply *assumed* he would be speaking someday, lightly. She would detest it if she were party to making Archie hate himself.

But Archie didn't love Miss Litchfield. And no matter what sort of woman she was, Lucy could not believe Miss Litchfield would want to marry a man who did not love her but another woman. What self-respecting woman would? By making Archie understand that he loved her, Lucy was saving two people from a terrible mistake and ensuring the future happiness of at least two others. So what if she was one of them?

Still . . . "Are you troubled about Miss Litchfield?"

He didn't answer. He had raked his hair back with his hand, in effect only tousling it more. He looked incredibly appealing.

"Archie? About Miss Litchfield."

"Hm?" He glanced up, still distracted. "What about missing a field?"

The tension left her on a sigh. Whatever was causing him unhappiness, it wasn't Miss Litchfield. Had he been thinking about her, her name would have been foremost in his mind.

Then he must be feeling guilty about me, Lucy decided.

Hadn't he realized by now that they were meant for one another? For a brilliant man he certainly didn't tumble to the obvious very quickly. She smiled. And it really was so very obvious.

They were both nomads at heart, both collectors of stories, both drawn to discovering what lay beyond the next horizon.

True, Archie's wanderlust had the added component of scientific curiosity, hers the lure of the exotic, but they both were drawn in the same direction by similar impulses.

Years ago she'd arrived at Robin's Hall hoping she would finally find her home, a place at which she would always belong, somewhere that would last forever. But even as a child she'd felt the lure of far-off places, the call of the unknown. It had confused her that she could love her great-aunts and Robin's Hall so much and yet still feel restless. That was probably why her favorite roles had always been exotic ones in which she could live out her dreams.

Now she realized that in Archie she had finally found her true home, and it wasn't a place but a companion to share in all the adventures, the mundane and the extraordinary, the struggles and the laughter, the roads and—God help her—if need be, the seas. Home meant shelter and refuge, passion and laughter, but above all being recognized as the person one was, not the person someone else wanted them to be.

No one had ever known her as well as Archie. He alone could differentiate playacting from reality, the fictional character from the person.

Just as she'd recognized him.

Her pirate. Her befuddled professor. Her chivalrous knight, spurned Gypsy beau, long-jumper, cat burglar, boxing champ. Lover.

Why couldn't he see what was so obvious to her?

The door to the cabin swung out and the tired-looking porter stuck his head in. "*Attention. Arrivee a la gare de Châtellerault.*"

Archie stood up and held out his hand. "We're there, Lucy."

Not yet, she thought. And took his hand.

CHAPTER

33

The minute they stepped down onto the train platform a sleek-headed hansom cabdriver sporting a trim black moustache hurried up to them, trailed by a lad of about ten.

"English, yes? I speak English. The clothes, little ma'am," he answered Lucy's unvoiced question. "No Frenchwoman . . ." His gaze fell tellingly on Lucy's clothing as he trailed off, shaking his head apologetically. "Allow me to introduce myself. I am Paul Herve. And I have the pleasure of addressing . . . ?"

"I am Lucy Eastlake and this is Archie Grant," Lucy replied, drawn into the formalities of making introductions.

"Miss Eastlake. Mr. Grant. Come, I will take you wherever you wish to go. If you extend your stay, I will be your guide. I know everyone and everything about Châtellerault. The best places to dine, the finest vineyards."

Archie met her glance. She shrugged.

The cabdriver turned as though their following him was a foregone conclusion and led them the short distance to the curb.

A pair of well-fed geldings waited patiently behind a large, black hansom carriage, its windows raised against the darkening sky.

"Here we are." The cabdriver beamed. "Now, where do you wish to go?"

"Is there a good hotel or inn in town?" Archie asked.

"But of course. The Hotel de la Post is a superior establishment and right across the street from our new theatre." He said this last with an unmistakable touch of civic pride before his neat little features collapsed in commiseration. "You have not traveled all this way to see Margery, I am hoping? Because Margery had only the one performance last night. Standing room only and even then, the crowds!" He kissed his fingertips by way of exclamation.

Lucy held her breath, willing Archie not to recognize the name from the evening they'd met at the Savoy. Luckily, he had other matters on his mind.

"No. We're not," he said.

"Then there is no problem. Those who came to town for the performance have left, too. I am sure the hotel can accommodate you. Now, where is your luggage?"

Archie looked down at the small leather satchel in his hand then wordlessly shoved it into the surprised cabdriver's arms.

"This is all?"

"That's it."

Once more he beamed and shook his head. "You English," he said. "So refreshing in your refusal to trouble yourself with transporting clothing appropriate for every occasion of the day."

Archie's black eyes narrowed, uncertain whether they had just been complimented or ridiculed. Lucy, who had no doubt at all, bit her lip to keep from laughing.

"Hm," Archie said. "Take us to the hotel." He shot her a determined expression; Lucy's heart sank. He meant to take advantage of the closed carriage to talk. She wasn't sure she was ready to talk.

"At once," the driver said, "but first I must collect my other passengers."

"What other passengers? I thought we'd just hired you."

"Now, now, monsieur. Châtellerault is a small town. There are not so many carriages for hire. It only makes sense to take as many passengers as wish to go to the town center all in one trip rather than back and forth and back and forth while the people left behind get tired and chilled. Like those small children," he pointed at their compartment companion and her wards. "The Favre's nurse is English like yourselves. You would not want her to stand about with those small children in the cold?"

"Of course not," Lucy exclaimed, relieved at this unanticipated reprieve.

"How do you know she wants to hire your cab?" Archie asked, looking a mite disgruntled.

"Because every time she returns from visiting the children's grandmama she takes my cab."

There was nothing left to discuss. Ever the gentleman, Archie handed Lucy up and then waited while the English nurse and her charges hurried over and piled in, followed closely by a prosperous-looking merchant and a reedy adolescent with a banded stack of books, clearly a student on his way home for a visit.

Unlike on the train, however, Archie sat next to Lucy. With a whistle and a snap of the driver's whip above the horse's backs, the carriage moved out on poorly sprung wheels, swaying like a rocking chair. Even through the horrid—and hourly becoming more horrid—skirt she could feel the heat of Archie's thigh, a potent reminder of the heat of the rest of him.

Archie kept his black gaze fixed ahead, but she could see a muscle working in his jaw as though he sought to contain some powerful emotion.

Less than fifteen minutes later they lurched to a stop. The cabbie leapt down from his perch as a lad scooted up. The two held a short conversation and the boy dashed off. The cabbie came round the side and opened the door. "My son. I have sent him to the hotel to see about readying you a room."

"Rooms," Archie corrected vehemently, climbing out of the carriage. "Two rooms."

The cabbie shrugged. "Yes, yes. I am sure they will oblige."

The merchant exited next, the school lad close behind him. At the last minute the poor boy dropped his bundle of books, breaking the strap and sending them scattering across the carriage floor. Turning beet red, he scrambled to collect them. He scooped them up in his arms and hurtled out of the carriage, chased by mortification.

Archie held out his hand. "Lucy?"

Instead of Lucy's hand, he found himself the recipient of a little boy. The nanny unceremoniously dumped the child in his arms, a matter he handled with admirable aplomb, accepting the boy with perfect equanimity before casually setting him on his feet.

"Bless you, sir," breathed the nanny as she climbed down. Shifting the baby to her hip, she grabbed hold of the boy's hand and headed down the street.

Lucy emerged from the door but rather than offer his hand again, Archie put both his hands round her waist and lifted her off the step. For an instant he held her above him. She braced her hands on his broad shoulders, her heart racing.

Then, ever so gently, he set her down, his hands lingering a second before he withdrew them to curl into fists at his side.

"That is the hotel there." The cabbie pointed across the street. "Beside it is the theatre. Next is our police station, and then a mercantile. On the other side, the apothecary." He turned and pointed down the street. "Down there is the school and the cricket field. Two streets over—"

"Yes. I see. Thank you," Archie broke in and thrust some francs into the man's hand. "*Merci.*"

Archie turned to Lucy, his expression grave. "Lucy, as soon as we are settled we need to talk."

He was entirely too somber. She tried giving him a gamin grin. "We're talking right now."

It wouldn't wash. "That's not what I mean and you know it."

Yes. She did. The jig, as the Americans said, was up. And in more ways than one. Soon he would meet Margery and realize just to whom she'd entrusted her great-aunts' care. "All right, Archie."

He picked up his kit and inclined his head toward the brick building the cabbie had indicated. "Shall we?"

They'd walked a short distance when Archie realized he'd left his hat in the carriage. Saying there was no need for her to wait in the cold while he hunted it up, he bid her go on ahead of him. She was halfway across the street when she noted a trio of uniformed men hurrying into the hotel, their batons in hand.

What would require three gendarmes to make use of their weapons in a small countryside hotel? Clearly they had been dispatched to deal with a problem.

The unpleasant possibility occurred to her that France might not be as forward thinking about men dressing up as women as they were England. Perhaps Margery stood in imminent danger of, if not arrest, deportation.

With this thought in mind, she sped up, arriving in the hotel lobby to find the gendarmes had taken up posts, one each on either side of the door and the other near the front desk. They held their batons at ready, their eyes flinty and their mouths grim.

Lucy's gaze flew about the lobby, looking for Margery. She had to warn him. It hadn't been that long ago that Oscar Wilde had been imprisoned for gross indecency and while Margery's proclivities off of the stage—which she did not, in fact, know—had always been a matter of unimportance to her, who knew what constituted indecency in France?

She hurried up to the reception desk where a fat, glistening-faced bald man stood nervously watching the door. The policeman next to the desk had adopted the attitude of a dog guarding a bone.

"Monsieur, please, do you speak English?" she asked the gendarme. He glanced at her, shook his head, and went back to staring fixedly at the front door.

She turned to the desk manager. "*Please* say you speak English."

"You should not be here, mademoiselle," he told her. "Come back later."

"What are those police doing there?"

"They are here to arrest a criminal," the fat man said, mopping his face with a delicate lawn handkerchief. His gaze narrowed on her accusingly. "An Englishman. It would be best if you came back here with me where you will be safe."

This man thought they needed protection from Margery? She could not imagine anything more absurd. "Where is he?"

"He will be coming through the door at any second. Please, mademoiselle. Behind the desk. We do not know of what this man is capable."

"He is *capable* of a stellar mezzo soprano. You are making a terrible mistake. He wouldn't do anything illegal. Unless it's illegal for a man to wear skirts in France."

"He wears skirts to facilitate his crimes?" The man's eyes widened. "Deplorable!"

"I am trying to tell you he would not commit a crime!"

The man shook his head sadly. "You carry national loyalty too far, mademoiselle. He already has. We have a telegram from his last victim, alerting us to his purpose."

"Victim? His *purpose*?"

"*Oui*, to take advantage of poor country innkeepers. Unless in your country it is legal to leave bills in excess of two hundred francs unpaid and sneak out in the middle of the night?"

Realization dawned with the speed of a lightning strike. *Oh, dear.*

The door opened and there stood Archie, his hat on his head, his mouth on the brink of a smile. "Did you find your great-aunts, Lucy?"

"*Run!*"

CHAPTER
34

Of course, Archie didn't run; he frowned at her.

"Run? Of course, I'm not going to—hey! What's going on?" he demanded as the gendarme on either side of the door grabbed an arm. "Let go of me." He jerked free of one, a middle-aged man who looked more concerned than confident.

The possibility that Archie might get angry and exacerbate an already very fragile situation prompted her to shout, "Don't hit him, Archie. Whatever you do, do not hit him!"

The gendarme next to her grabbed her and pulled her back, not to restrain her so much as to keep her safe from big bad Archie. She had to concede he did look rather dangerous, with his two-day's growth of beard, tousled black hair, and collarless, stained shirt beneath the rumpled tweed jacket.

Archie froze, staring at her in astonishment. "*Hit* him? What on earth are you talking about, Lucy. I have no intention of hitting anyone. I just want to know . . ." His black eyes narrowed on her from behind their thicket of long black lashes.

"Lucy. What have you done?" He turned to address the younger, grimmer policeman. "Whatever she's done, I swear she didn't mean any harm."

"Nothing! I swear . . . well, I *have,* technically, but nothing these men know about. They're arresting *you,* Archie."

His expression grew even more dangerous. "So it would appear." The way he said it, so vehemently calm, made her shrink back a little. Apparently believing she was no longer likely to run pell-mell toward danger, the gendarme let her go.

"The question," Archie continued, "is why?"

"I'm not *exactly* certain. But I believe it is, maybe, for running out on the hotel bill in Saint-Malo." She racked her brain. There had to be some way out of this mess that would not endanger what she'd worked so hard to achieve. She couldn't think of one, not straight off. She needed time to think, plan. *Plot.*

The dangerous expression evaporated from Archie's face. He unleashed a torrent of French at the young policeman. From his intonations, Lucy could tell he was asking questions. From the inflections in the policeman's voice, he apparently took a grim, official pleasure in his replies.

When Archie had finished, he simply shook his head, his brow furrowed, as though puzzled about something. In the meantime, the officer nearest her was in close conversation with the hotel manager.

"Archie?" she asked tentatively.

"Hm?" He sounded distracted.

"What did he say?"

He looked up at her, his dark eyes searching her face as if looking for answers there. "It's just as you surmised."

"If you are arrested, I should be, too," she said staunchly. She still hadn't figured a way out of this mess. But if she shared his difficulty, he might forgive her. Maybe. Hopefully.

"Lucy, don't," Archie said, sounding tired. "You weren't the one who promised Navarre full payment. I was. They won't arrest you."

She turned to the gendarme. "Monsieur, I insist you arrest me, too!" He spared her a quick, exasperated glance before asking the hotel manager a question. At the reply, he gave a snort and let fly a rapid stream of French. Oh, *why* hadn't she actually learned the dratted language?

"But you didn't steal anything!" she protested, her sense of doom increasing by the second.

"Technically, I did. They're right, I stand guilty as accused. I . . . I can't quite believe this—no," he said, firmly, "I can. What I *can't* believe is that I didn't foresee this would happen. Of course Navarre would wire ahead to the authorities. He knew where we were going. Why wouldn't I have thought of that?"

"Because you intended to pay him as soon as circumstances allowed."

"That may be true, but it's no excuse," he said. "As for why I didn't think things through clearly, well, the answer to that is obvious. I haven't thought clearly since I embarked on this . . . this madness.

"You have a way, Lucy, of making whatever comes out of your mouth sound reasonable, even when it's not. Maybe even *especially* when it's not. Or maybe it's not you, but me?" The idea seemed to find some merit with him for he nodded sadly. "There's some part of my thought process that is broken where you are concerned."

The officer by the desk, apparently the man in charge, had finished talking to the hotel manager. He spoke to the other two uniformed men, gesturing for them to take Archie elsewhere.

She couldn't let them arrest Archie.

But there was only one way to stop them. "No, let him go. Please!"

The gendarmes on either side of Archie hesitated, deferring to their commander.

Lucy swiveled, seizing the fat manager's hand and wringing it. He stared at her, aghast. "*Please.* Please tell them this is all my fault!"

Archie shook his head. "Lucy, it's not—"

She couldn't bring herself to look at him. "Yes, it is, Archie," she said, keeping her back to him because she knew she couldn't face him and say it. She tried to blink away the tears that sprang to her eyes, tears of remorse. And of fear. What would he do? What would he *say*?

"Mademoiselle, if you would kindly release my hand?" the manager said, pulling at it until she let go. "Now, what would you have me say?"

"Tell them it's all a mistake," she said. "Tell them we will repay the bill."

"Mademoiselle," the innkeeper said not unkindly, "you miss the point. Even if you could afford—"

"I can!" she said desperately and, fumbling deep down into her skirt's pocket, pulled out the wallet.

Archie's wallet.

A terrible silence met this revelation. No one moved. No one breathed. It was as if time itself had stopped. She closed her eyes in misery, waiting to hear Archie say something, say *anything*, to break the awful silence.

And when he didn't and she could stand it no longer, she gathered her courage and turned around to face him.

It was so much worse than she could ever have anticipated.

He looked lost, utterly betrayed, his expression dazed and uncomprehending.

"Archie, please."

"You had it all along," he said wonderingly. "All this time."

"Yes. I—"

"Found it?" His eyes were bleak, his tone unhopeful.

She swallowed. As much as she wanted to, she couldn't lie to him. "No. I took it."

He closed his eyes briefly, as if the mere sight of her was painful, but she plowed ahead, unwilling to let anything remain undisclosed. "At the restaurant, when I excused myself at the end of dinner. I picked your pocket when I bumped into you."

At the look on his face, she began trembling and once she started she could not stop. She hadn't realized . . . She'd never meant . . . *Oh, no. No. No. No. Please, no.*

She raised a shaking hand toward him in entreaty, pain and panic racing headlong through her, lancing straight to her heart.

"I see," he said, then, "I hadn't realized your talents extended that far."

"Archie . . ." She took a step toward him but he was already turning away, murmuring something to the officers. Then, without another word to her, he let them lead him away.

The town hall had just three cells, each occupied by a prisoner guilty of a felony of some degree or other. At the end of the corridor that accessed them, a door swung open. The guard who'd opened it stepped aside, allowing Lucy to enter.

Archie rose slowly to his feet from the narrow bed that was the only furnishing in the cell. "What is she doing here?" he demanded in French. "Get her out."

The guard shrugged. "She has the commander's permission. Also, she paid."

"It must be true that all Englishmen are mad," said the prisoner in the next cell, an unclean antique of a man with the bulbous, red-mapped nose of the perpetual drunkard.

"Obviously," concurred the youth occupying the far end cell, a good-looking lad with overlong hair whose socialist ideals had

led him to leaving a flaming pile of excrement on the mayor's doorstep. "Why else would he want her to leave? She's beautiful."

Archie ignored them. The last thing in the world he wanted
right now was a solicitous call from Lucy Eastlake. "I don't care
whose permission she has or what she's paid," he told the guard, "I
do not want to see her. Don't prisoners in your country have any
rights?"

The guard shrugged. "No."

Lucy, who didn't understand any of this exchange, regarded
him owlishly, looking vulnerable and small and exquisite. How
could she have done this to him? And why did his heart still jump
at the sight of her?

Madness. But then he'd been headed for madness the moment
he'd met her. He'd suspected it; he just hadn't heeded the warning
bells his higher faculties had rung.

It was long past time he did.

He had spent the last days in some weird altered state of consciousness where folly had became the norm. But seeing his wallet
in her hand and realizing that she had purposefully turned him
into a criminal, engineered a trip that had organically changed his
life, and very possibly ruined any hopes of returning to his former
one, had catapulted him back to his senses. *Finally.*

It didn't matter that enough vestiges of the madness remained
so that his pulse quickened at the sight of her and his chest constricted painfully, and that something inside him leapt, ready and
willing to dive back into the lunacy. He ruthlessly ignored the
drive. As he understood it, a drug addict experienced much the
same sort of thing upon withdrawal; it didn't mean drugs were
good for him. Eventually they destroyed you.

The guard beckoned her in. She hurried down the corridor,
past the ogling gazes of the other prisoners.

"What are you doing here, Lucy? You should be with your great-aunts on your way to Saint-Girons."

"They're not here. They left a letter with the hotel manager. My friend is escorting them to Saint-Girons and I'm to meet them there."

"Then you should go."

"No. It isn't right that a moment of reckless abandon keeps you in jail."

He burst out in bitter laughter.

"A *moment* of reckless abandon?" he echoed. "My dear girl, the entire week has been one episode of recklessness after another. Please, just go."

She shook her head vehemently. She stepped closer and gripped the bars. "No. Not until you are free."

He might have anticipated something like this. Her sense of drama had been engaged. "You have to join your great-aunts. There should be enough money left of that boxing purse to pay for a train ticket."

"It's not my money, it's yours."

"I cannot believe that you of all people are sticking at that."

At least she had the grace to blush.

"I won't touch a *sou* of that money, Lucy. Not one *sou*. So you can throw it in the river, give it to the town drunk, or pay the hotel bill. I personally recommend the last option, seeing how the French seem radically opposed to people not paying their hotel bills."

Her blush grew brighter. "Fine. But I still can't leave you here like this."

"Like what? I'm hardly doing hard labor, Lucy. Look, they've telegrammed my family's lawyer and he's sent word he'll be here Monday. I should be in front of the judge by midweek. If I am lucky, he will allow me to repay what is owed along with whatever fine he deems appropriate and then let me return to London."

"Midweek?" she exclaimed in horror. "That's not fair. If anyone should be behind bars it should be me."

"Doubtless true, but probably in another sort of facility. One with inmates rather than prisoners."

"Now, that is simply unkind."

His anger faded. "You're right. It isn't you who put their life's work at risk for a rash and ill-considered scheme. Perhaps I should look into renting a room at one of those barred establishments myself when I get back to England."

At this, she went still. "What do you mean, your life's work at risk?"

He sighed and dropped down on the bunk, his forearms resting on his thighs, his head bowed tiredly.

"Archie? What do you mean?"

He looked up, vexed by her heedlessness. "As hard as it is to imagine—and I concede that judging from my recent activities it may be damn near impossible—I am a well-respected scholar. Some people, like my fellow professors, students, and research colleagues, actually look up to me. Not to mention the directors and trustees at St. Phillip's where I am employed." He paused, considered his last words. "But perhaps I should say *was* employed."

She stared at him, stricken. "But Archie, surely once you explain—"

"Have you ever heard of St. Phillip's, Lucy?" he broke in conversationally. "It is a very old, very conservative college with a very old, very conservative board of directors.

"They are vigilant in squelching any threats, real or imagined, to the college's reputation for dignity and rectitude. What do you imagine their reaction will be when they discover that the man whom they had anticipated making the director of their newly minted anthropology department has been arrested for fleeing a foreign hotel with an unknown woman in the dead of night in order to avoid paying his bill?"

"They wouldn't like it?" she asked in a small voice.

He nodded thoughtfully. "No, I daresay they wouldn't." He tipped his head, regarding her. "Do you suppose they will still offer me the directorship of the department?"

She shook her head.

"No? Neither do I." He mused in silence for a few seconds; he could hear her unsteady breath.

"Which leaves only a few unanswered questions, the first being will I have a job at all when I return to England?" He met her eyes. They shimmered with tears and he reminded himself of his pledge not to be swayed by emotions.

He had spent a good part of his adolescence being extricated from one sort of trouble or another, disappointing his parents and thwarting his own aspirations. Subsequently, he'd spent an even better part of his young adulthood learning to keep his passions under control. And it had worked. Vigilant self-control had facilitated his successes. *Why* had he abandoned those hard-learned lessons? What about *her* had made him forget them?

Did it matter? Abandon them he had and look where it had got him. He might as well be fourteen again, trying to explain to the dean of students why he'd thought spelunking in the school's abandoned well had been a good idea. Only this time rather than a corporal punishment, he stood at risk of losing his life's work. The only thing that ever mattered to him, the only thing that had garnered him respect while still allowing him to do something he relished.

No, he would not be led by impulse and emotion again. Not his, God help him, not even by hers. They only led to imminent destruction. Hadn't that been his life's early lesson?

So now, he looked her dead in the eye and asked her, "Well, Lucy, what do you think? Will I have a job? Is my career effectively over? The career you once took pains to point out that I loved?"

At the barely sustained amiability in his voice, she broke down. Tears spilled from her eyes and trailed down her cheeks. Her hands gripped the bars so tightly her knuckles shone white. "Oh, Archie, I am sorry! I am so, so sorry. Maybe if I talk to your directors, I am sure I can make them understand—"

"Oh, no. No. For *God's* sake, no. I beg you, spare me your help."

"But—"

"*No*. Can you *at least* do this one thing for me?"

Her lips trembled but after a second she nodded miserably. "All right. But you must believe me, Archie, when I tell you that I never meant any of this to happen. I swear I would never have—I wasn't thinking—"

"Exactly!" Even to his own ears, the word came out with whiplash cruelty. He saw her flinch but still could not stop the words from coming. All his frustration, his sense of betrayal, his outrage and confusion came pouring out, demanding to be heard. "You were *not thinking*. What the hell *were* you doing, Lucy?"

"Why in God's name would you steal my wallet and then convince me to take off in the middle of the night leaving a bill, a bill I could have paid, behind? I'm not blaming you solely for that part. I could have said no. I didn't and that responsibility falls squarely on me, but I need to understand why you would take my money. Why would you risk a virtual stranger's entire life work like that?"

She paled. Her hands fell limply to her sides. "Stranger?"

"Yes," he said, his anger carrying him along while, inside, alarms were clanging madly. "What else would you call someone you didn't know existed a month earlier?"

Which really wasn't what he wanted to know at all. But he charged on, bent on getting an answer to his question. *The* question. "Was it simply a lark? On a whim? What? *Why?*"

Her head drooped, a flower too heavy for its slender stalk.

"Did you ever stop to consider the risks? Not to me—clearly I didn't rate that sort of consideration—but to your great-aunts? Lavinia stood a very real chance of not arriving in Saint-Girons by the proscribed date. If it hadn't been for this friend of yours—"

The friend. The man to whom she'd entrusted her great-aunts so she could play havoc with his life. "Who is he? How could you play so fast and loose with your great-aunts' future?" He plowed his fingers through his hair, trying to make sense of it.

"No," she said tragically. "*No.* I would never have let it get to that point. I swear it. If things got too tight I would have—"

"Would have what? Suddenly 'found' my wallet? You may think I'm dense, Lucy, and heaven knows I've provided ample evidence to support that idea, but even I am not as gullible as that."

"No." She sniffed. The tears were still streaming down her cheeks. She made no effort to wipe them away and against all reason he found his hand twitching to do just that. "No, I would have told you what I'd done."

"Really? You mean as in told the truth? No fabrication, none of your stories?"

"I'm not sure."

He turned away from her with a sound of disgust. "Well, there's an honest answer at last."

"Monsieur, please. How can you treat the girl so? You are breaking her heart!" exclaimed the young socialist.

"Shut up," Archie said tiredly. He was drained, wrung dry, nothing left in him to give, neither anger nor understanding.

"I thought I knew exactly what I risked," he heard her say softly.

"Then why?" he asked the wall, not really expecting an answer.

"I did it because I'd fallen in love with you."

Something deep inside of him leapt at the soft declaration, like a deeply buried ember, uncovered by a thready, chance wind and blown to life. A small warmth seeped through the chill engulfing him.

No. No more burning and glowing for him. Ruthlessly, he forced himself to view her words as the delusional, romantic fantasy they were.

"That's ridiculous. People don't fall in love at first sight."

She laughed a little at this, forlornly, sounding much older, much more worldly than him.

"Of course they do. They do it all the time. Why, my grandparents fell in love after one dance. Lavinia fell in love with your grandfather within days of meeting him.

"But I knew you wouldn't believe that. So I tried to buy us some time, so you might realize that you were in love with me, too."

"In love with you?"

She nodded somberly.

"I don't *know* you!"

"Yes, you do." She sounded so certain, so sure of herself, and he reacted against her conviction because it threatened everything he'd been taught to believe.

"No. I *know* Cornelia. I *know* my grandfather. My parents. My brothers and sisters. Not you.

"And as for love? Love doesn't pounce on you like some overly friendly puppy or catch you unsuspecting when your resistance is down like a bad head cold. It's a process. It comes from a slow discovery, from the security of knowing how someone is going to react or what they are going to say, to shared ambitions and a common base of experiences. And from trust. *Trust*, Lucy. As in not lying to another person or manipulating them or playing havoc with their lives . . ."

He closed his eyes, the sight of her anguish acutely painful even though the scientist in him affirmed what he said as true, firmly grounded in good sound reasoning.

"I see," he heard her murmur.

And when he opened his eyes again, she was gone.

CHAPTER

35

The nine o'clock a.m. train from Châtellerault climbed into the Pyrenees foothills rocking gently, the rhythmic sound of the steel wheels against the rails singing a lullaby. Most of the passengers had disembarked earlier, leaving only a handful bound for the route's end point, Saint-Girons. Lucy was among them. But while the thin-haired old man in the cheap new suit across from her snored gently, sleep eluded Lucy.

She had telegrammed the Bergerac hotel, which Margery named in the note the fat innkeeper in Châtellerault had held for Lucy, and received a reassuring message in return. Having grown fond of her great-aunts but also because he simply *had* to satisfy his curiosity about how this particular chapter of their story would end, he'd arranged for the Misses Litton and himself to travel on to Saint-Girons. They would meet Lucy there. And where in the name of mercy had she been?

She had stayed an additional day in Châtellerault to buy a decent set of ready-mades, using the money left over from the boxing purse Archie had refused. She left her raggedy skirt and jumper in the fire grate of the hotel. The next day she had returned to the town jail, only to be informed that Archie refused to see her. She did not try to bribe the guard again. She could not see any good in forcing herself on Archie. So, with no other recourse, she had done as he'd bid her and bought a ticket to Saint-Girons.

Now, she stared hollow-eyed at the passing scenery. Once Lucy would have delighted in the sight of shepherds whistling up their sleek-coated dogs to herd fat, fluffy sheep along the mountainside; or the snow-covered shoulders of the great peaks looming ahead; or the charming chatter of the Basque ladies who for a short while shared her compartment and plied her with cheese sandwiches they pulled from the baskets at their feet.

But those pleasures belonged to another Lucy, a Lucy who had not ruined the life of the man she loved and did not carry that incontrovertible knowledge with her every waking moment, along with the devastating recognition that nothing she could do or say could set it right. She had robbed Archie of the one thing that he'd kept for himself, the one passion he had allowed himself. That knowledge plagued her even more than having lost any hope of a future together.

Because she loved him. She loved him and yet she had hurt him in a way that would echo throughout his life and she could not forgive herself that, for not foreseeing the ramifications of her actions.

She couldn't even console herself with the age-old excuse that she was in love and she wasn't thinking. Because wasn't loving someone, really *loving* someone, actually thinking *more*? Wasn't it putting another's best interests ahead of your own, making their happiness your priority? She hadn't. And now, when it was too late, she realized she should have. If she only had the chance to go back and make different decisions, she would. She would make better choices.

A sad smile flickered across her face. She had been so arrogantly certain Lavinia had erred in not pursuing her English lord, that emotional cowardice had robbed her of a happily-ever-after. But perhaps Lavinia had been right. Perhaps blind pursuit of one's heart desire only left collateral damage behind. At least Lavinia had not ruined Lord Barton's life.

Her spine straightened with a burgeoning sense of resolve. As soon as she returned to London she would go to St. Phillip's and explain to the trustees—no. She would only make it worse. Her shoulders slumped. There was *nothing* she could do to make amends or atone. She would simply have to bear her guilt. All she could do by way of reparation was to stay out of Archie's life.

"Mademoiselle?" The conductor appeared in the doorway. "We will be arriving soon."

She nodded. When he slid the door closed again, she wearily rummaged through her purse for her small, mirrored compact and opened it, studying her face. She sighed and tried on a smile. She would have to do better than that.

It was time to don another mask for another role, rehearse the lines for a new act in a new show, this one about a happy-go-lucky niece who finished an amusing but grueling set of misadventures just in time to find her great-aunts before the triumphant climax of their story.

How odd, she realized, that Bernice and Lavinia did not even know Archie had been with her. There was no reason they ever should. A few fabrications, a little evasion, and perhaps a small head cold to explain the red-trimmed eyes and the dark circles beneath them, and they would be satisfied. She was good at manufacturing a role for a discriminating audience. The only person she had never fooled, who had known what she contrived and what was truth, had been Archie.

Except for once.

The train whistle blew, signaling the approach to the tiny mountain station. The old man across from her woke with a start and smacked his lips loudly. He leaned forward eagerly to peer out the window.

Smoke billowed up from beneath the carriage as the engineer applied the brakes. When it cleared she saw a small, neat building separated from the tracks by a broad platform. The door to the station opened and a passel of children streamed out, faces bright with excitement and welcome.

The old man stood up and yanked down the carriage window, hanging his upper torso outside and waving his hat gaily as the children gathered beneath shouting, "*Grand-pere! Bienvenue chez vous!*"

Their mutual joy in the reunion was palpable. Lucy could not help but smile, then her gaze moved beyond the family scene to the station doorway and the two elderly ladies anxiously scanning the train's compartments. They saw her and their faces bloomed with relief.

They must never know what had transpired. It would only worry and sadden them. She must keep it close, her own personal siege of Patnimba, but one never to be shared.

The train stopped and Lucy stood up.

It was showtime.

"I did not worry for an instant!" exclaimed Bernice. "Not a second. I knew you would prove up to any challenge." She said this last a shade too heartily, which led Lucy to conclude that she had in actuality worried a great deal. Poor Bernice, she lied so poorly. Perhaps Lucy should offer her lessons?

She rejected the bitter thought. She would not be bitter. Bitterness was the dubious preserve of those who had been wronged, not those who had wronged others.

"Nor I," Lavinia said, coming forward and clasping Lucy's hands tightly in hers, then pulling her in and pressing her cheek to hers, surprising Lucy. Lavinia was not generally given to shows of emotion. "My main concern was about our taking your luggage with us and leaving you without any clothing."

"I'm afraid it was a matter of make-do," Lucy said brightly. She could do this. Act Three, Scene One: Juvenile girl engages in small talk with elderly aunt prefatory to arrival of principal performers. "Not at all your situation, I can see," she said admiringly. Lavinia looked lovely in a beautiful suit of gray and navy-blue striped wool. "I don't recall ever seeing this. Is it a recent purchase?"

Lavinia's thin cheeks pinked up becomingly. "No. It is on loan from Mrs. Martin. She has been advising me."

"You could not have a better guide," Lucy said sincerely. There was something different about Lavinia, even aside from the new clothes and the soft chignon tucked beneath an elaborate hat. She exuded an air of newly found confidence. *Feminine* confidence.

"She has been delightful company, Lucy," Bernice put in. "We have had a marvelous time. Not as marvelous as if you had been with us, of course," she hastily added.

Nope. No talent for lying at all.

And now that she looked at Bernice, she noted small changes about her, too, and not only the saucy red toque. Lucy tended to think of Bernice as the mouse that roared: timid in public, but perhaps a wee bit strong-willed behind closed doors. But today she seemed both more relaxed and more animated, with a lively and appealing energy.

"Really?" she said. "Tell me about it."

Bernice beamed. "Oh, the adventures I've had! Why, I actually bought a little trinket from a Gypsy." She leaned forward. "She told my fortune."

"Bernice!" Lavinia exclaimed, scandalized. It was a good thing Lavinia would never know about her sojourn; if the thought of a little ball-gazing scandalized her she'd probably die of mortification if she learned her great-niece had spent two days as the chief attraction in some Gypsies' nightly performance.

Amazingly, rather than looking chastised, Bernice simply lifted her shoulders dismissively.

"And what did the Gypsy say?" Lucy asked.

"That I would take a long trip," Bernice said softly, her face aglow with pleasure, her gaze already fixed on some distant horizon.

"Aunt Bernice," Lucy exclaimed. "I never knew you wanted to travel."

"Oh, *always*. Though I must admit that Lavinia's single experience with overseas travel rather put me off the mark for quite a few years. But after our trip here I am feeling quite intrepid."

"You mean all those the *National Geographic* magazines were wish lists of a sort? And here I just thought you liked to read."

"Me, too," Lavinia piped in. "You always seemed so content to stay at Robin's Hall."

Bernice tipped her head. "Well, I don't see as I had any choice, did I?" she said without rancor. "I mean, we hadn't the wherewithal for anyone to go anywhere, so why bring it up?"

"To share your dreams?" Lucy offered gently.

Bernice smiled. "Sharing dreams is for young people and lovers, and rightfully so. You share dreams to validate them with those whose opinions you respect, or to compare and examine them though another's eyes, to see if others' dreams might be more enticing and worth adopting. Or, in the case of potential lovers, to discover if you are compatible and whether your future hopes and goals align.

"But once you reach a certain age, you don't need to examine the validity of a dream. You know it to the very core of you."

Lucy's heart leapt in recognition. "Or who," she said softly.

Bernice eyed her curiously. "Yes, well, we were talking about dreams. A person is not a dream. A person is an exquisitely complicated assembly of fears and hopes, strengths and weaknesses. Why, even a beloved sister can never fully understand what a sibling has endured or"—she glanced fondly at Lavinia—"wants. Romantic relationships are a little too much work for me, I'm afraid." She spoke with no visible regret.

When had Bernice become so astute? Or perhaps she had always been so and Lucy had simply not been listening carefully enough. Perhaps she, too, had changed, at least enough to know wisdom when she heard it.

"Darling girl!" A voice hailed her.

She turned and her eyes went wide as she spied Margery striding across the platform. Except this was Margery dressed as a man, in a smart cashmere coat, leather driving gloves, and bowler hat.

"Oh, the look on your face! Priceless!" he said. "I am sorry," he said, then immediately recanted, "No, I'm not. You know I have never been able to resist making an entrance."

He grabbed her by the shoulders and pulled her toward him to whisper in her ear. "Sweetie, where the *hell* have you been? And who is this man you've been gallivanting about with? Now, don't worry. The great-aunties know nothing about him. I covered for you. But darling, I must say, I am *so* impressed! I didn't think you had it in you!"

He pushed her away to his arm's length, looking her up and down and beaming benevolently. Lucy didn't know whether to be more surprised that Margery knew about Archie, or that her great-aunts knew about *him*.

"But, how . . . I mean . . . when . . ."

He turned toward Lavinia and Bernice, wagging a finger at them. "They are too cunning by half. I don't doubt they suspected right from the start."

"But we didn't!" denied Lavinia. "The verisimilitude of your impression is in every manner convincing. I would never have known but for the innkeeper in Châtellerault." She turned to Lucy. "The fellow was fortunate enough to have seen Mr. Martin's show the previous evening and congratulated him on his performance in the morning. But he used the masculine pronoun in reference to Mr. Martin.

"Now, I may not have spoken French in fifty years but I was always rather good at it. An aptitude we were always sad you did not inherit. All that money to Madame de Barge." She shook her head. Bernice clucked her tongue sympathetically. Lucy felt heat rise in her face.

"But that's of no matter now. After I heard the innkeeper's comments, well, certain things became, if not apparent, at least noticeable, to one who had cause to look."

"The damned Adam's apple," Margery said sadly. "I should have never removed my scarf."

"But," Lucy said, her gaze moving between her great-aunts, "you weren't . . . offended? Distressed? Affronted?"

"By Mr. Martin's willingness to remain in female character despite undoubted personal discomfort and only in order to make himself a more acceptable companion to two maiden ladies? I should hope we could never be so ungrateful. I think I might be rather offended you even think it possible."

"I'm sorry," Lucy said, feeling disoriented. If she had a propensity for the unexpected, she apparently came by it naturally.

"Really. It was no problem," Margery said modestly. "Besides, it was an excellent opportunity to hone my craft."

"And now that we know his gender, there's no reason we shouldn't attend his show in Toulouse," Bernice proclaimed.

"Toulouse?"

"Yes, we thought that after our business here was finished we might go with Mr. Martin to Toulouse where his next performance is scheduled. You did suggest we make a holiday of our excursion, didn't you? I mean, if that's all right with you?"

Why not? It wasn't as if there was anything, or anyone, waiting for her England.

"It sounds delightful," she said.

CHAPTER
36

The only other occupants of Saint-Girons Inn's public taproom sat at the bar, well away from the table where Margery and Lucy sat, allowing as private a conversation as possible.

"And the old man with the suspiciously black hair sitting at the bar alongside a handsome middle-aged woman is Bento Oliveria and his wife. I suspect that particular marriage was predicated on his eventually taking possession of his share of the rubies."

"Why would you say such a thing?" Lucy asked, taking a sip of the aperitif Margery had ordered for her.

"She has the look of one whose ship has finally come in after a long, long, long voyage. And see what an eagle eye she keeps on how much he is drinking? She won't have him dropping dead hours before that ship makes port, so to speak."

"You're awful."

"I'm a pragmatist. And the old gasser bending his ear and plying Bento with drinks? That is Luis Silva, the other surviving member." He nodded at a small, energetic-looking man in a flamboyant cape and slouch hat. "Everyone is here for the big reveal tomorrow afternoon."

He rubbed his hands together. "I can hardly wait to clamp eyes on those rubies. Lavinia is not given to exaggeration and from what she described I daresay she will be swimming in gravy by this time tomorrow."

"*Lavinia?*" she echoed, startled.

"Oh, yes. We are all quite chummy." He nodded, correctly reading her expression. "I *know*. Rather amazing. But then, people are always surprising, aren't they? You imagine the worst and then they surprise you with unexpected generosity.

"I admit that if I had been told the old girls would tumble to my being a man I would have guessed they'd be appalled. But they were quite accepting of it, even sanguine. Especially Bernie, who is filled with questions—though, as you would expect, none of a personal or indelicate nature." He smiled. "But enough about me. Who is this man, Lucy? I insist you tell me."

She could say, "What man?" but Margery would not believe her and she didn't have any faith at all in his ability, or interest, in taking a hint that she'd rather not discuss it. Not only was he a confirmed gossip, he sincerely believed that anything having to do with anyone of whom he was fond was categorically and indisputably his business. It was a trait that either charmed or irritated depending on one's mood and what secret he was intent on prizing out. Why fight it?

"Arch—Ptolemy Grant. Professor Ptolemy Grant."

"Grant." He frowned. "Where do I know that name?"

"He's the grandson of one of the original members of the tontine, Lord Barton."

"Not *Lavinia's* Lord Barton?"

"Lavinia told you about Lord Barton?" Lavinia hadn't revealed his name to Lucy until she'd been sixteen and now she was divulging her lifelong secrets to a relative stranger? As soon as the thought was completed, she realized its error. Of course, Lavinia and Margery could form a deep and abiding friendship in a matter of days.

Hadn't she fallen in love?

"Oh, yes. Livie and I had quite a few girlish confabs before she realized I wasn't a girl. She's quite an interesting woman, your great-aunt. And quite a stunner. Not in the accepted mode, of course, but it's been scads of fun teasing out her long-ignored vanity.

"She's something of a clotheshorse, you know, and is finding it all sorts of fun to know she is the object of men's admiring glances—though would die before she would admit such."

"Lavinia?"

Margery nodded. "But she's not half as interesting as Bernice who, while not as elegant, is twice as naughty and you know how I love the naughty ones. She's got the heart of an adventurer. As a matter of fact, I do think she means to go to Egypt this winter. She wants me to go with her and damned if I mightn't just." He looked pleasantly surprised by the notion until he caught her smile. "Oh, no you don't. You shan't sidetrack me. Back to your young man. What does he look like?"

"First, he's not mine, and second, you've seen him."

"I have? When?"

"At the Savoy earlier this month. He was the fellow whose pen you nipped."

His eyes widened. "Say not so? The gorgeous black-eyed brute in the fabulously cut tuxedo?"

She nodded miserably.

"Well, if he's not yours why the *hell* not?"

"Because I scotched it, Margery. I made him loathe me."

Margery, bless him, scoffed. "My darling girl, I doubt you have the wherewithal to make anyone loathe you."

"No. I mean it. I ruined his life."

"Ah, I see."

"I did."

"Or so you think now." Margery sighed. "I can't tell you how many lives I've 'ruined' only to years later encounter the individual and discover they had been pottering along as happy as a pig in a peach orchard without me. The truth is few people are *ruined* because they are turned down. Thank God." He lifted his glass in salute then took a long drink.

She took a deep breath. "I didn't turn him down."

"Oh?" He looked at her over the rim of his glass. His eyes widened. "Ohhhhh."

"I *pray* he does potter happily along but I doubt he can or will because it's not losing me that's ruined his life—he made it very clear that he was quite looking forward to that prospect."

"The bounder!" Margery breathed, slamming down his drink and sending the liquor sloshing onto the table. "Look here, Lucy. I'm not the dueling-pistols-at-dawn sort. Or even the fisticuffs in the alley." He shuddered. "But I know quite a lot of people and some of them are that latter type and if you'd like—"

"No! Good heavens, Margery, I don't want him hurt. I love him! And he hasn't done anything wrong. Were I in his position I'd wish to be well rid of me, too."

"What did you do?" Margery asked worriedly.

"I . . . I got him into a bit of a fix. I . . . there was this situation. I sort of orchestrated a plan that had . . . Aw, hell. I got him arrested."

This apparently was not enough to sway Margery's opinion that she was the offended party. He was a loyal, if not particularly discriminating, friend.

"So now, not only is it very likely he will lose the appointment he's being nominated for, the head of an entire new department at his college, but almost as likely that he will lose his position at the college altogether."

He straightened to protest but then, upon seeing her expression, drooped. "Oh, Lucy."

Tears started in her eyes. And here she'd thought she had none left. "I know."

"And you love him, you say?"

"Oh, Margery, so very much."

"I'm sorry."

For a long moment they communed in silence. "Have you ever been in love? I mean, really deeply in love?" she finally asked.

"Yes. Once."

"Did you ever get over it?"

"I learned to live with it."

"Do you wish you hadn't fallen in love?"

"Oh, no," he said at once. "No. No, my dear. Never. Those were the very best months of my life."

"What happened?" It said much about Margery's friendship that he did not hesitate in answering. When asked about his history by either acquaintances or the press, he always gave a pat and unrevealing answer: he'd say he was exactly what he appeared to be—or not. Then he'd laugh. It generally served to stopper any more questions.

Lucy had never asked. She figured he'd tell her whatever he wanted her to know.

"I was young. I had only just begun to achieve acclaim for my impersonations. We met at a party. I would like to say we fell in love all at once, but it took time. We kept running into one another at mutual friends' homes, various parties, that sort of thing. Somehow, we always ended up together, laughing and sharing jokes, eventually trading dreams. Canny Bernice scored a hit about that.

"And had much in common. We both loved music, word play, fashion, good food, and good company. A match made in heaven, you might say." His gaze was fixed on his hands folded on the tabletop in front of him, his voice soft and poignant.

"But you couldn't marry."

"Couldn't?" He looked up. "*Wouldn't*. How could I ask her to marry me knowing what her life would be like wed to a female impersonator and *why* do people always look like that whenever I reveal that I am interested in girls? And *only* girls. You'd think I'd just grown another head."

"I . . . I . . . I," she stuttered.

He waved her down. "Oh, calm down. I'm having a bit of sport. It's not as if I don't know what people think. But yes, my beloved was a young lady, a bit of a *bon vivant*, but from a very respectable family. We talked about the possibility of marrying, but we both knew it would never take. She might put up with the sniggers but she could never expose her children, *our* children, to all the ugliness of which people are capable. Thankfully, the vast majority of people are like your great-aunts, but those few others always seem to be the most vocal, don't they?"

"Did you ever consider not . . . doing what you do?"

"You mean take infrequent male roles, singing an octave below my natural voice in inferior productions for a tenth of the pay?" He snorted.

"For about a day, but that same night she arrived to go to one of our last dinners together. She wore a sable cape and a parure of pearls and diamonds, and I realized that we both enjoyed rarified air too much. I don't know that we would breath as easily in lesser climes.

"And, too, I love what I do, Lucy." Her chest constricted at the familiar words, words Archie had spoken to her on Sark. "I love the saucy humor and the dresses, the applause and the music, the wink and the nod . . . all of it. Give up Marjorie with her flamboyance, her *joi de vive* and sophistication, for Jasper Martin, unlisted so-so tenor in knickers? I don't think so."

"Do you ever regret your decision?" she asked thinking of Archie. "Do you ever wish you had chosen . . . love?"

"But I did," Margery said. "I chose the real love of my life, my career. And while she's a bitch of a mistress, we've been happy together."

CHAPTER

37

The gendarme opened the door to Archie's cell and jerked his head in the direction of the corridor. "Time to go."

Relieved at not being required to listen to another rambling dissertation on the coming revolution by his young fellow inmate, Archie leapt to his feet. "Where?"

"Wherever you wish, my friend, as long as you appear on Monday. But for the time being you are being released on your own recognizance."

Having recently learned from an exemplary teacher not to look a gift horse in the mouth, he snatched up his jacket and followed the gendarme, offering his erstwhile companion a somewhat ironic, "Long live the revolution," on his way past the boy's cell.

"*Adieu, mon frère!*" the boy called out fervently, assuming he had recruited Archie to his glorious cause.

The only cause Archie had right now was apologizing to Lucy.

He'd been furious when she'd come to see him, locked in on what he saw as a betrayal of trust. He'd known even as he'd made the accusation that she hadn't meant to ruin his life on a lark. She hadn't a frivolous bone in her body. Odd, outspoken, exuberant, joyful, whimsical bones, but not frivolous. A girl as young as she was when she took over the physical and financial care of two elderly great-aunts could hardly be accused of irresponsibility.

No, she had meant to woo him. In her own weird, unsettling way she had simply been courting him and he'd been too stupid to realize it.

The gendarme opened the door leading into the police station's main room and stepped aside.

If he only could—

Cornelia Litchfield stood beside the captain's desk, flanked by his family's middle-aged lawyer, Oliver Tuttiddle, and Lionel Underwood. Her gaze raked him up and down and found him wanting. "Oh, Ptolemy. Look at you."

"What are you doing here?"

"I am here in an unofficial capacity, acting on behalf of St. Phillip's."

"How did you find out?" he asked, confounded.

"I went to your grandfather's house to discover your whereabouts. Lord Blidderphenk has moved up the dates he will be interviewing the candidates and I knew you would want to return to London immediately in order to prepare. When I arrived at Lord Barton's house he had just received the telegram saying you'd been arrested." She frowned a little. "I must say he was most forthcoming about it all. In fact, I had the distinct notion he took pleasure in showing it to me."

Archie just bet he had.

"Anyway, of course, I immediately went to Father. He was apoplectic. As your chief sponsor with the chancellor and Lord Blidderphenk, your actions reflect directly on him. He would be a laughingstock if this got out. I convinced him you must have suffered from some sort of fit and persuaded him I was the best person to fetch you and see if I could make this all disappear." She looked about the tiny police office with a grimace of distaste.

"*You* bailed me out?"

"Yes. Not only bailed you out, but I am in negotiations with the judge to have all charges against you dropped."

Archie narrowed his eyes on Tuttiddle. "Then what are you doing?"

"Your grandfather sent me."

"Never mind him, Ptolemy. You only need to stand before the judge on Monday and apologize. Say you were sadly influenced by the bad company you'd fallen in with—"

"Bad company?"

Her lips pursed into a tight line of exasperation. "This girl you were chasing about with, Ptolemy. This *actress*." There was no hurt in her eyes, just exasperation and a sort of long-suffering acceptance. In the same situation, he couldn't imagine Lucy reacting in any way but passionately. Passionately angry.

"Why are you smiling?"

"Was I?"

"Yes. And I must say, Ptolemy, it indicates a decided lack of sobriety. A decided lack. Doesn't it, Lionel?"

Lionel, silently standing in the background wearing an odd expression that somehow managed to convey both glee and disillusion, gave a curt nod.

"What is *he* doing here?"

"He is here to provide the benefit of his sound advice."

"Advice about what?"

Once more he'd exasperated her. "Whatever comes up. What is wrong with you, Ptolemy?"

"Sorry."

She sniffed. "After you apologize to the judge, should anyone look into the matter of your arrest, they would only find out that a rural French policeman had made a mistake and that the case had been summarily dismissed."

"But he didn't."

"Ptolemy. Please. What does that matter? You are this close"—she lowered her voice and raised an elegantly gloved hand, holding her forefinger and thumb a half inch apart—"to losing the Blidderphenk professorship. Do you understand that? Now, can we *please* leave this place?"

Though they'd been conversing in English, the police captain had been watching the exchange from his chair with avid interest. But at Cornelia's words he got heavily to his feet. "I agree. Fascinating as this has been, I would like to enjoy my breakfast in peace. Until Monday."

Cornelia either didn't have the grace or the imagination to look embarrassed. With a regal tilt of her head, she led the way out of the office, Lionel springing forward to open the door for her.

"Why is it that you are here, Lionel?" Archie asked, abruptly stopping at the bottom of the steps.

"To, ahem, to support Miss Litchfield." He turned brick red.

My God, why hadn't he seen it before? "Ahuh."

He turned to the lawyer. "And have you earned even a penny of the fee you are undoubtedly charging by the hour, Tuttiddle?"

"Miss Litchfield has arranged matters so adroitly there hasn't been any need for me to step in," the lawyer said admiringly. "Though I will, of course, be submitting my bill based on time I've made myself accessible."

Cornelia sighed heavily. "If there isn't anything else, I'd like to remove to the hotel."

"There is something else," said Archie. "Did you read the telegram I sent?"

She raised her eyes heavenward. "Yes. I didn't pay it much attention. All you did was rhapsodize about the world being too magnificent or fascinating or some such thing to explore from behind a desk and that you thought you ought to withdraw from consideration for the Blidderphenk professorship."

"What did you think?"

She stopped walking and spun around and now, finally, there was a flash of real anger in her fine, blue eyes. "Honestly?"

"Yes."

"I thought it self-indulgent nonsense. It might have been written by some overly sentimental, quixotic and impetuous *boy*. It was . . . off-putting."

He stared at her, feeling as though someone had just shown him the obvious answer to a problem he'd thought impossible to solve. "Then why did you come?" he asked, though he thought he already knew the answer.

She scowled.

"I already told you," she said, "Father's reputation." It took a few heartbeats for her to remember to add, "as well as your career."

He'd been right. He wanted to kiss her.

"Despite everything, Ptolemy, I assume you will act rationally once you've returned home."

Home? Yes. He needed to go home.

"Now, are you coming or not?" she asked, clearly having had enough of the conversation.

"Yes, yes. Of course. What time is it?"

She looked at her wristwatch. "It's eight thirty."

He started past her and heard her release a sigh of relief. But once in front of the hotel he didn't enter, he kept walking right past it. Cornelia scurried to catch up. "Where are you going?"

"I'm going to buy a train ticket."

"We don't need to do that now. We can purchase them on Monday."

"I won't be here Monday."

"What? Are you mad?"

"Possibly."

Now, for the first time, she looked truly bewildered and maybe a little frightened; no, more like unnerved, like the world was turning upside down and she hadn't even known it was tilting. He knew the feeling. Luckily, Lionel would be there to catch her. Still, Archie was fond of her. She'd have made a crackerjack Blidderphenk professor.

He turned and came back to her, taking one of her hands between both of his. It lay there limply as she stared up at him. "Dear Cornelia. I can't thank you enough for helping me understand."

"Understand what?"

"That I'm an overly romantic, quixotic, impetuous man. Or should be."

"Ptolemy, listen to yourself. *Look* at yourself." She pointed to his reflection in the window of the store they'd stopped in front of. "Disheveled and unshaven and wild-eyed. I swear I don't recognize you!"

He didn't need to look. He knew what he'd see. "I know. That's the problem, isn't it? That, and that for the first time since I was lad I finally recognize myself.

"This is who I am and I like this person a good deal more than the one you think so highly of. Too highly, truth be told. I would have made an awful Blidderphenk professor and I'm definitely not someone you'd want to marry."

"*Marry?*" she stammered. "I would not presume—"

"I know, God bless you. Be happy, Cornelia." He looked beyond Cornelia to where Lionel stood shuffling, looking decidedly dog-in-the-mangerish. "*Bon chance*, Lionel."

He grabbed Cornelia by the shoulders and pulled her close, bussing her soundly on the cheek. "Thank you."

"For what?" she asked, startled.

"For *not* recognizing me," he said and started past her.

"But where are you going?" she called after him. "What about the judge?"

"I'm afraid he'll have to wait for his apology. I'm going home."

CHAPTER
38

Saint-Girons's only bank had a small, windowless anteroom furnished with a round table and leather-upholstered chairs reserved for the use of its clients, should they feel the need for privacy in their financial dealings with bank officials. Around this table now sat three of the four surviving members of the siege of Patnimba and Bernard DuPaul, Junior, the son and namesake of the now deceased banker who'd inherited the task set before them from his father.

Sitting a little distance from the table, along the perimeter of the room, was a gallery of relatives. They had been adjured by Monsieur DuPaul to bear in mind the solemnity of the proceedings, a comment occasioned by Señora Oliveria's squeal of delight upon seeing the size of the pouch the security guard had brought in and set in the center of the table.

Lucy sat between Margery and Bernice. Their interest had long since begun to wane. In fact, Margery had dozed off a half hour earlier and was snoring gently. They had been sequestered in this room all afternoon as various lawyers and bank officials brought in stacks of legal documents to be explained and signed. They'd been there so long, in fact, that afternoon tea had been brought in through the discreetly curtained door leading to the bank's public areas. But now, finally, the grand finale was in sight.

"Let me summarize," said Monsieur DuPaul in perfectly accented English. It turned out he had been attached to a French bank in London for decades, only returning to France to retire after his father had died. "As you have already been informed, the individual stones have been assessed by four of France's most reputable gemologists. After conferring with one another they have assigned a value to each.

"As agreed upon, my bank is going to arrange for the immediate sale of the stones. After the deduction of our nominal fee, the money realized will be divided into four equal shares, two of which, of course, will be assigned to Miss Litton. Earlier today, in anticipation of this sale, a sum of roughly one hundred thousand English pounds was deposited into individual accounts in your names."

Señora Oliveria stifled another giggle.

"Now I imagine you would like to see the gems."

"I don't suppose it much matters," said Lavinia, looking from one to the other of her fellow siege survivors.

"Not really. But I should like to see if my memory holds up to the reality," Señor Silva said. Oliveria nodded.

Lucy nudged Margery in the ribs. "Wake up. It's the final act."

Margery shifted upright in his seat as DuPaul carefully untied the leather pouch and then, with an unexpected touch of showmanship, upended it. Beneath the soft illumination of old-fashioned gaslight dozens of rubies spilled out in a glimmering cascade, a crimson Milky Way winking and sparkling across the deep blue baize-lined table.

"Voila!"

The only sounds were hushed gasps followed by a long moment of silence.

"Yes," Señor Silva said. "That's pretty much how I remembered them." He rose heavily to his feet, aided by a quick helping hand from a grandson who jumped forward from his chair, and looked around. "Mesdames et Messieurs, let us adjoin to the tavern. The drinks are on me!"

Light, excited laughter and agreement answered his invitation as all those in attendance, including Bernice and Margery, rose and followed Señor Silva. Bernard DuPaul began carefully counting the rubies into piles of ten with a flat silver wand. Lavinia was the last to get up, her gaze soft in reflection. Lucy waited for her near the curtains.

As he saw Lavinia rise, DuPaul paused. "But, Miss Litton, surely you'll want the letter."

She regarded him quizzically. "Letter? What letter?"

"I thought you knew. There's a letter in here, too, addressed to you."

She sat back down. "From whom?"

"I don't know. The letter is sealed." He reached into the leather pouch and withdrew a small envelope, the excellent quality paper turned ivory with age. "I supposed you would know."

He turned it over. A strong but elegant hand had written *Miss Lavinia Litton* across the center. He rose and brought it to her, bowing as he retreated.

The color rose and fled her face in quick succession. Her hand fluttered at the base of her throat.

"What is it, Aunt Lavinia?" Lucy asked in concern.

"I'm not sure."

Having finished counting the rubies, DuPaul swept the gems back into the leather pouch. "I will leave you to your memories, Miss Litton." He nodded at Lucy. "Miss Eastlake."

Lucy waited until he was gone before taking the chair next to Lavinia. "Do you know who wrote it?"

"I believe I do. Yes."

"Would you rather just burn it?" Lucy asked. She heard the curtain move, the clerks coming to clear the dishes, no doubt. "Please wait," she called to them. "We'll just be a few minutes."

She softly touched the back of her great-aunt's hand. "Lavinia?"

Lavinia shook her head. "No. No. It's all long ago now and I'm curious." She reached for the wand DuPaul had left behind and slid it beneath the sealed flap, slicing it neatly open, and blew into the envelope. She turned it upside down. A single sheet of paper glided out. She eyed it as though it might turn into a snake and bite her. Then, taking a deep breath, she picked it up and opened it. Her gaze fell to the signature.

"I was right," she murmured. She scanned the contents quickly, a frown furrowing the space between her brows, and then she abruptly held it out toward Lucy. "I'm afraid my eyesight is not what it used to be and the light in here is fading. Would you be so kind as to read it to me?"

Doubtfully, Lucy took it. "Are you sure? It might be of a personal nature."

"It assuredly is," Lavinia replied with a gentle smile. "But it also references two very young people who no longer exist. Whatever was said to Lavinia Litton, age eighteen, no longer matters except as a point of historic interest. Rather like the geological record."

By heaven, Lucy believed her great-aunt Lavinia had just made a joke. At Lucy's expression Lavinia's smiled broadened. "There. That was just the thing. I feel quite up to hearing whatever it is that letter contains. Read on, Lucy."

So Lucy read.

My dear Miss Litton, my own Lavinia,

You cannot imagine such pleasure as I take in writing what I cannot say: that in my heart, you are and will ever be my own, my dearest, my beloved Lavinia. I write these words in the fragile hope

that someday you will read them and that in the coming years I will
be able to take some comfort in imagining that in one respect at least
I was able to speak my heart and that perhaps you heard me.

I am pledged to marry another. Craven though I know myself to
be, the longer I knew you the more reluctant I was to tell you. For a
short time I wanted to pretend that I was free and so I did but now I
must return to the future others planned for me. Ours will be a marriage arranged by our parents at our births. I cannot recall a time when
I was not aware of the identity of my future bride. She is a fine, intel-
ligent girl, also raised to expect and accept our eventual marriage and,
though there was never a question of this being a love match, I never
had cause to oppose our union.

That is, until I met you.

"What a caddish thing to do!" Lucy exclaimed.

"Not necessarily," Lavinia murmured. Her attention was fixed
upon her hands, folded together atop the blue baize table covering.
"Remember, I never gave him any reason to believe my heart had
been engaged. He would not want to presume. Go on."

My darling, compassionate, brave, and valiant Lavinia, how was
I to know that amidst the brutal carnage of this God-awful rebellion
I would encounter a heart that beat so close in unison with my own,
a mind that so easily understood and reflected my own best self, a spirit
so sublime? But I did.

How many nights have I lain awake trying desperately to find
some way out of this hellish predicament? You will never know how
close I have come, not once but a dozen times, to asking you if you
could love me and, should you say yes, of begging you to elope. But I
dared not ask you, fearing the answer. Either answer. The one would
break my heart and the other would make us pariahs. For how could

an honorable man ask you to turn your back on all you know, the people you love and who love you?

It is only this that keeps me mute, the knowledge that loving me would reduce you—though never in my eyes!—in the eyes of the world. What sort of man would I be if I asked the woman I love to sacrifice her good name for me?

"Oh, how could he?" Lucy exclaimed.

"He was doing what he thought was best. Honorable."

"But he didn't love her."

"He'd made a promise."

"How can you defend him?"

"I'm not. But that doesn't mean I don't understand. It was a different time, Lucy. A different world. We saw things very much as black and white. One's honor was inviolable." Lavinia sounded so composed, so calm. Would Lucy be so relaxed about Archie someday?

No. Never.

She read on.

So I am left with nothing but to wish you happiness, my darling, to hope that any hurt I engendered healed quickly, that someone worthy of you won your heart and made you happy. If I were a better man I would hope that you forgot me. But I am not. I hope you remembered me, infrequently but kindly, because I know every day for the rest of my life I will have thought of you.

And now, at last and forever, let me write the words I cannot say: I love you. I love you. I love you.

Lucy's head jerked up. She could have sworn that as she read his last declaration, she heard another voice softly echoing her own.

"Aunt Lavinia?" Her great-aunt had risen to her feet and was staring behind Lucy, her hands twisting before her.

She swung around. A handsome elderly man with a thick head of silvered hair and a still-firm cleft chin stood leaning heavily on a silver-headed cane. All his attention was focused on Lavinia, his expression tense but resolute.

"Lavinia?"

"Hello, John."

She was older—but then, so was he. She wore age well, with a grace and sureness he should have expected. She'd never been a beauty, but time and experience had revealed something far more appealing: her character.

"What are you doing here, John?"

"I could not help myself. I tried . . ." He trailed off in despair before straightening his spine. "I came to see if . . . if there was any hope."

She tipped her head. "Hope of what?" He would swear there was warmth in her blue-gray eyes, but was it merely the warmth of a fond recollection? Or dare he look for something more?

He took a deep breath. "A future."

"Oh, John," she murmured and sank down heavily. "Now, after all these years of silence?"

The girl, Lucy, rushed to her side, glaring at him like a young tigress prepared to eviscerate her foe.

"I have loved you for fifty years, Lavinia. I never stopped loving you. But I was married. How could I communicate with you when every word I said, no matter how mundane or trivial, would be a betrayal of my vows, for no other reason than they were spoken to you? How could I bear to see you? My love would be apparent to anyone. My wife deserved better. You deserved better.

"And after she died, I waited the requisite year before making my plans. I had left you to satisfy honor and though I could never love her, I could at least give her memory its due respect. But now I am here and what I feel for you has not changed. It has never changed."

"So you came to discover if I had feelings for you?" Lavinia asked quietly.

"Yes." Hope hushed his voice.

"Yes, John, I did."

"Did."

She smiled oddly. "We hardly know one another now, do we? We are, both of us, so much changed from the people who took refuge together in that fortress."

No. This could not be. He had anticipated this moment for so long. "Do you think people really change so much?" he asked. "Don't you still love the color pink?"

"Not really. Lavender is more flattering to a more mature woman."

He smiled at that. "But you still like Wagner."

"I like Gilbert and Sullivan better."

"Really?" the girl piped in, coloring when Lavinia shot her a quelling glance.

He held his hand out. "Why are you so determined to show yourself to be different than the girl I fell in love with?"

"Because I *am* different."

He regarded her steadily, refusing to believe there was no hope. He had spent fifty years imagining this moment and it was not at all what he'd envisioned. Poignant, tragic, passionate, ecstatic, filled with recrimination, denunciation, or declarations; they were all scenes he'd envisioned at one time or another. But not this: quieter, but richer and far more complicated.

She smiled softly and added, "As are you."

He gazed helplessly at Lavinia, uncertain where to go from here, or how. She returned his regard with complete equanimity, reminding him sharply of the girl who'd lived through five months of siege without ever losing her hope or nerve. A girl with courage and resolve, who had been sent to India because she hadn't taken with British society, but who somehow had never undervalued herself. She'd been exceptional then; she was magnificent now.

And as simply as that he understood.

"You're right. I am," he agreed. "So let us see, my darling, if these two different people we've become can fall in love. Let us build on the past. Not to re-create it, but to make something new. Please."

He held out his hand.

She took it.

CHAPTER
39

She'd been right.

What she had just witnessed turned her sad little plan on its ear and put to rest all the nonsense she'd been thinking for the last two days. Furiously, Lucy shoved her few bits of clothing into the rucksack she'd bought on the way back from the bank. Her pulse beat in time to an inner resolve.

Lord Barton had married a woman he didn't love and spent fifty years pining after the one he did. Where was the sense in that? Who'd won in that little trade? Honor? And as for Lavinia, Lucy wasn't sure if she would fare better or worse in accepting Lord Barton's long-postponed proposal.

Lucy didn't have an answer for Lavinia but she sure as shambles had one for herself. She would have been furious. Lord Barton should have told Lavinia about his fiancée and then he should have told Lavinia he loved her. He should have given her a choice in her future instead deciding for her. To hell with stiff upper lips! And to hell with maidenly dignity! Had Lucy been Lavinia she would have followed Lord Barton straight to his ancestral home and declared her love.

Which was just what she intended to do with Archie. She'd pay the guard whatever bribe he required and then she'd sit outside Archie's cell door and drone on and on and on about how much she loved him and why she had done what she had and how he must forgive her because *they belonged together*, damn it, and she was not waiting fifty years for Miss Litchfield to die in order to be with him.

So, she was right back where she had started, though having come about it from a different direction. She was not going to give Archie up without a fight. And a bloody good one, too.

Indeed, she could hardly believe she'd left Châtellerault in the first place. And why? Simply because Archie had told her to? When had she *ever* done anything simply because she'd been told to? *Never.* She'd always followed her own sound judgment and if it sometimes led her on circuitous routes, it had never yet failed to get her to her desired destination, and that place first and foremost, now and forever, would be Archie.

She set her hands on her hips and looked around the room, spied her hairbrush, and shoved it in the pack. Then she latched the satchel shut and jammed her arms through her much-abused coat then headed out the door. She looked both ways in the hall, and seeing no one who'd require an explanation, darted down the stairs and past the tavern pub where the celebration was still going strong, aided by the presence of the reunited lovers.

At the front desk, she paid her bill and asked the clerk to give her great-aunts the letter she'd written explaining where she'd gone. After one final peek into the tavern where Bernice was singing her heart out alongside fifty strangers led by Margery, and Lavinia was fluttering as she pretended not to notice Lord Barton's rapt gaze, she struck out.

Though the train station was set at the far end of town, it didn't take her ten minutes to make it there. She bought a ticket from the drowsy-looking clerk, who informed her that the train would be arriving in a quarter hour give or take, and thanked him. Outside the office, she took a seat on the bench and settled in to wait.

And wait.

And wait.

After half an hour she got up and approached the clerk who was playing a solitary card game. "Where's the train?"

He shook his head. "It's a mystery."

She went back to her seat.

And waited another half hour.

It was going on twilight. In the distance, the mountainsides were blistered by extravagant shades of magenta and salmon, and a dark blue canopy was spreading overhead. A fog seeped up from the lower valleys, blanketing the road into town in swirling effervescence.

She caught the clerk's eye. He shrugged again and went back to his card game. Exasperated, she got up and started pacing back and forth along the platform, craning her neck to peer down to where the train tracks curved into a copse of pine trees, a thready-looking footpath running alongside them.

"Where is the train?" she asked again.

The ticket agent sighed and put down his cards, regarding her dolefully. "Sometime there is problems with the engine, or a flock of sheep on the track, or a tree falls across . . ." He shrugged.

She made an exasperated sound. She didn't have time for this; Archie was in jail, waiting for her. Even if he didn't realize he was waiting for her.

Finally, unable to stand the waiting any longer, she set off along the footpath, intent on finding out what had happened to the blasted train that should have been taking her to Archie's side by now. At once, with the simple act of doing something, she felt better. She smiled into the gloaming.

The air was still warm and soft, the scent of autumn rising underfoot from a cushion of fallen leaves and moist, flinty ground. The fog was growing thicker, a shifting curtain on a phantom play, while ghost birds wept and trilled from a barely discernible forest's shelter. An owl passed overhead, sifting the air on silent wings so low she could have reached up and brushed it with her fingertips.

And then a figure materialized on the path ahead of her, striding out of the fog like a pirate coming up from the churning sea. It was a man, his coattails swinging at his sides, his collarless white shirt open at the throat, head bare and black curls gleaming with condensation.

Archie.

Lucy froze, unable to believe her eyes, certain she had conjured him through sheer longing.

She couldn't tell if he saw her; he came on towards her without a check in his stride, without the slightest change in his speed, inexorably, like the tide pulled by the moon, until he was right in front of her and his hands rose to cup her face, and his head was bending down and his mouth found hers in a kiss so tender, so filled with yearning, and so passionately restrained that her eyes filled with tears.

Her eyelids squeezed shut and she threw her arms around his neck, kissing him back, fear and relief and love and hunger all jumbled together in her passionate response. And finally, when she felt certain she would swoon, he broke off the kiss and set his forehead against hers, breathing heavily, his hands still bracketing her face.

"I love you, Lucy. I've been such a fool but you have to forgive. You have to because I love you and I know you love me, God knows why, but I'm sure as hell not going to question it. I'm simply going to do my damnedest to make sure you never stop."

She started to smile but then recalled a very good reason not to smile. "Miss Litchfield."

He shook his head. "She's not you. How could I . . . ? If I'm a cad then so be it. But at least I'm not the sort of cad who would marry one woman when I'm in love with another."

She should stop now, while she was ahead. After all, everything she wanted was right here in her arms. She shouldn't muck it up by asking stupid, irrelevant questions like, "What about your job?"

But she did. Because she did love him.

"I don't need to work, Lucy. I'm disgustingly well-heeled. I *do* need you. With you, I'm the man I want to be, the person I want to be. I was never interested in recognition or acclaim, I work because I find it fascinating. Whether I'm a professor at St. Phillip's or not won't make it any more or less so."

Something in her expression made him drop a kiss on her lips and once there, linger longer before reluctantly lifting his head again.

She told herself to be satisfied but restraint had never been her strong suit. "You said you didn't know me."

He laughed. "I was angry. I knew it for a lie the second it left my lips. True, I may not know what cake you like best, or the name of your first crush. But I do know you don't speak French. I know you are the most audacious storyteller I have ever seen"—his beautiful mouth quirked with humor—"that you sing like a fallen angel and dance like a Gypsy's fantasy.

"I *know* you in my very bones, Lucy. You're no more a stranger to me than my own breath, the sun in the sky, or the sound of my heartbeat and no less a part of me. So, please say you'll marry me, Lucy. And pray God, say you'll marry me soon."

For a split second Lucy thought of Lavinia boldly telling Lord Barton that he would have to court her. But then she looked at Archie, his rumpled black locks and cleft chin under his unshaven cheeks, his black-lashed pirate eyes, and the strong throat bared to the night air, and his mouth . . . oh my, his mouth . . .

Waiting had never been her strong suit, either.

"Yes," she said as he caught her up in his arms.

And didn't have to wait at all.

AUTHOR'S NOTE

What could be more delicious, exciting, or evocative than the Edwardian age? I've been hooked ever since binging on *Downton Abbey* one snowy Minnesota winter day.

The Songbird's Seduction takes place a wee bit earlier than Season One of the wonderful BBC production, but I have been ruthless in making sure that I faithfully represented the clothing, the idioms, the theatrical productions, the music, the technology, and the ferry transportation of 1908 and, hopefully, how women were enjoying newfound freedoms.

Because I'm a history geek, I have to share some of this über-cool stuff. Better to do so here, I believe you'll agree, than in the middle of a scene. Here are but a few things you might find interesting: Margery is based on an American female impersonator, Julian Eltinge, whose onstage alter ego was Vesta Tilley. At one time, he was the highest-paid actor in New York, and toured the continent to rave reviews.

Written in the mid-nineteenth century, the song "Dark Eyes," though Ukrainian, has long and traditionally been associated with Russian Romani. Over the years it has had so many lyrics attached to it, to so many ends, that I settled on using a jumble of several. If you hear it, I'm sure you'll recognize it. It's the quintessential passionate Gypsy ballad.

I have strived for verisimilitude in my down-and-dirty portrayal of the siege of Patnimba. While there is no hill station called Patnimba, the Indian Mutiny of 1857 claimed many lives, both innocent and otherwise, and looting on both sides was rampant. But for the purposes of the story, I made up the fortress and the siege.

Finally, the first Olympic boxing match was held in St. Louis in 1904.

I think Archie won.

Minnesota, 2013

ABOUT THE AUTHOR

New York Times and *USA Today* bestselling author Connie Brockway has received starred reviews from both *Publishers Weekly* and the *Library Journal,* which named *My Seduction* as one of 2004's top ten romances.

An eight-time finalist for Romance Writers of America's prestigious RITA award, Brockway has twice been its recipient, for *My Dearest Enemy* and *The Bridal Season.* In 2006 Connie wrote her first women's contemporary, *Hot Dish,* which won critical raves. Connie's historical romance *The Other Guy's Bride* was the launch book for Montlake Romance.

Today Brockway lives in Minnesota with her husband—a family physician—and two spoiled mutts.